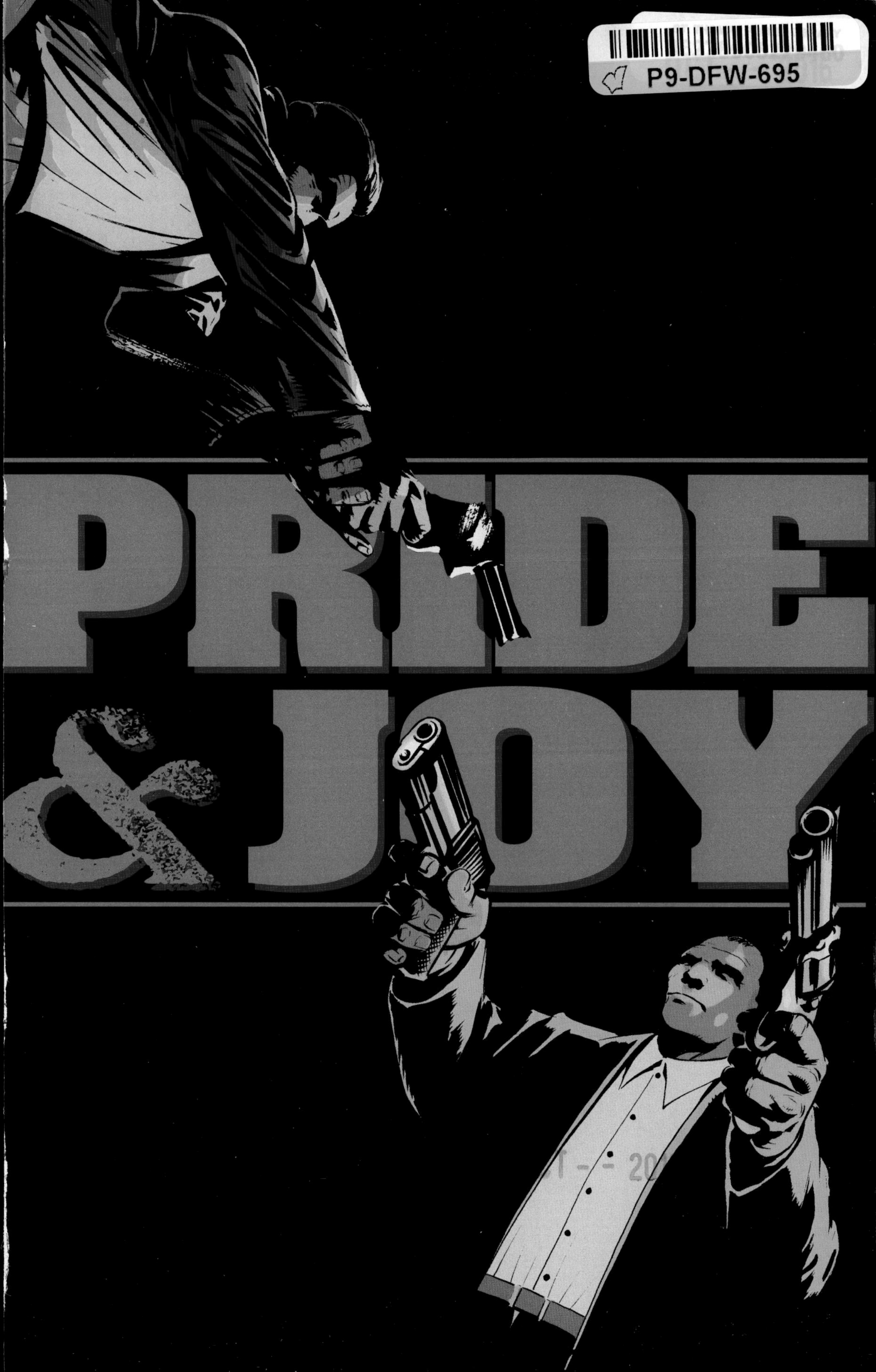
PRIDE
& JOY

IMAGE COMICS, INC.
Robert Kirkman – Chief Operating Officer
Erik Larsen – Chief Financial Officer
Todd McFarlane – President
Marc Silvestri – Chief Executive Officer
Jim Valentino – Vice-President

Eric Stephenson – Publisher
Corey Murphy – Director of Sales
Jeff Boison – Director of Publishing Planning & Book Trade Sales
Jeremy Sullivan – Director of Digital Sales
Kat Salazar – Director of PR & Marketing
Emily Miller – Director of Operations
Branwyn Bigglestone – Senior Accounts Manager
Sarah Mello – Accounts Manager
Drew Gill – Art Director
Jonathan Chan – Production Manager
Meredith Wallace – Print Manager
Briah Skelly – Publicity Assistant
Sasha Head – Sales & Marketing Production Designer
Randy Okamura – Digital Production Designer
David Brothers – Branding Manager
Ally Power – Content Manager
Addison Duke – Production Artist
Vincent Kukua – Production Artist
Tricia Ramos – Production Artist
Jeff Stang – Direct Market Sales Representative
Emilio Bautista – Digital Sales Associate
Leanna Caunter – Accounting Assistant
Chloe Ramos-Peterson – Administrative Assistant

PRIDE & JOY. First printing. May 2016. Published by Image Comics, Inc. Office of
publication: 2001 Center Street, Sixth Floor, Berkeley, CA 94704. Copyright © 2016
Garth Ennis & John Higgins. All rights reserved. Contains material originally published in
single magazine form as PRIDE & JOY #1-4. "Pride & Joy," its logos, and the likenesses
of all characters herein are trademarks of Garth Ennis & John Higgins, unless otherwise
noted. "Image" and the Image Comics logos are registered trademarks of Image
Comics, Inc. No part of this publication may be reproduced or transmitted, in any form
or by any means (except for short excerpts for journalistic or review purposes), without
the express written permission of Garth Ennis, John Higgins, or Image Comics, Inc.
All names, characters, events, and locales in this publication are entirely fictional. Any
resemblance to actual persons (living or dead), events, or places, without satiric intent,
is coincidental. Printed in the USA. For information regarding the CPSIA on this printed
material call: 203-595-3636 and provide reference #RICH-675131. For international
rights, contact: foreignlicensing@imagecomics.com ISBN: 978-1-63215-801-7

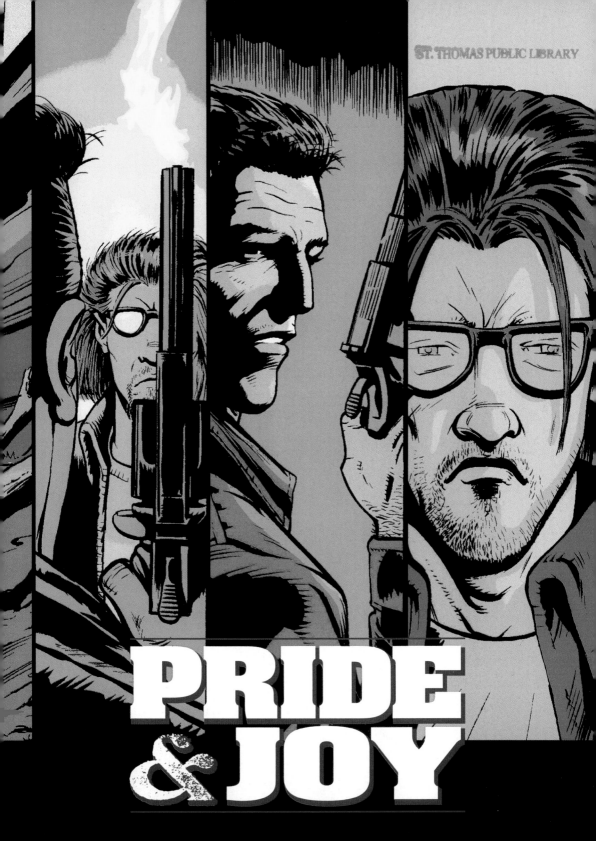

PRIDE & JOY

Garth Ennis Writer **John Higgins** Artist & Colorist **Annie Halfacree** Letterer

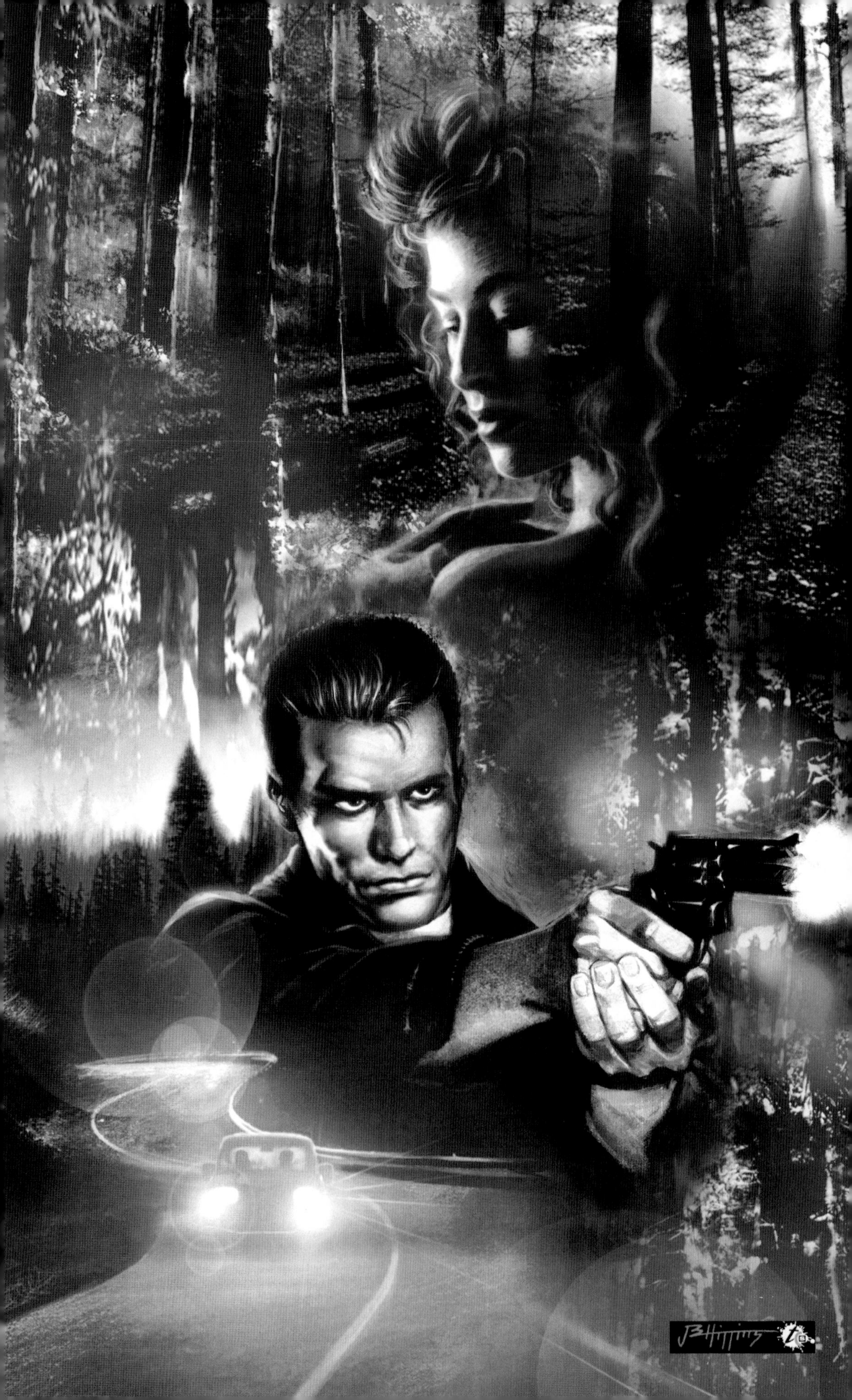

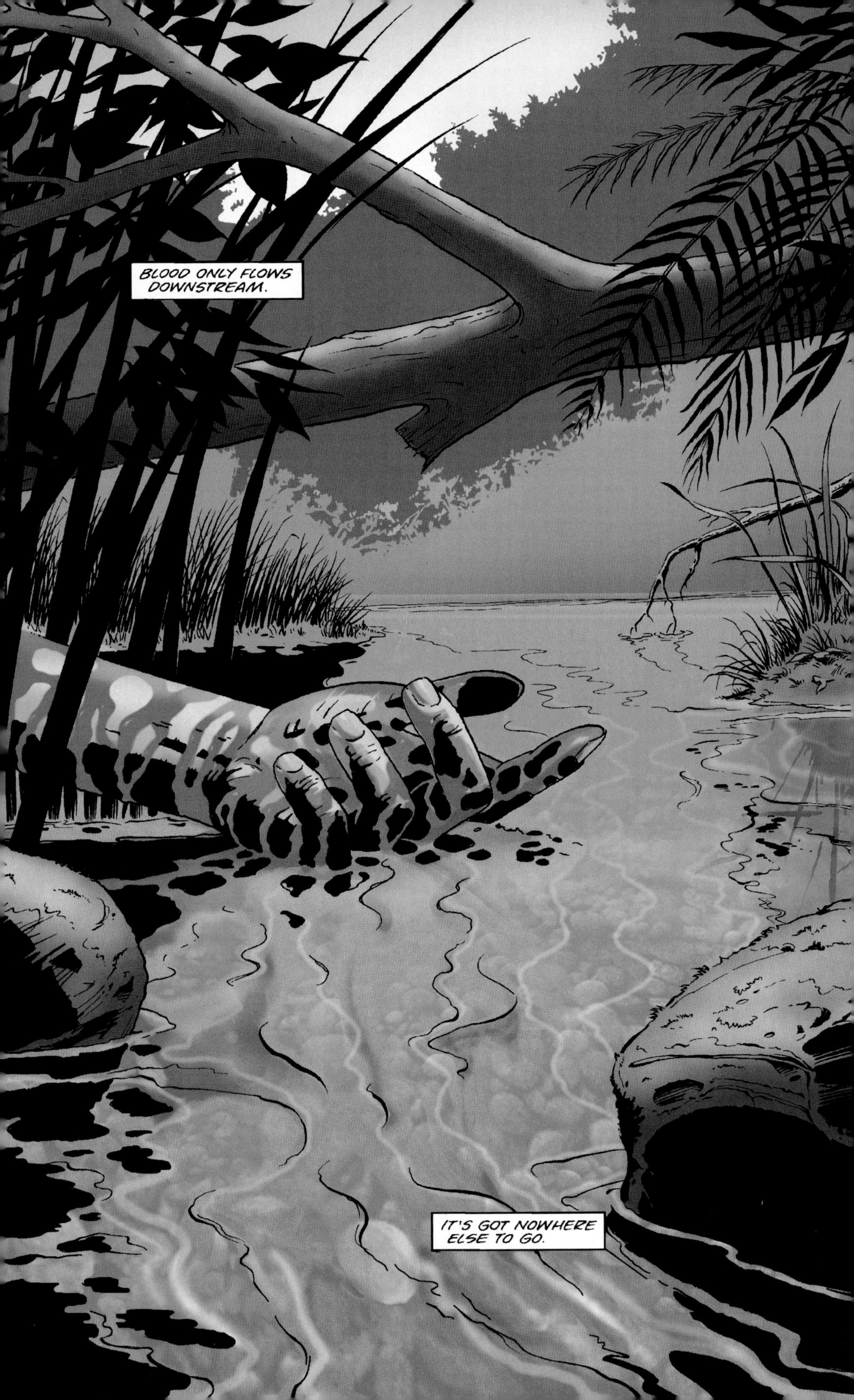
BLOOD ONLY FLOWS DOWNSTREAM.
IT'S GOT NOWHERE ELSE TO GO.

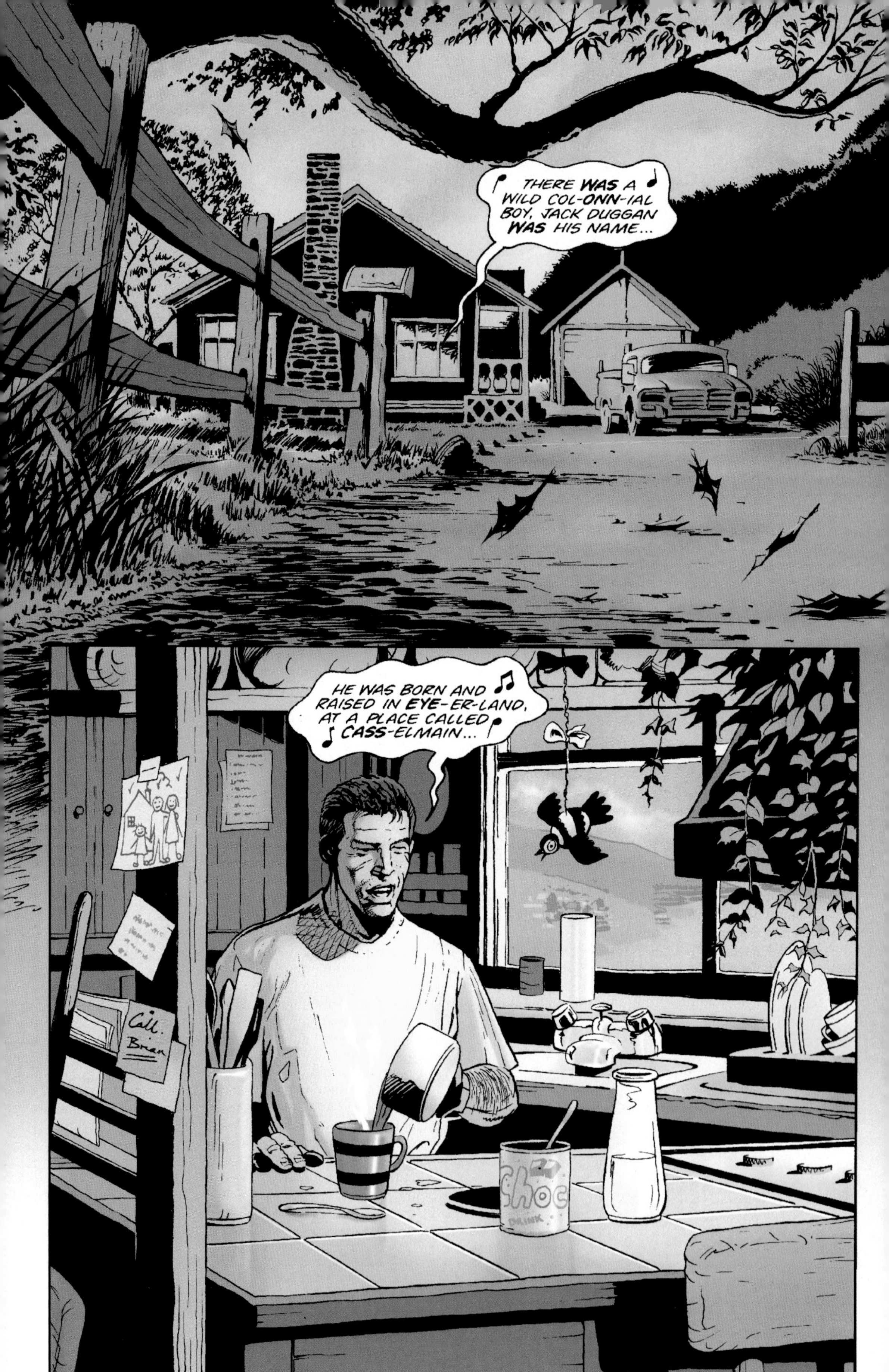
THERE WAS A WILD COL-ONN-IAL BOY, JACK DUGGAN WAS HIS NAME...
HE WAS BORN AND RAISED IN EYE-ER-LAND, AT A PLACE CALLED CASS-ELMAIN...
Call. Brian
Choc
DRINK

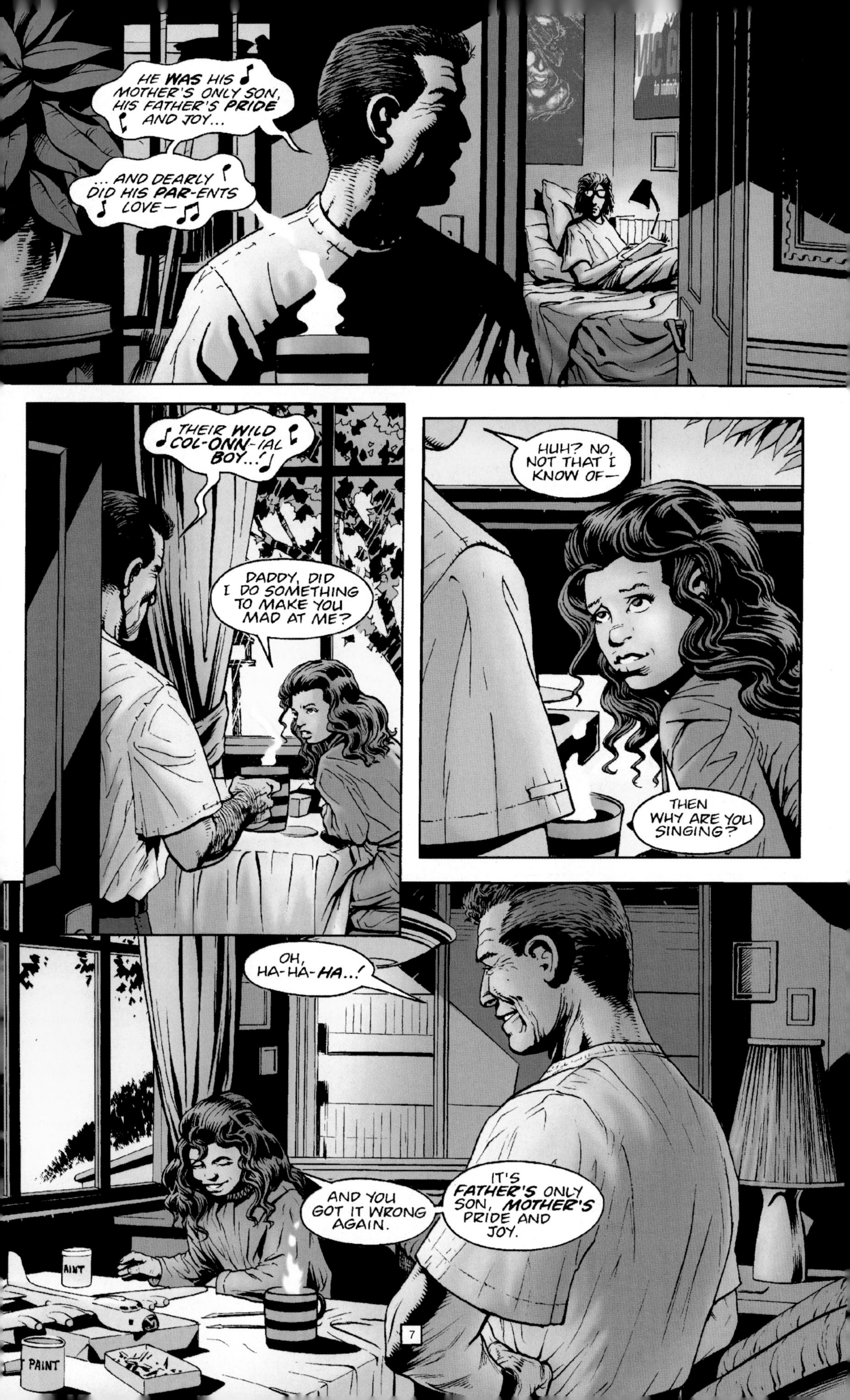
HE WAS HIS MOTHER'S ONLY SON, HIS FATHER'S PRIDE AND JOY...
... AND DEARLY DID HIS PAR-ENTS LOVE—
THEIR WILD COL-ONN-IAL BOY...!
DADDY, DID I DO SOMETHING TO MAKE YOU MAD AT ME?
HUH? NO, NOT THAT I KNOW OF—
THEN WHY ARE YOU SINGING?
OH, HA-HA-HA...!
AND YOU GOT IT WRONG AGAIN.
IT'S FATHER'S ONLY SON, MOTHER'S PRIDE AND JOY.
PAINT
PAINT

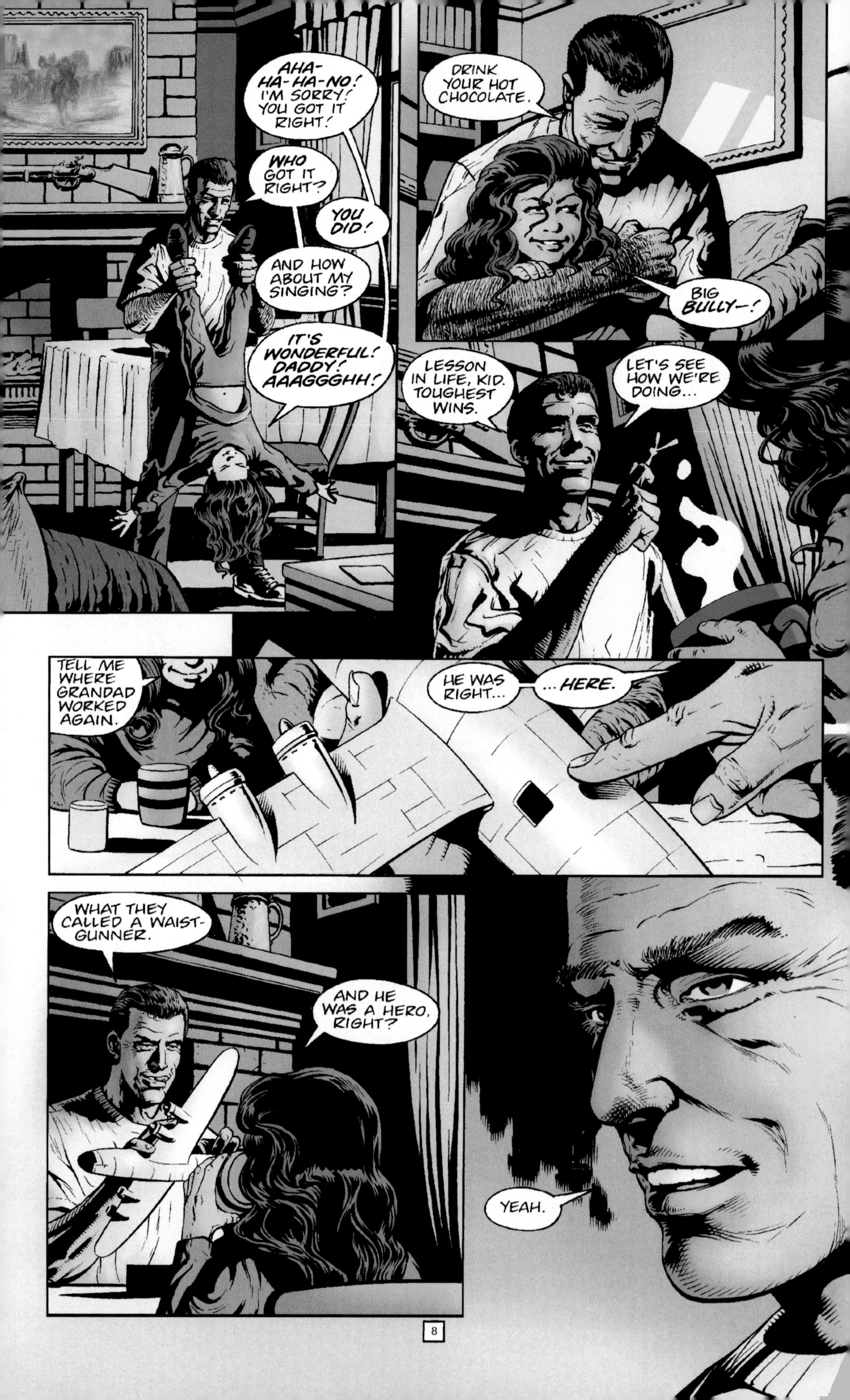
AHA-HA-HA-NO! I'M SORRY! YOU GOT IT RIGHT!
WHO GOT IT RIGHT?
YOU DID!
AND HOW ABOUT MY SINGING?
IT'S WONDERFUL! DADDY! AAAGGGHH!
DRINK YOUR HOT CHOCOLATE.
BIG BULLY--!
LESSON IN LIFE, KID. TOUGHEST WINS.
LET'S SEE HOW WE'RE DOING...
TELL ME WHERE GRANDAD WORKED AGAIN.
HE WAS RIGHT...
...HERE.
WHAT THEY CALLED A WAIST-GUNNER.
AND HE WAS A HERO, RIGHT?
YEAH.

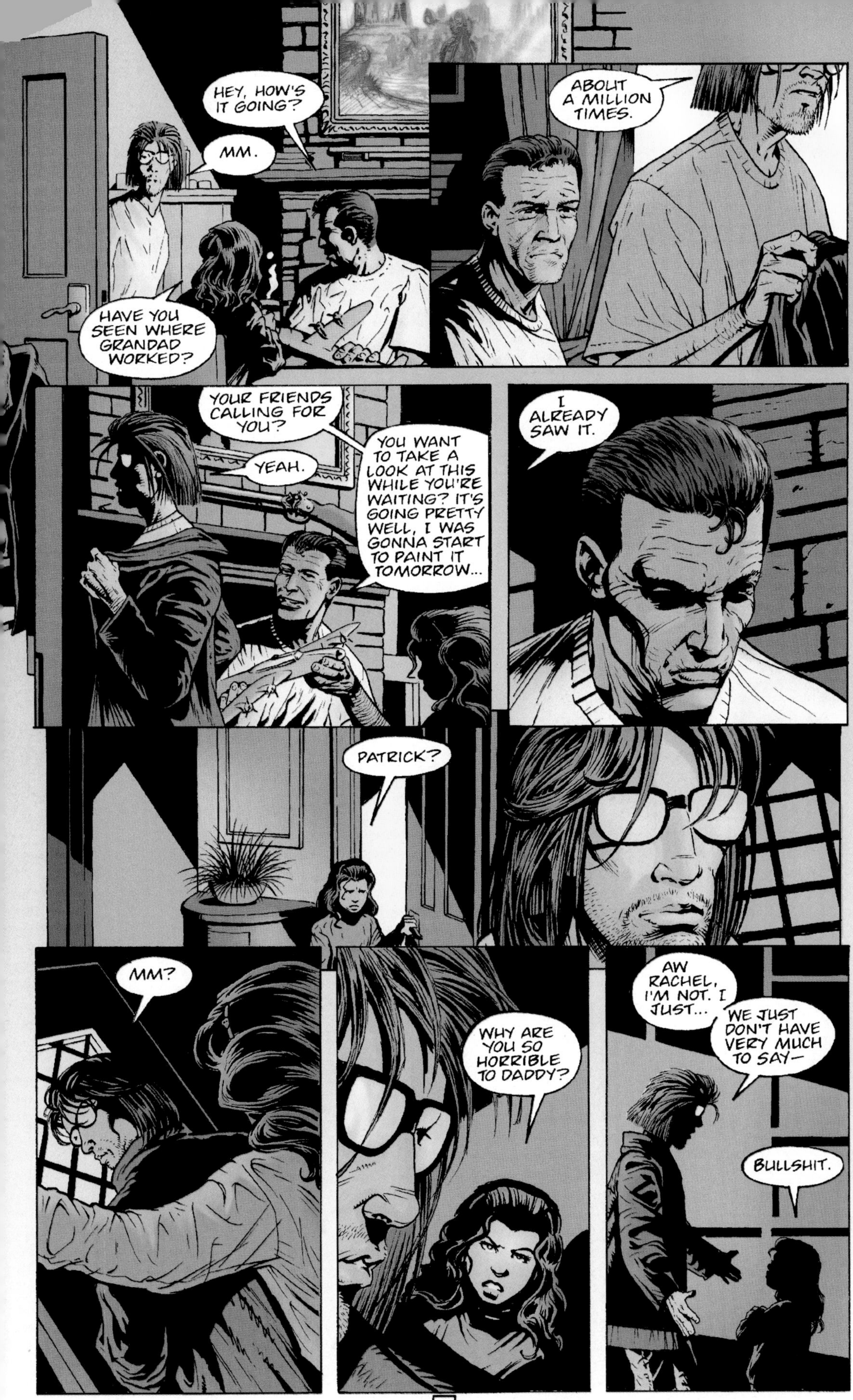
HEY, HOW'S IT GOING?
MM.
HAVE YOU SEEN WHERE GRANDAD WORKED?
ABOUT A MILLION TIMES.
YOUR FRIENDS CALLING FOR YOU?
YEAH.
YOU WANT TO TAKE A LOOK AT THIS WHILE YOU'RE WAITING? IT'S GOING PRETTY WELL, I WAS GONNA START TO PAINT IT TOMORROW...
I ALREADY SAW IT.
PATRICK?
MM?
WHY ARE YOU SO HORRIBLE TO DADDY?
AW RACHEL, I'M NOT. I JUST...
WE JUST DON'T HAVE VERY MUCH TO SAY—
BULLSHIT.

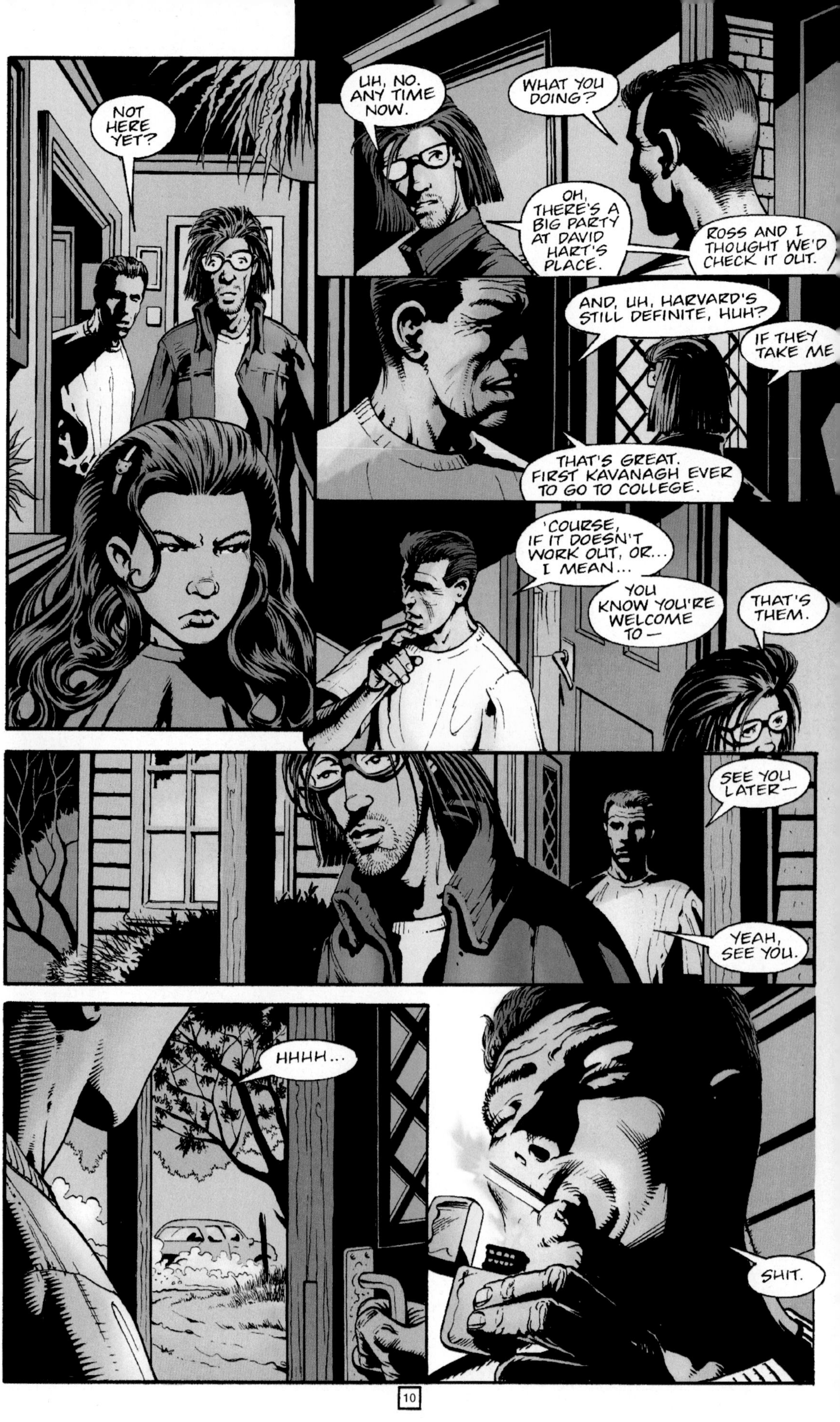
NOT HERE YET?
UH, NO. ANY TIME NOW.
WHAT YOU DOING?
OH, THERE'S A BIG PARTY AT DAVID HART'S PLACE.
ROSS AND I THOUGHT WE'D CHECK IT OUT.
AND, UH, HARVARD'S STILL DEFINITE, HUH?
IF THEY TAKE ME
THAT'S GREAT. FIRST KAVANAGH EVER TO GO TO COLLEGE.
'COURSE, IF IT DOESN'T WORK OUT, OR... I MEAN...
YOU KNOW YOU'RE WELCOME TO—
THAT'S THEM.
SEE YOU LATER—
YEAH, SEE YOU.
HHHH...
SHIT.

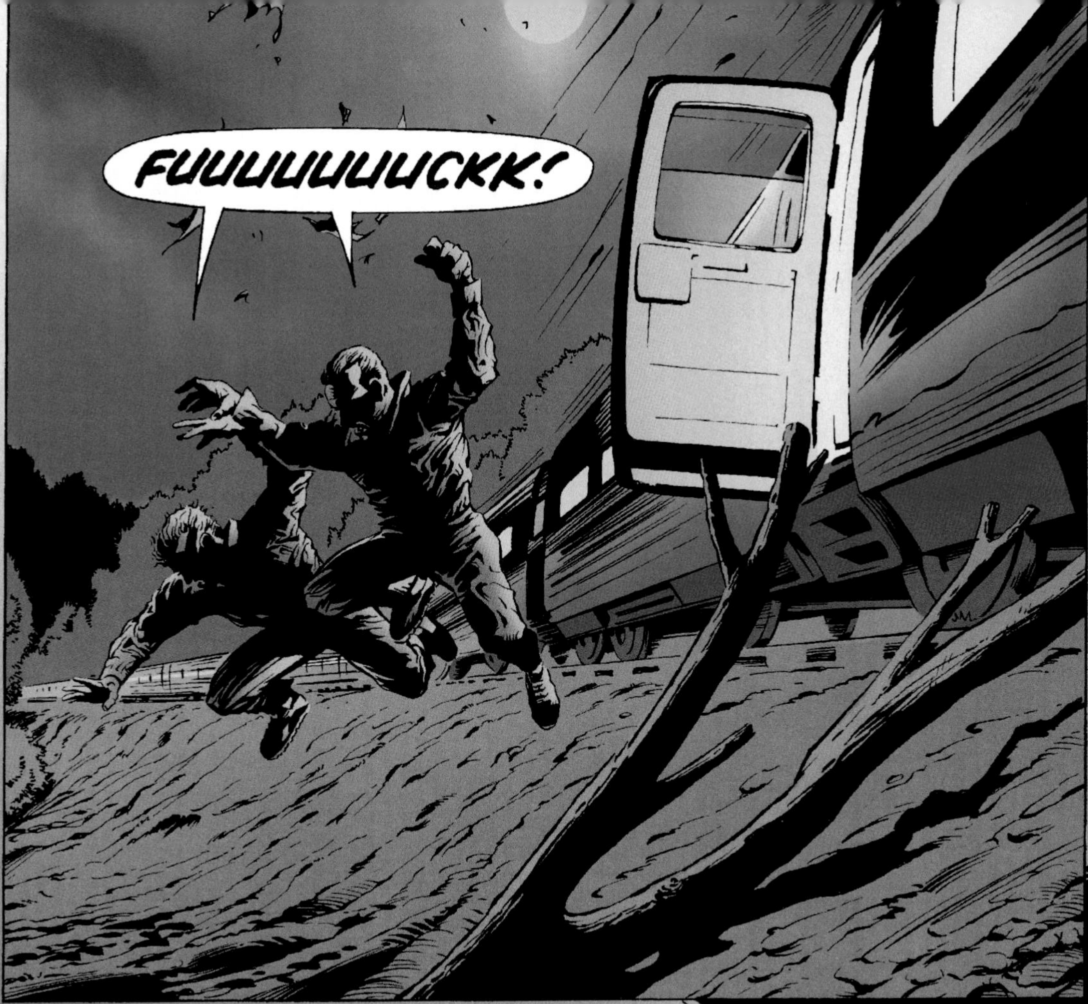
FUUUUUUUUCKK!

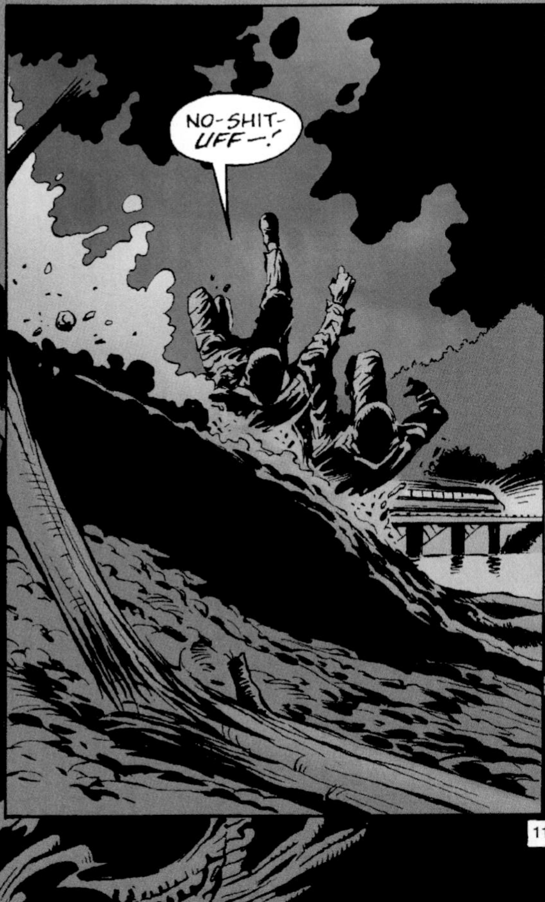
NO-SHIT-
UFF--!

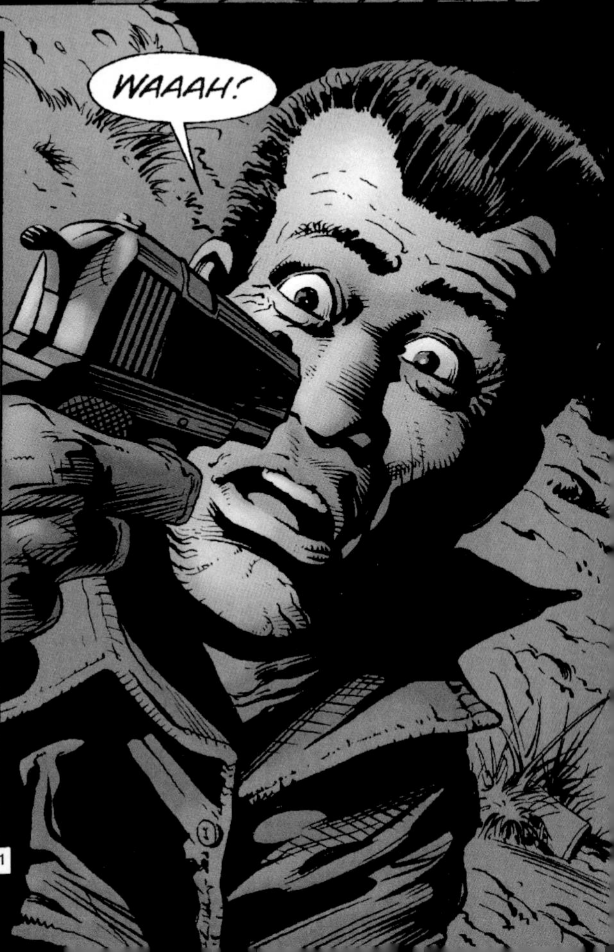
WAAAH!

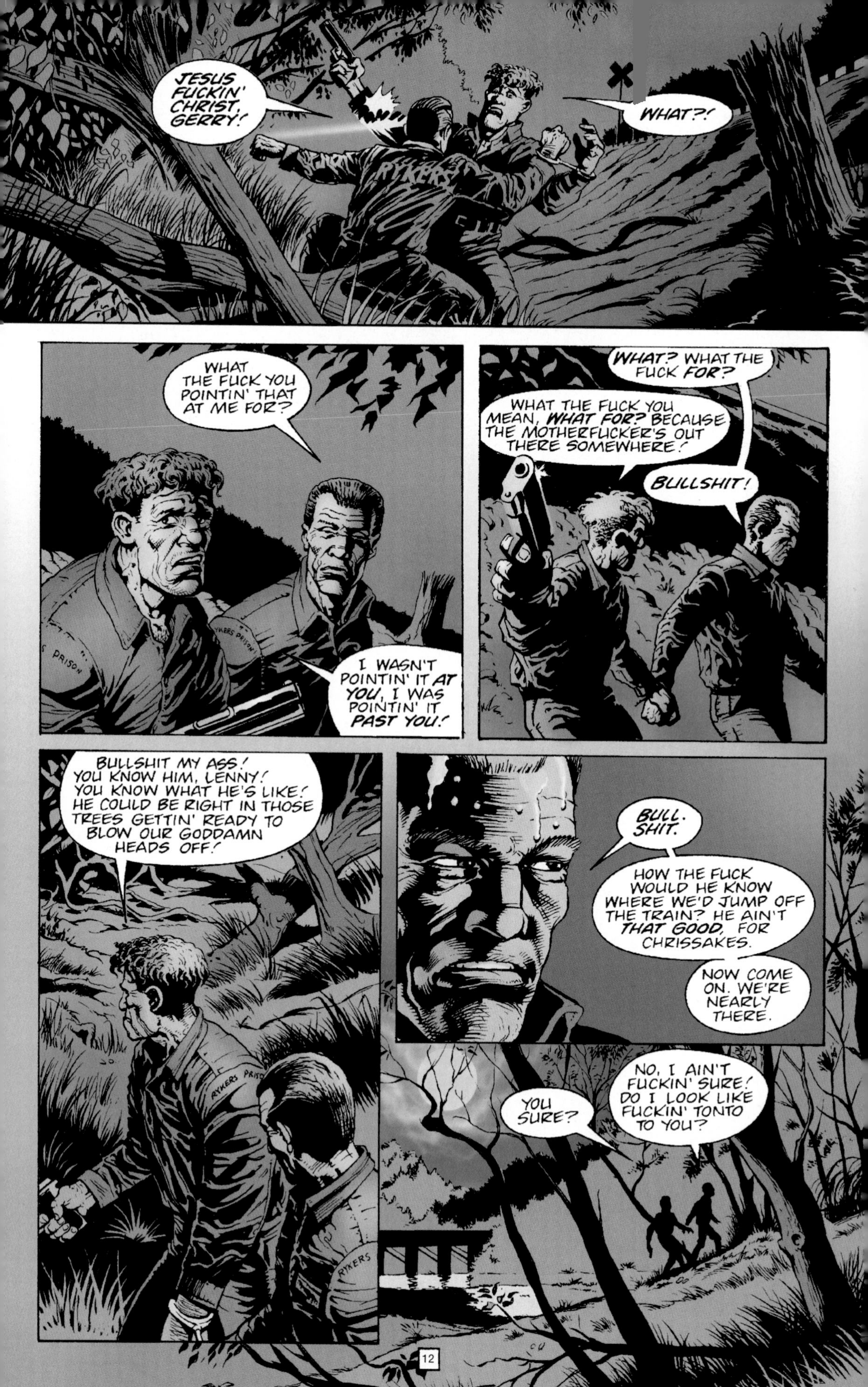

JESUS FUCKIN' CHRIST, GERRY!
WHAT?!
WHAT THE FUCK YOU POINTIN' THAT AT ME FOR?
I WASN'T POINTIN' IT AT YOU, I WAS POINTIN' IT PAST YOU!
WHAT? WHAT THE FUCK FOR?
WHAT THE FUCK YOU MEAN, WHAT FOR? BECAUSE THE MOTHERFUCKER'S OUT THERE SOMEWHERE!
BULLSHIT!
BULLSHIT MY ASS! YOU KNOW HIM, LENNY! YOU KNOW WHAT HE'S LIKE! HE COULD BE RIGHT IN THOSE TREES GETTIN' READY TO BLOW OUR GODDAMN HEADS OFF!
BULL. SHIT.
HOW THE FUCK WOULD HE KNOW WHERE WE'D JUMP OFF THE TRAIN? HE AIN'T THAT GOOD, FOR CHRISSAKES.
NOW COME ON. WE'RE NEARLY THERE.
YOU SURE?
NO, I AIN'T FUCKIN' SURE! DO I LOOK LIKE FUCKIN' TONTO TO YOU?

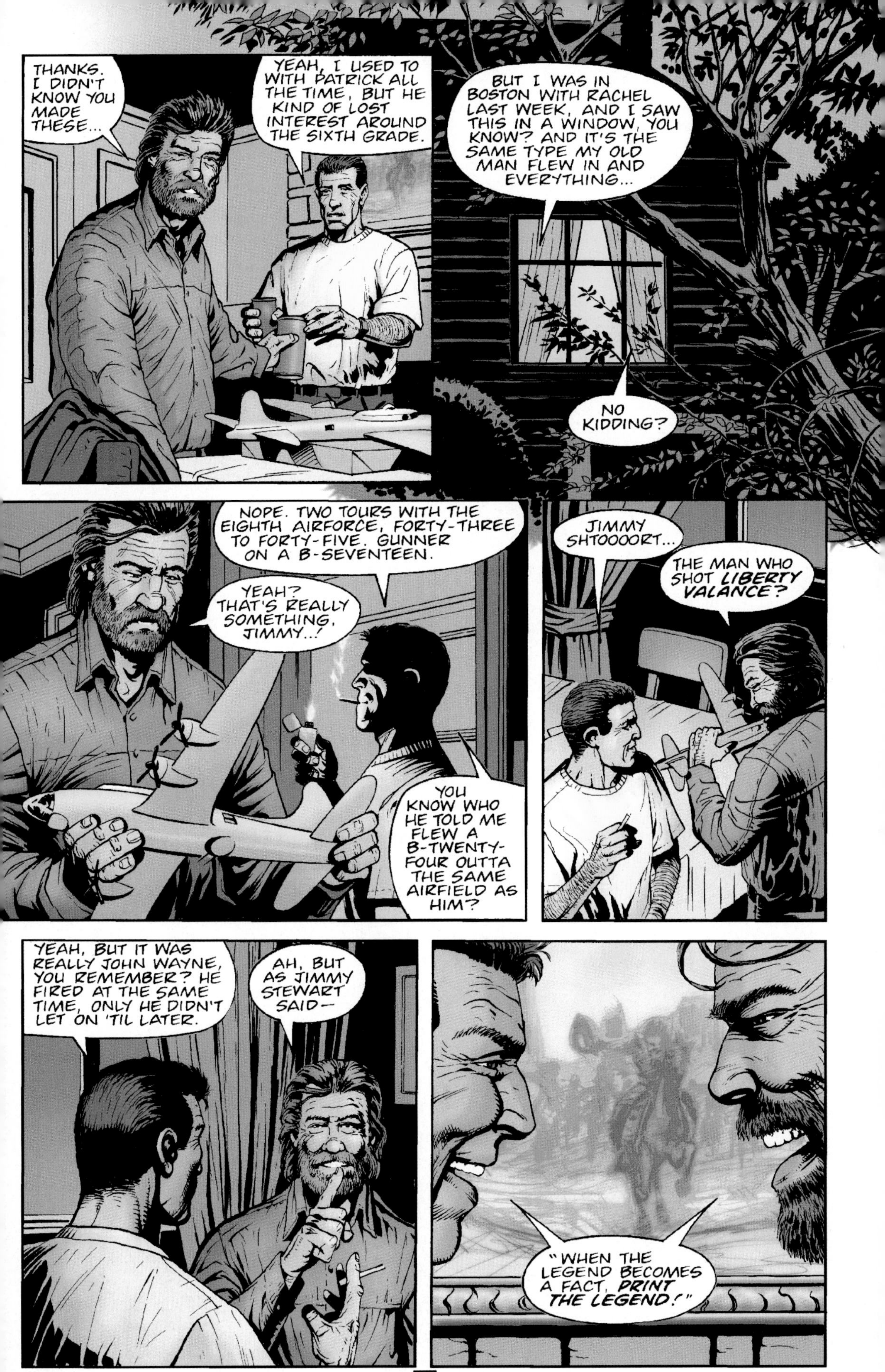
THANKS. I DIDN'T KNOW YOU MADE THESE...
YEAH, I USED TO WITH PATRICK ALL THE TIME, BUT HE KIND OF LOST INTEREST AROUND THE SIXTH GRADE.
BUT I WAS IN BOSTON WITH RACHEL LAST WEEK, AND I SAW THIS IN A WINDOW, YOU KNOW? AND IT'S THE SAME TYPE MY OLD MAN FLEW IN AND EVERYTHING...
NO KIDDING?
NOPE. TWO TOURS WITH THE EIGHTH AIRFORCE, FORTY-THREE TO FORTY-FIVE. GUNNER ON A B-SEVENTEEN.
YEAH? THAT'S REALLY SOMETHING, JIMMY...!
YOU KNOW WHO HE TOLD ME FLEW A B-TWENTY-FOUR OUTTA THE SAME AIRFIELD AS HIM?
JIMMY SHTOOOORT...
THE MAN WHO SHOT *LIBERTY VALANCE?*
YEAH, BUT IT WAS REALLY JOHN WAYNE, YOU REMEMBER? HE FIRED AT THE SAME TIME, ONLY HE DIDN'T LET ON 'TIL LATER.
AH, BUT AS JIMMY STEWART SAID—
"WHEN THE LEGEND BECOMES A FACT, *PRINT THE LEGEND!*"

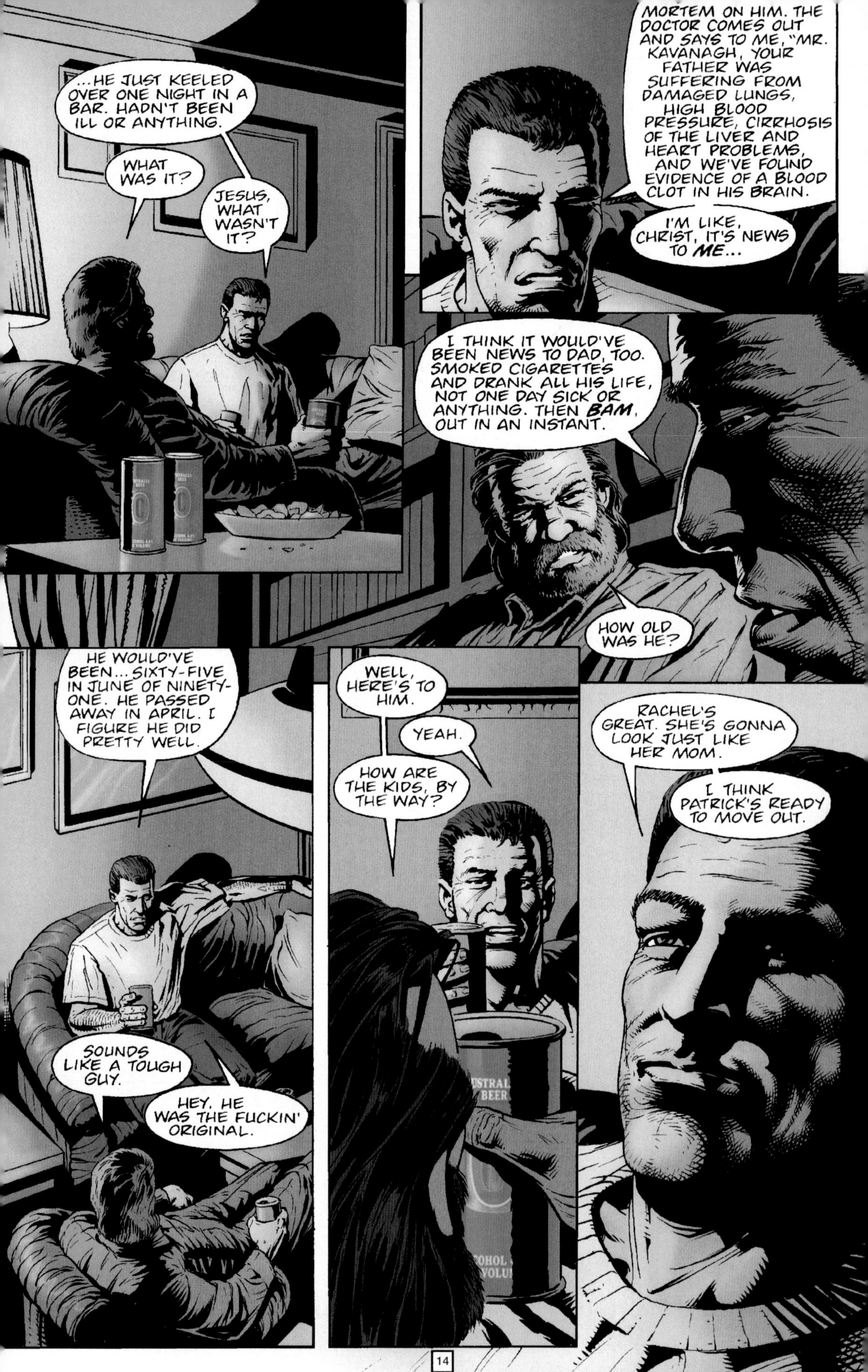

...HE JUST KEELED OVER ONE NIGHT IN A BAR. HADN'T BEEN ILL OR ANYTHING.
WHAT WAS IT?
JESUS, WHAT WASN'T IT?
MORTEM ON HIM. THE DOCTOR COMES OUT AND SAYS TO ME, "MR. KAVANAGH, YOUR FATHER WAS SUFFERING FROM DAMAGED LUNGS, HIGH BLOOD PRESSURE, CIRRHOSIS OF THE LIVER AND HEART PROBLEMS, AND WE'VE FOUND EVIDENCE OF A BLOOD CLOT IN HIS BRAIN.
I'M LIKE, CHRIST, IT'S NEWS TO ME...
I THINK IT WOULD'VE BEEN NEWS TO DAD, TOO. SMOKED CIGARETTES AND DRANK ALL HIS LIFE, NOT ONE DAY SICK OR ANYTHING. THEN BAM, OUT IN AN INSTANT.
HOW OLD WAS HE?
HE WOULD'VE BEEN... SIXTY-FIVE IN JUNE OF NINETY-ONE. HE PASSED AWAY IN APRIL. I FIGURE HE DID PRETTY WELL.
SOUNDS LIKE A TOUGH GUY.
HEY, HE WAS THE FUCKIN' ORIGINAL.
WELL, HERE'S TO HIM.
YEAH.
HOW ARE THE KIDS, BY THE WAY?
RACHEL'S GREAT. SHE'S GONNA LOOK JUST LIKE HER MOM.
I THINK PATRICK'S READY TO MOVE OUT.

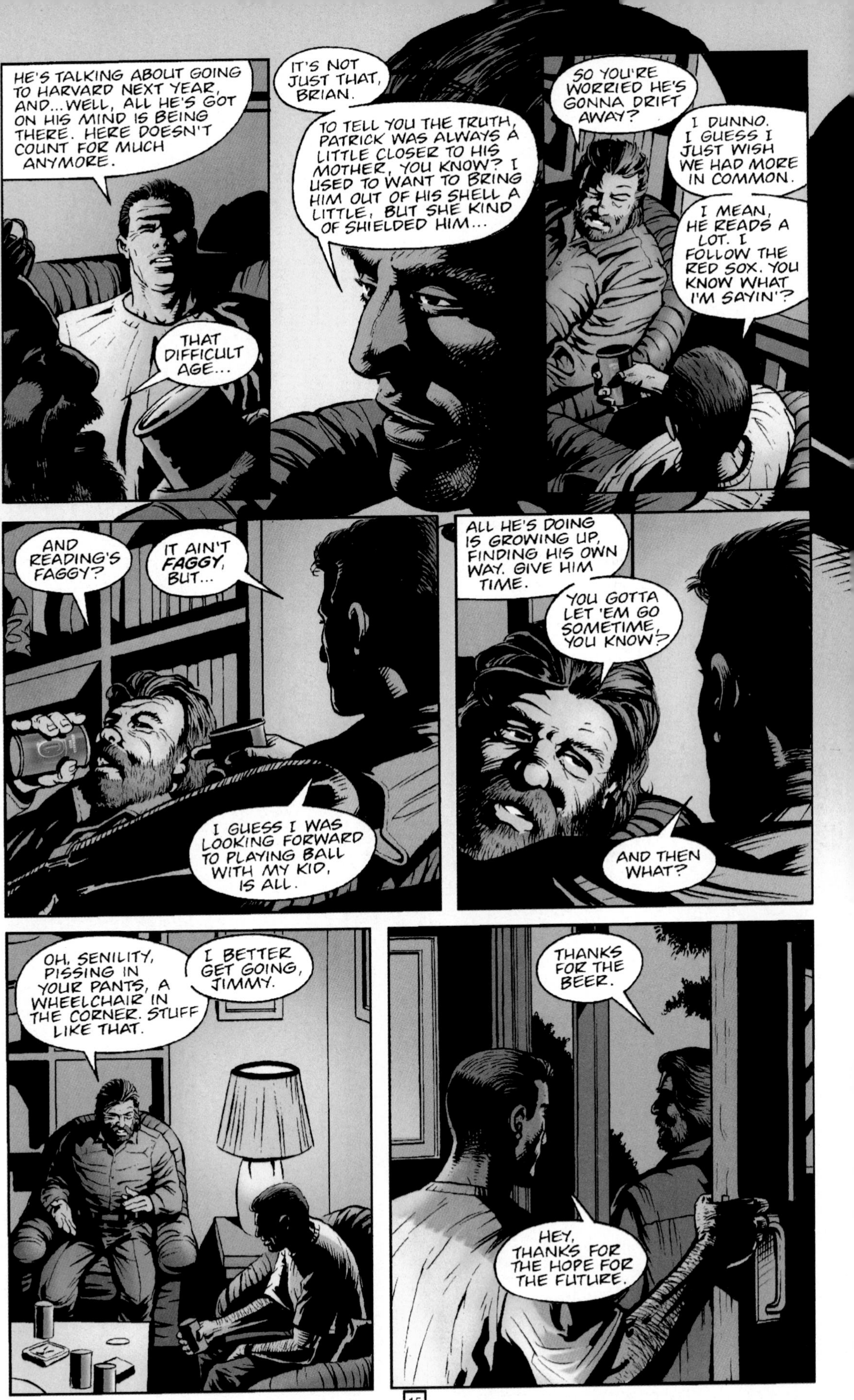

HE'S TALKING ABOUT GOING TO HARVARD NEXT YEAR, AND...WELL, ALL HE'S GOT ON HIS MIND IS BEING THERE. HERE DOESN'T COUNT FOR MUCH ANYMORE.
THAT DIFFICULT AGE...
IT'S NOT JUST THAT, BRIAN.
TO TELL YOU THE TRUTH, PATRICK WAS ALWAYS A LITTLE CLOSER TO HIS MOTHER, YOU KNOW? I USED TO WANT TO BRING HIM OUT OF HIS SHELL A LITTLE, BUT SHE KIND OF SHIELDED HIM...
SO YOU'RE WORRIED HE'S GONNA DRIFT AWAY?
I DUNNO. I GUESS I JUST WISH WE HAD MORE IN COMMON.
I MEAN, HE READS A LOT. I FOLLOW THE RED SOX. YOU KNOW WHAT I'M SAYIN'?
AND READING'S FAGGY?
IT AIN'T **FAGGY**, BUT...
I GUESS I WAS LOOKING FORWARD TO PLAYING BALL WITH MY KID, IS ALL.
ALL HE'S DOING IS GROWING UP, FINDING HIS OWN WAY. GIVE HIM TIME.
YOU GOTTA LET 'EM GO SOMETIME, YOU KNOW?
AND THEN WHAT?
OH, SENILITY, PISSING IN YOUR PANTS, A WHEELCHAIR IN THE CORNER. STUFF LIKE THAT.
I BETTER GET GOING, JIMMY.
THANKS FOR THE BEER.
HEY, THANKS FOR THE HOPE FOR THE FUTURE.

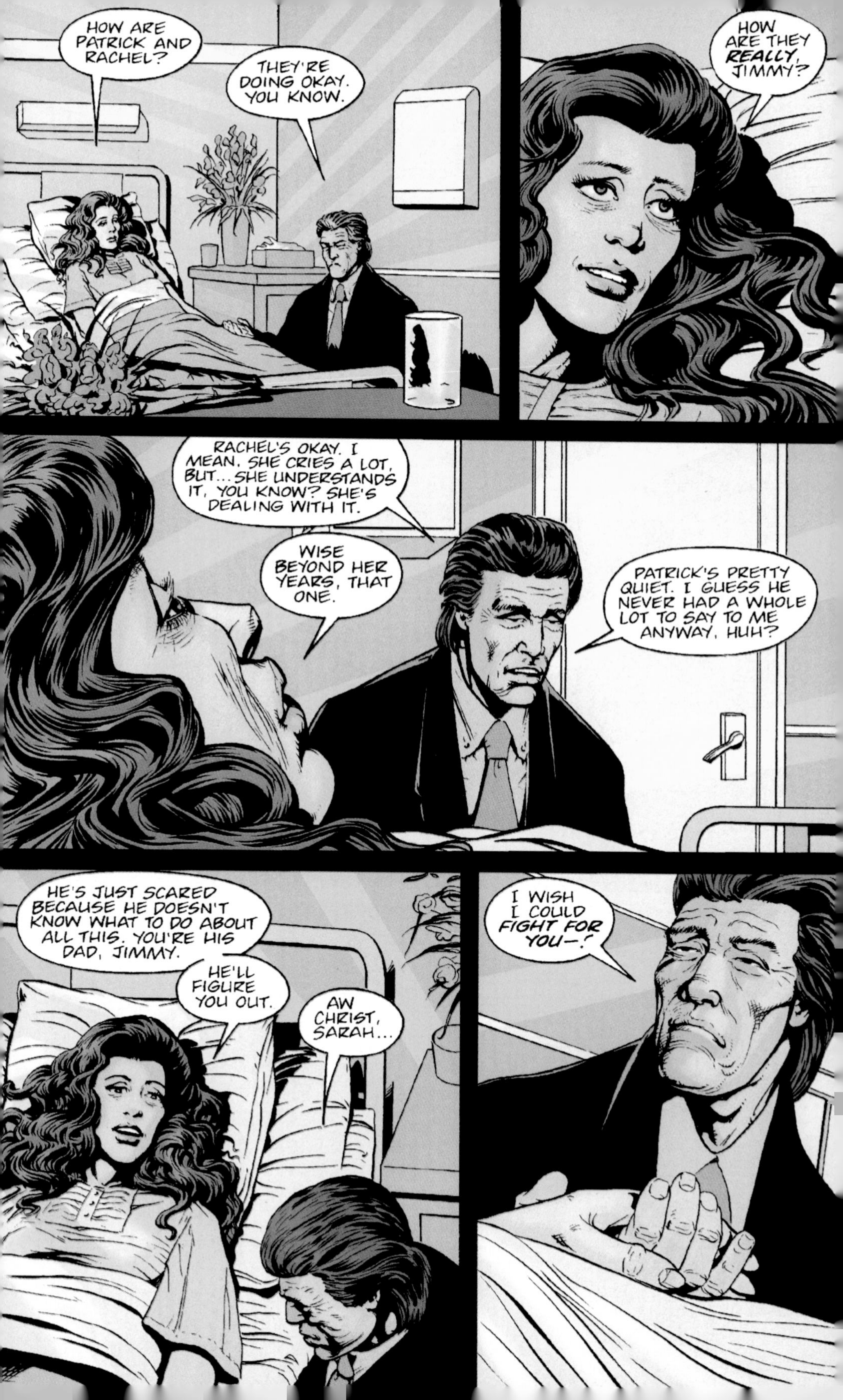

HOW ARE PATRICK AND RACHEL?
THEY'RE DOING OKAY. YOU KNOW.
HOW ARE THEY *REALLY*, JIMMY?
RACHEL'S OKAY. I MEAN, SHE CRIES A LOT, BUT... SHE UNDERSTANDS IT, YOU KNOW? SHE'S DEALING WITH IT.
WISE BEYOND HER YEARS, THAT ONE.
PATRICK'S PRETTY QUIET. I GUESS HE NEVER HAD A WHOLE LOT TO SAY TO ME ANYWAY, HUH?
HE'S JUST SCARED BECAUSE HE DOESN'T KNOW WHAT TO DO ABOUT ALL THIS. YOU'RE HIS DAD, JIMMY.
HE'LL FIGURE YOU OUT.
AW CHRIST, SARAH...
I WISH I COULD *FIGHT FOR YOU*--!

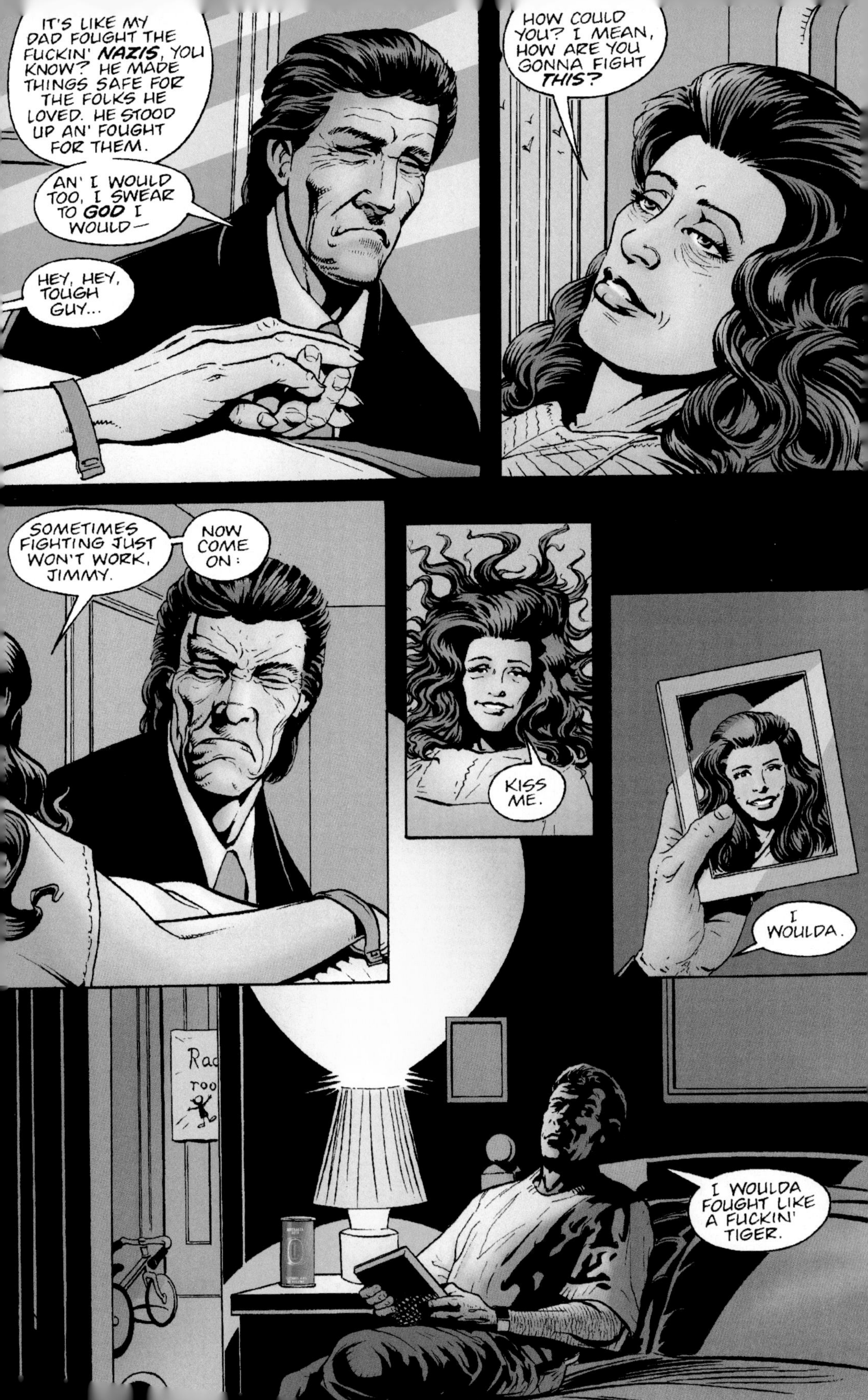
IT'S LIKE MY DAD FOUGHT THE FUCKIN' NAZIS, YOU KNOW? HE MADE THINGS SAFE FOR THE FOLKS HE LOVED. HE STOOD UP AN' FOUGHT FOR THEM.
AN' I WOULD TOO, I SWEAR TO GOD I WOULD—
HEY, HEY, TOUGH GUY...
HOW COULD YOU? I MEAN, HOW ARE YOU GONNA FIGHT THIS?
SOMETIMES FIGHTING JUST WON'T WORK, JIMMY.
NOW COME ON:
KISS ME.
I WOULDA.
I WOULDA FOUGHT LIKE A FUCKIN' TIGER.

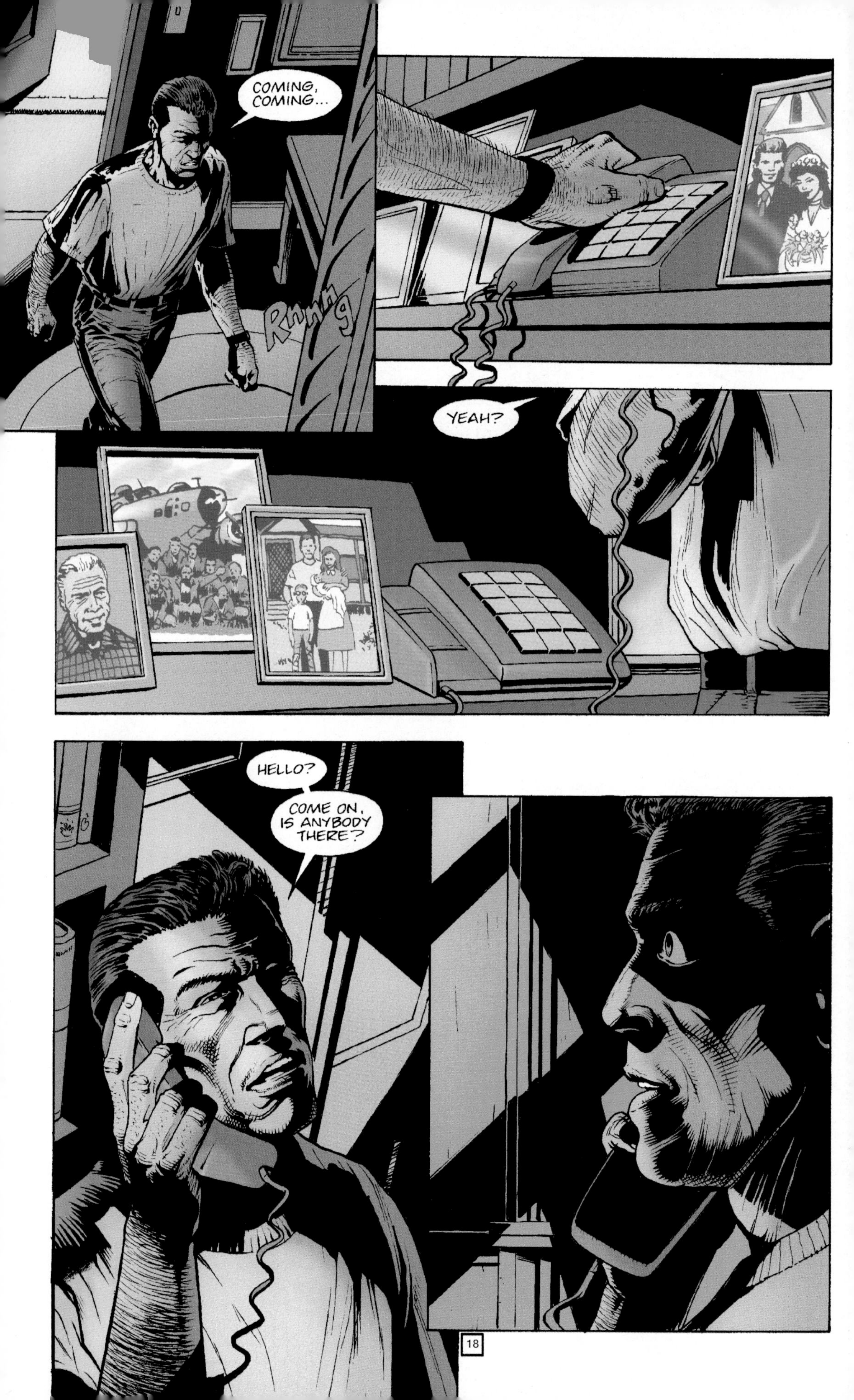
COMING, COMING...
Rnnng
YEAH?
HELLO?
COME ON, IS ANYBODY THERE?

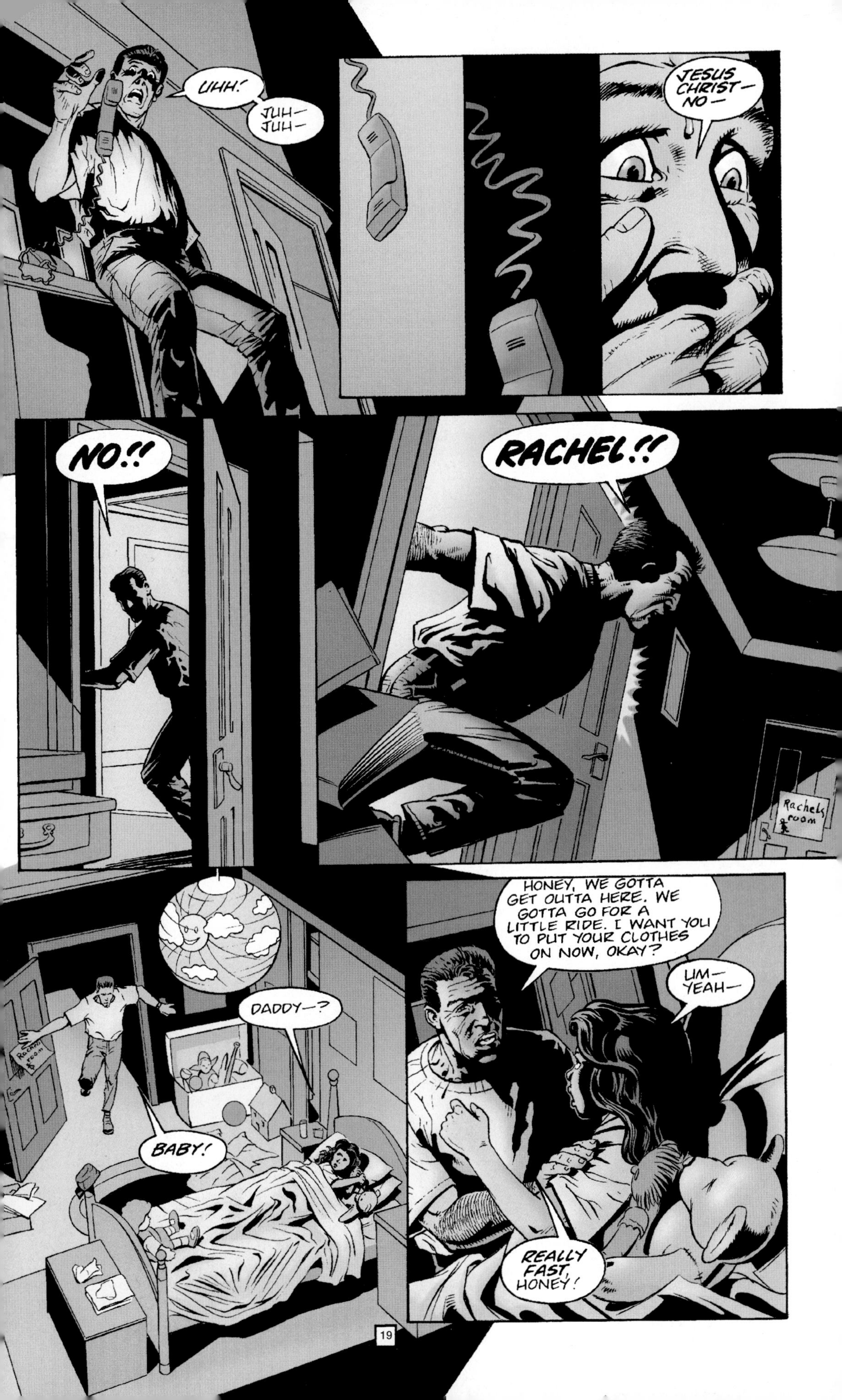
UHH!
JUH-
JUH-
JESUS CHRIST- NO-
NO.!!
RACHEL.!!
Rachels room
DADDY-?
BABY!
HONEY, WE GOTTA GET OUTTA HERE. WE GOTTA GO FOR A LITTLE RIDE. I WANT YOU TO PUT YOUR CLOTHES ON NOW, OKAY?
UM- YEAH-
REALLY FAST, HONEY!

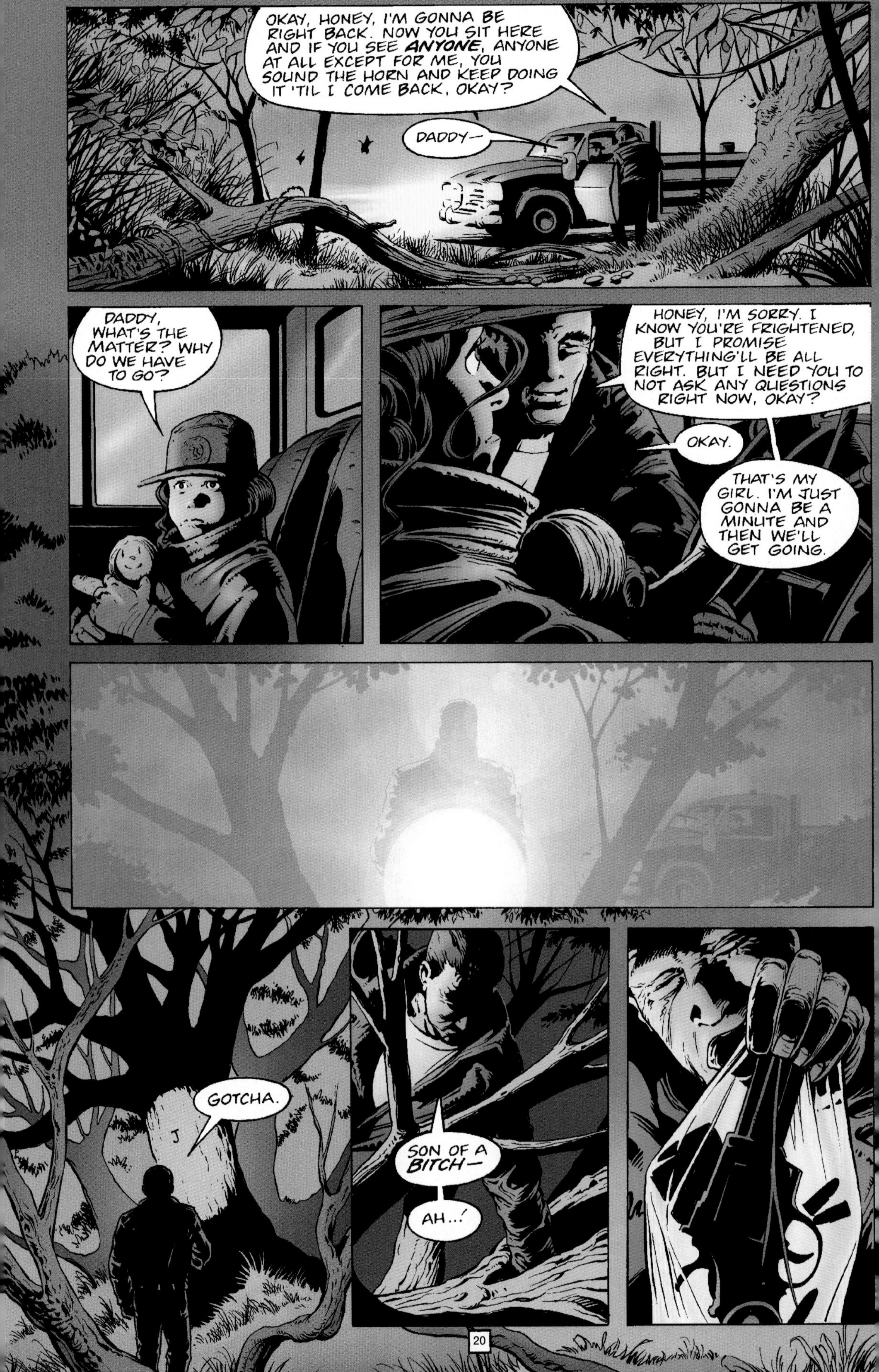
OKAY, HONEY, I'M GONNA BE RIGHT BACK. NOW YOU SIT HERE AND IF YOU SEE ANYONE, ANYONE AT ALL EXCEPT FOR ME, YOU SOUND THE HORN AND KEEP DOING IT 'TIL I COME BACK, OKAY?
DADDY--
DADDY, WHAT'S THE MATTER? WHY DO WE HAVE TO GO?
HONEY, I'M SORRY. I KNOW YOU'RE FRIGHTENED, BUT I PROMISE EVERYTHING'LL BE ALL RIGHT. BUT I NEED YOU TO NOT ASK ANY QUESTIONS RIGHT NOW, OKAY?
OKAY.
THAT'S MY GIRL. I'M JUST GONNA BE A MINUTE AND THEN WE'LL GET GOING.
J
GOTCHA.
SON OF A BITCH--
AH...!

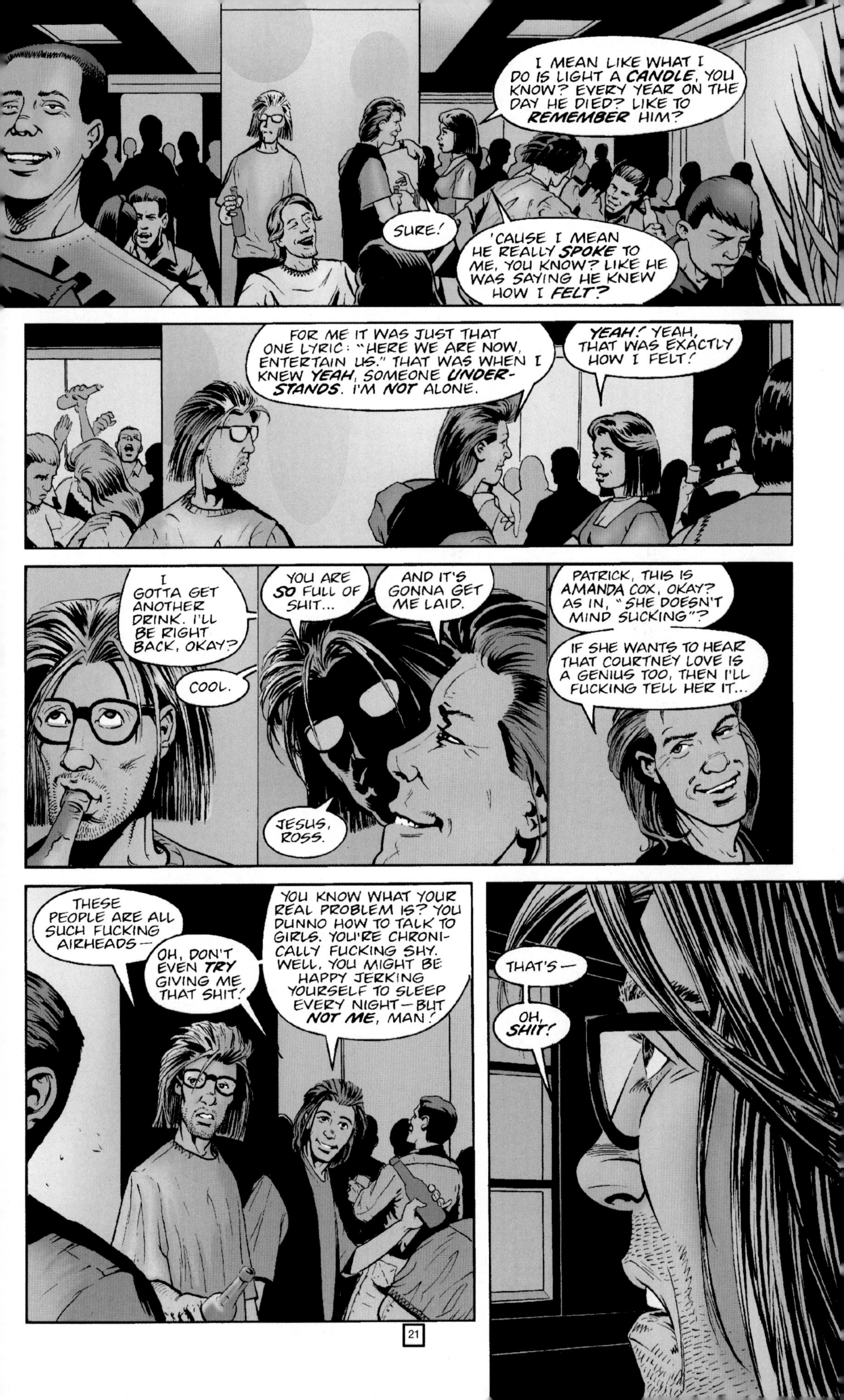
I MEAN LIKE WHAT I DO IS LIGHT A CANDLE, YOU KNOW? EVERY YEAR ON THE DAY HE DIED? LIKE TO REMEMBER HIM?
SURE!
'CAUSE I MEAN HE REALLY SPOKE TO ME, YOU KNOW? LIKE HE WAS SAYING HE KNEW HOW I FELT?
FOR ME IT WAS JUST THAT ONE LYRIC: "HERE WE ARE NOW, ENTERTAIN US." THAT WAS WHEN I KNEW YEAH, SOMEONE UNDER-STANDS. I'M NOT ALONE.
YEAH! YEAH, THAT WAS EXACTLY HOW I FELT!
I GOTTA GET ANOTHER DRINK. I'LL BE RIGHT BACK, OKAY?
COOL.
YOU ARE SO FULL OF SHIT...
AND IT'S GONNA GET ME LAID.
JESUS, ROSS.
PATRICK, THIS IS AMANDA COX, OKAY? AS IN, "SHE DOESN'T MIND SUCKING"?
IF SHE WANTS TO HEAR THAT COURTNEY LOVE IS A GENIUS TOO, THEN I'LL FUCKING TELL HER IT...
THESE PEOPLE ARE ALL SUCH FUCKING AIRHEADS—
OH, DON'T EVEN TRY GIVING ME THAT SHIT!
YOU KNOW WHAT YOUR REAL PROBLEM IS? YOU DUNNO HOW TO TALK TO GIRLS. YOU'RE CHRONI-CALLY FUCKING SHY. WELL, YOU MIGHT BE HAPPY JERKING YOURSELF TO SLEEP EVERY NIGHT—BUT NOT ME, MAN!
THAT'S—
OH, SHIT!

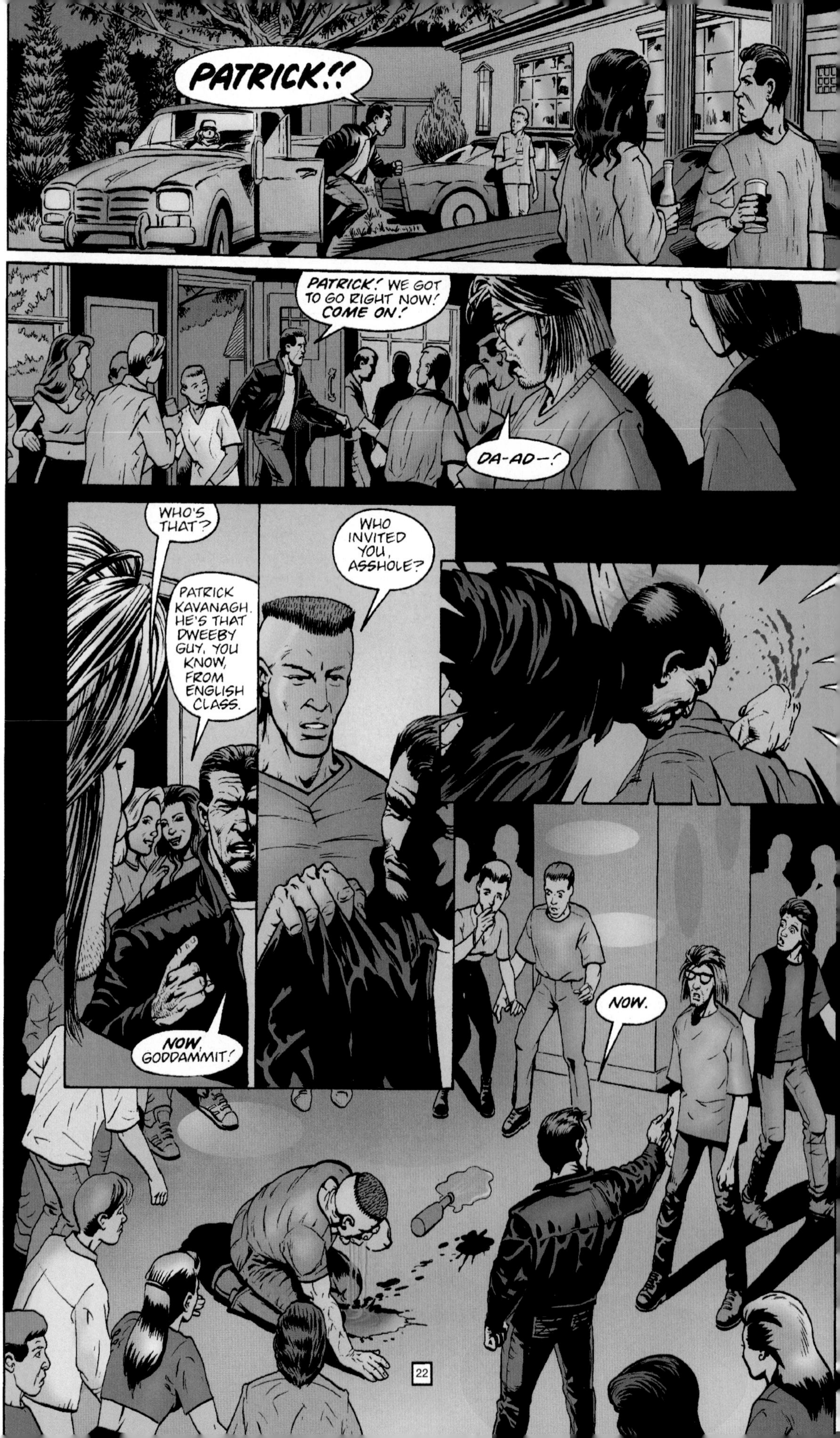

PATRICK!!
PATRICK! WE GOT TO GO RIGHT NOW! COME ON!
DA-AD--!
WHO'S THAT?
PATRICK KAVANAGH. HE'S THAT DWEEBY GUY, YOU KNOW, FROM ENGLISH CLASS.
WHO INVITED YOU, ASSHOLE?
NOW, GODDAMMIT!
NOW.

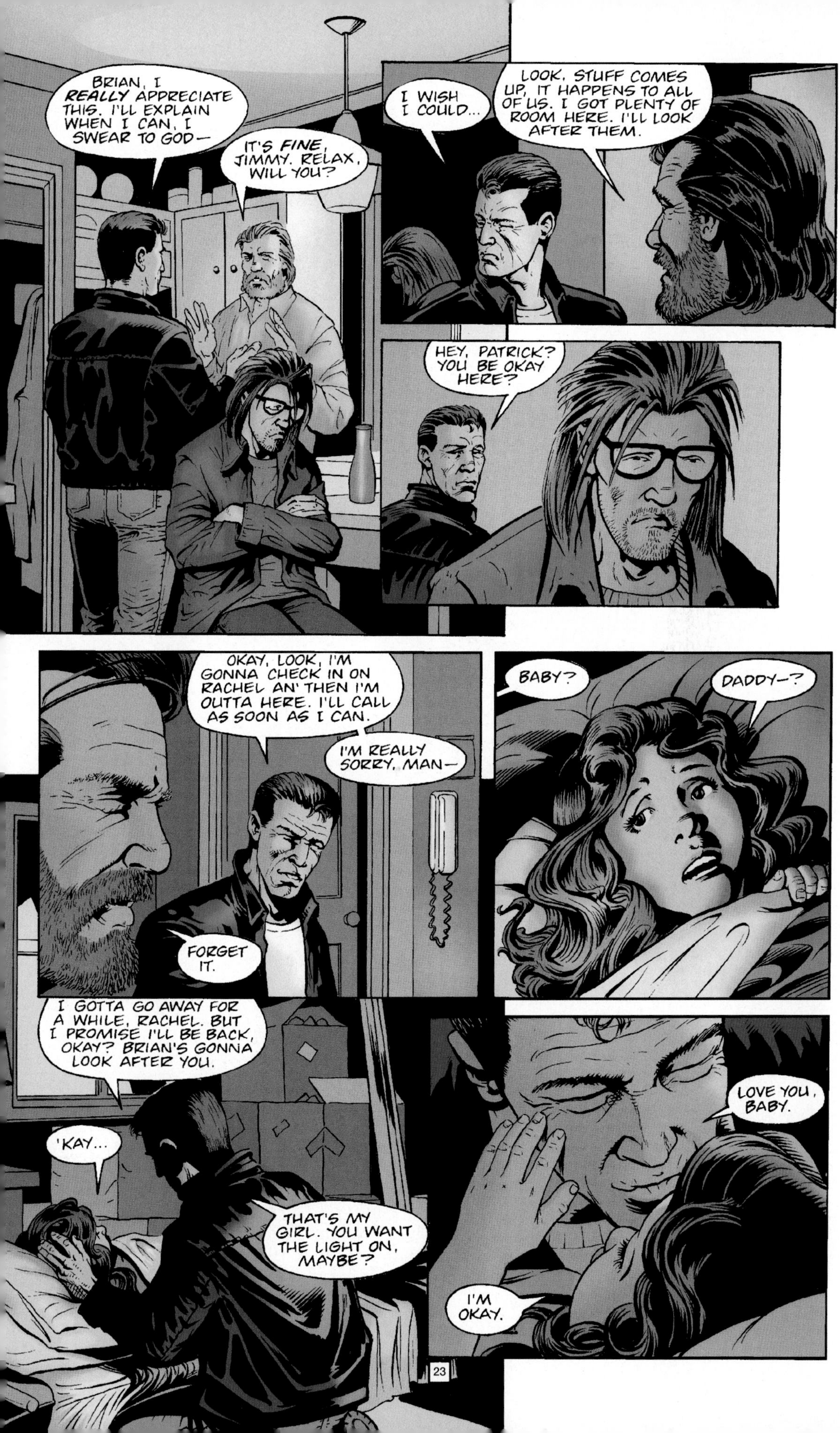
BRIAN, I *REALLY* APPRECIATE THIS. I'LL EXPLAIN WHEN I CAN, I SWEAR TO GOD—
IT'S *FINE*, JIMMY. RELAX, WILL YOU?
I WISH I COULD...
LOOK, STUFF COMES UP, IT HAPPENS TO ALL OF US. I GOT PLENTY OF ROOM HERE. I'LL LOOK AFTER THEM.
HEY, PATRICK? YOU BE OKAY HERE?
OKAY, LOOK, I'M GONNA CHECK IN ON RACHEL AN' THEN I'M OUTTA HERE. I'LL CALL AS SOON AS I CAN.
I'M REALLY SORRY, MAN—
FORGET IT.
BABY?
DADDY—?
I GOTTA GO AWAY FOR A WHILE, RACHEL. BUT I PROMISE I'LL BE BACK, OKAY? BRIAN'S GONNA LOOK AFTER YOU.
'KAY...
THAT'S MY GIRL. YOU WANT THE LIGHT ON, MAYBE?
LOVE YOU, BABY.
I'M OKAY.

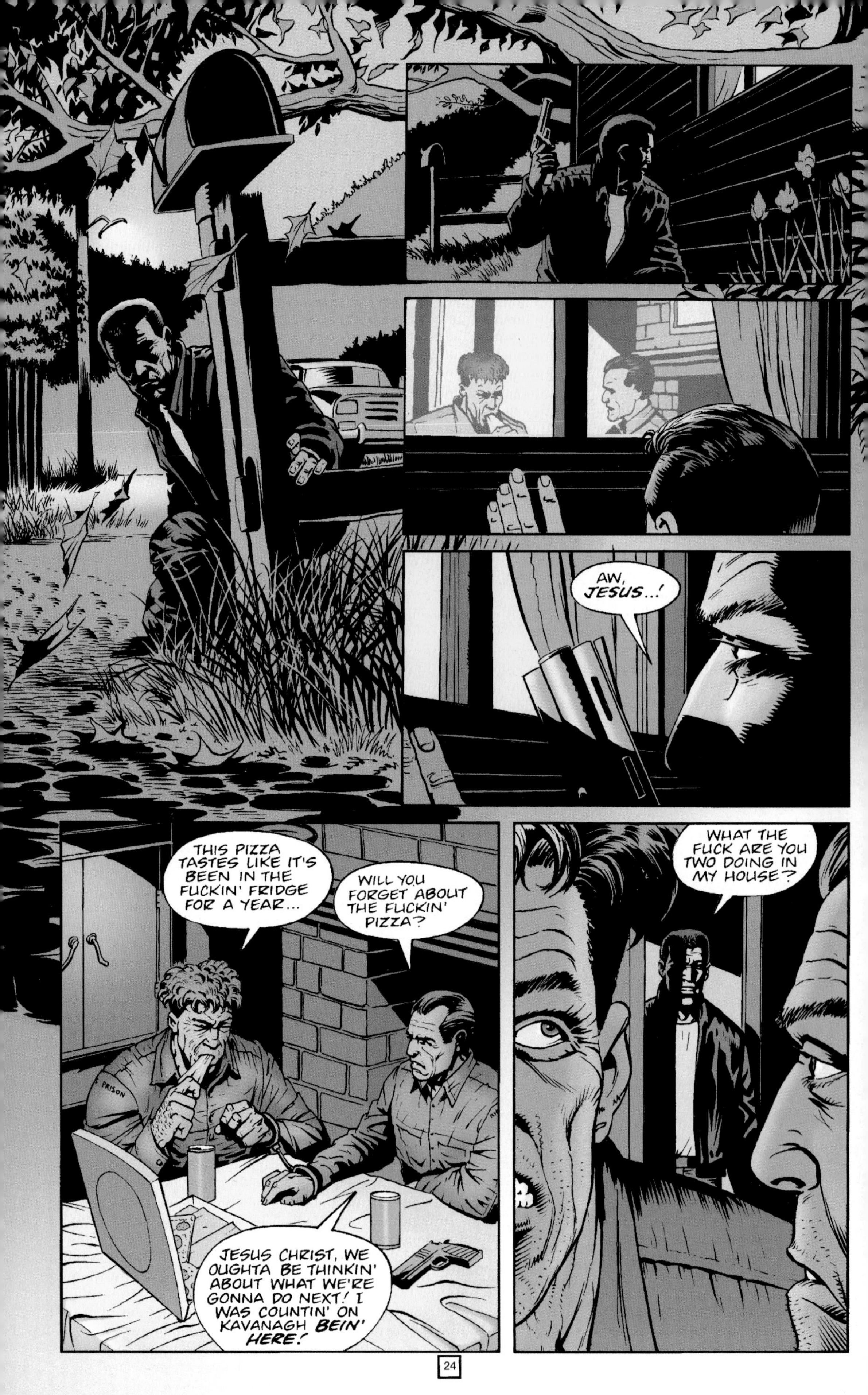
AW, JESUS...!
THIS PIZZA TASTES LIKE IT'S BEEN IN THE FUCKIN' FRIDGE FOR A YEAR...
WILL YOU FORGET ABOUT THE FUCKIN' PIZZA?
JESUS CHRIST, WE OUGHTA BE THINKIN' ABOUT WHAT WE'RE GONNA DO NEXT! I WAS COUNTIN' ON KAVANAGH BEIN' HERE!
WHAT THE FUCK ARE YOU TWO DOING IN MY HOUSE?

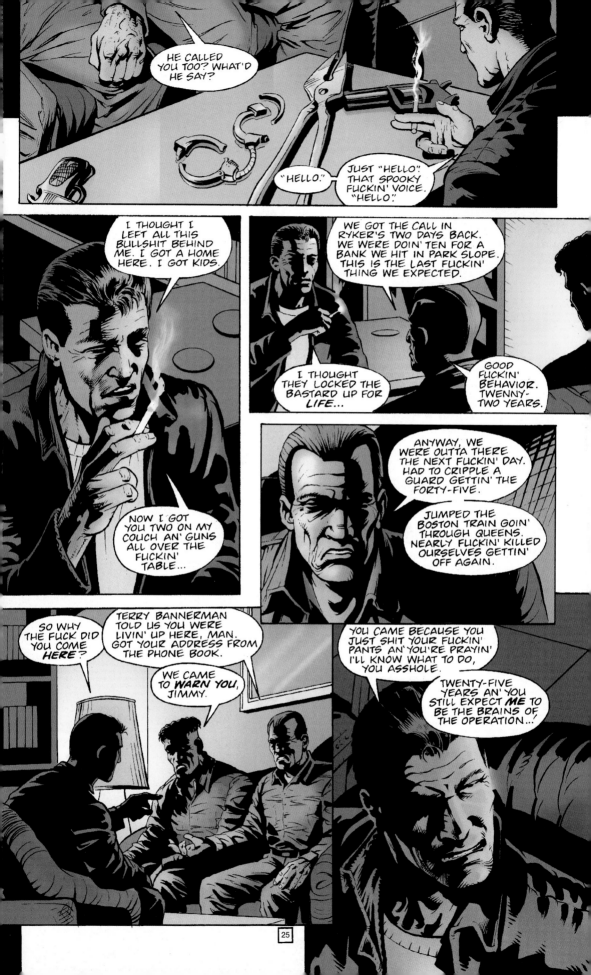

HE CALLED YOU TOO? WHAT'D HE SAY?

"HELLO."

JUST "HELLO." THAT SPOOKY FUCKIN' VOICE. "HELLO."

I THOUGHT I LEFT ALL THIS BULLSHIT BEHIND ME. I GOT A HOME HERE. I GOT KIDS.

WE GOT THE CALL IN RYKER'S TWO DAYS BACK. WE WERE DOIN' TEN FOR A BANK WE HIT IN PARK SLOPE. THIS IS THE LAST FUCKIN' THING WE EXPECTED.

I THOUGHT THEY LOCKED THE BASTARD UP FOR LIFE...

GOOD FUCKIN' BEHAVIOR. TWENNY-TWO YEARS.

NOW I GOT YOU TWO ON MY COUCH AN' GUNS ALL OVER THE FUCKIN' TABLE...

ANYWAY, WE WERE OUTTA THERE THE NEXT FUCKIN' DAY. HAD TO CRIPPLE A GUARD GETTIN' THE FORTY-FIVE.

JUMPED THE BOSTON TRAIN GOIN' THROUGH QUEENS. NEARLY FUCKIN' KILLED OURSELVES GETTIN' OFF AGAIN.

SO WHY THE FUCK DID YOU COME HERE?

TERRY BANNERMAN TOLD US YOU WERE LIVIN' UP HERE, MAN. GOT YOUR ADDRESS FROM THE PHONE BOOK.

WE CAME TO WARN YOU, JIMMY.

YOU CAME BECAUSE YOU JUST SHIT YOUR FUCKIN' PANTS AN' YOU'RE PRAYIN' I'LL KNOW WHAT TO DO, YOU ASSHOLE.

TWENTY-FIVE YEARS AN' YOU STILL EXPECT ME TO BE THE BRAINS OF THE OPERATION...!

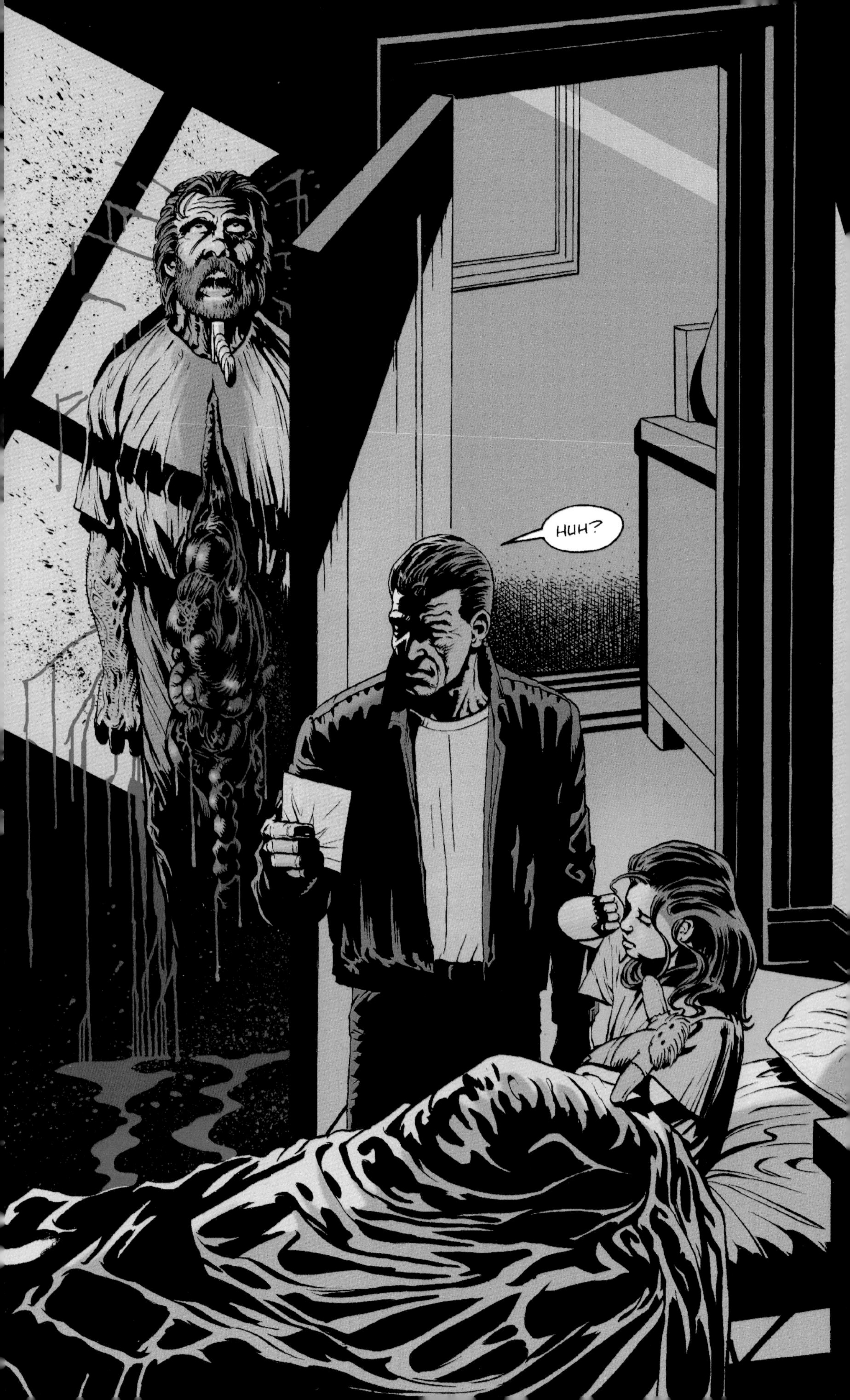
HUH?

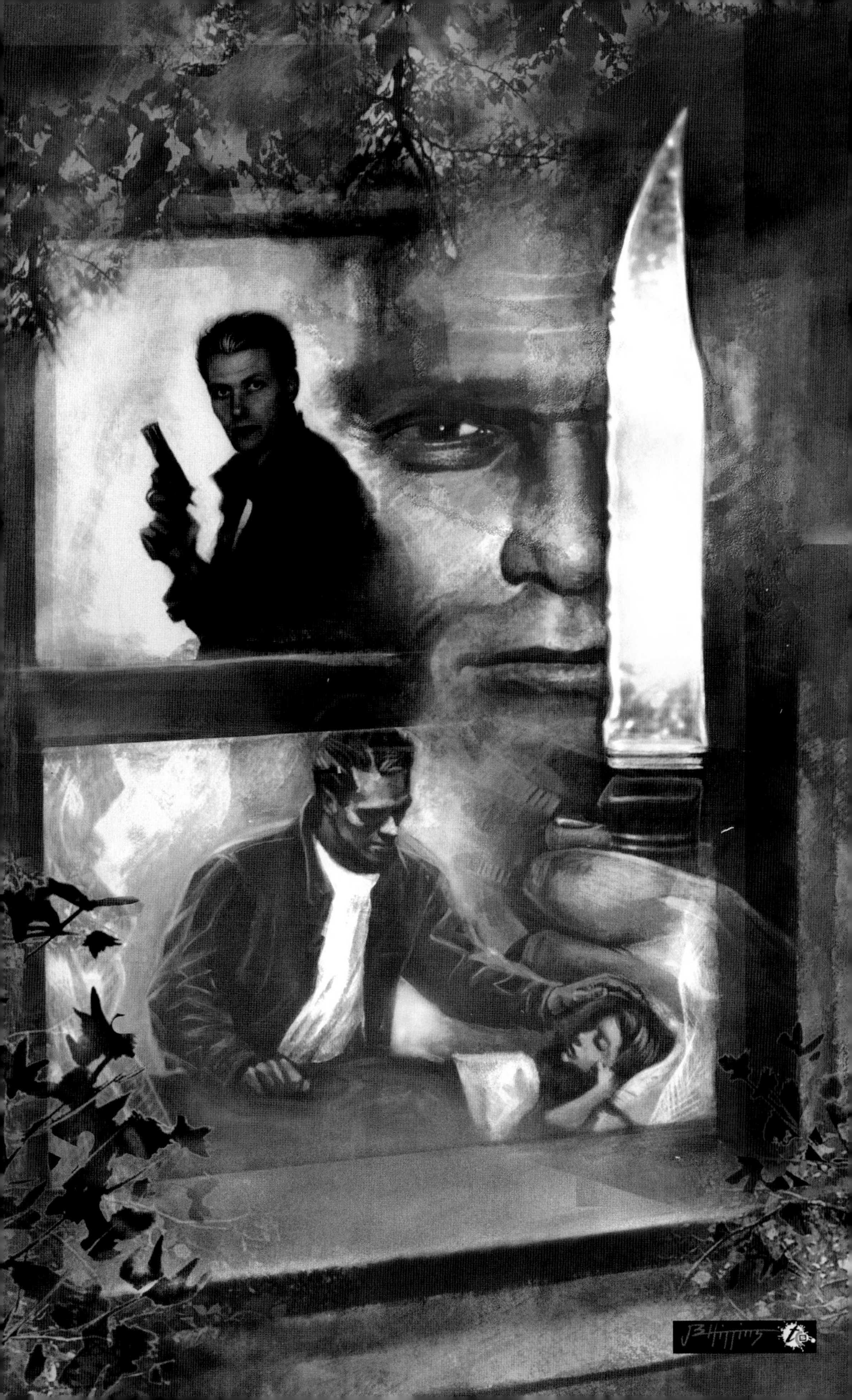

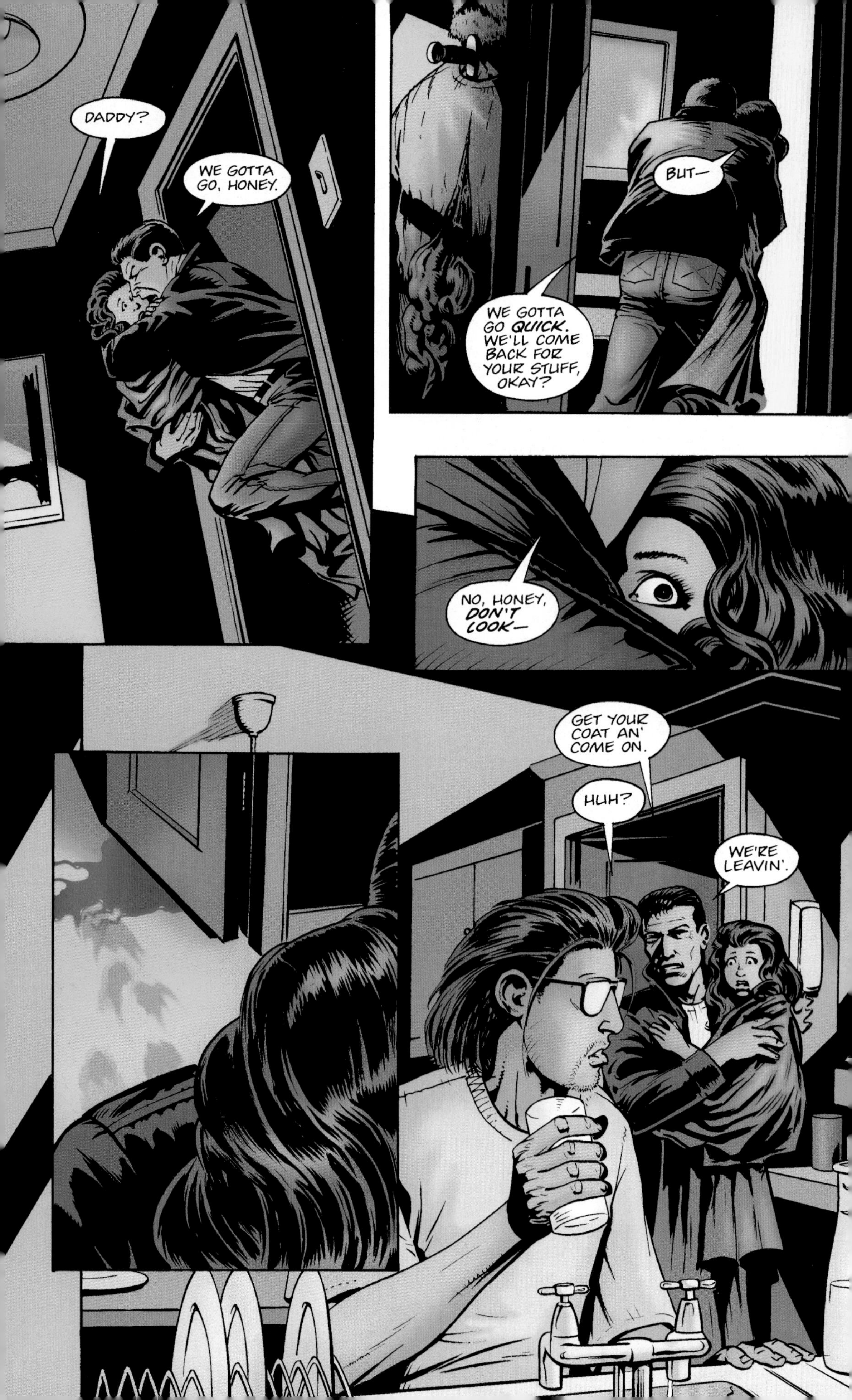
DADDY?
WE GOTTA GO, HONEY.
BUT—
WE GOTTA GO QUICK. WE'LL COME BACK FOR YOUR STUFF, OKAY?
NO, HONEY, DON'T LOOK—
GET YOUR COAT AN' COME ON.
HUH?
WE'RE LEAVIN'.

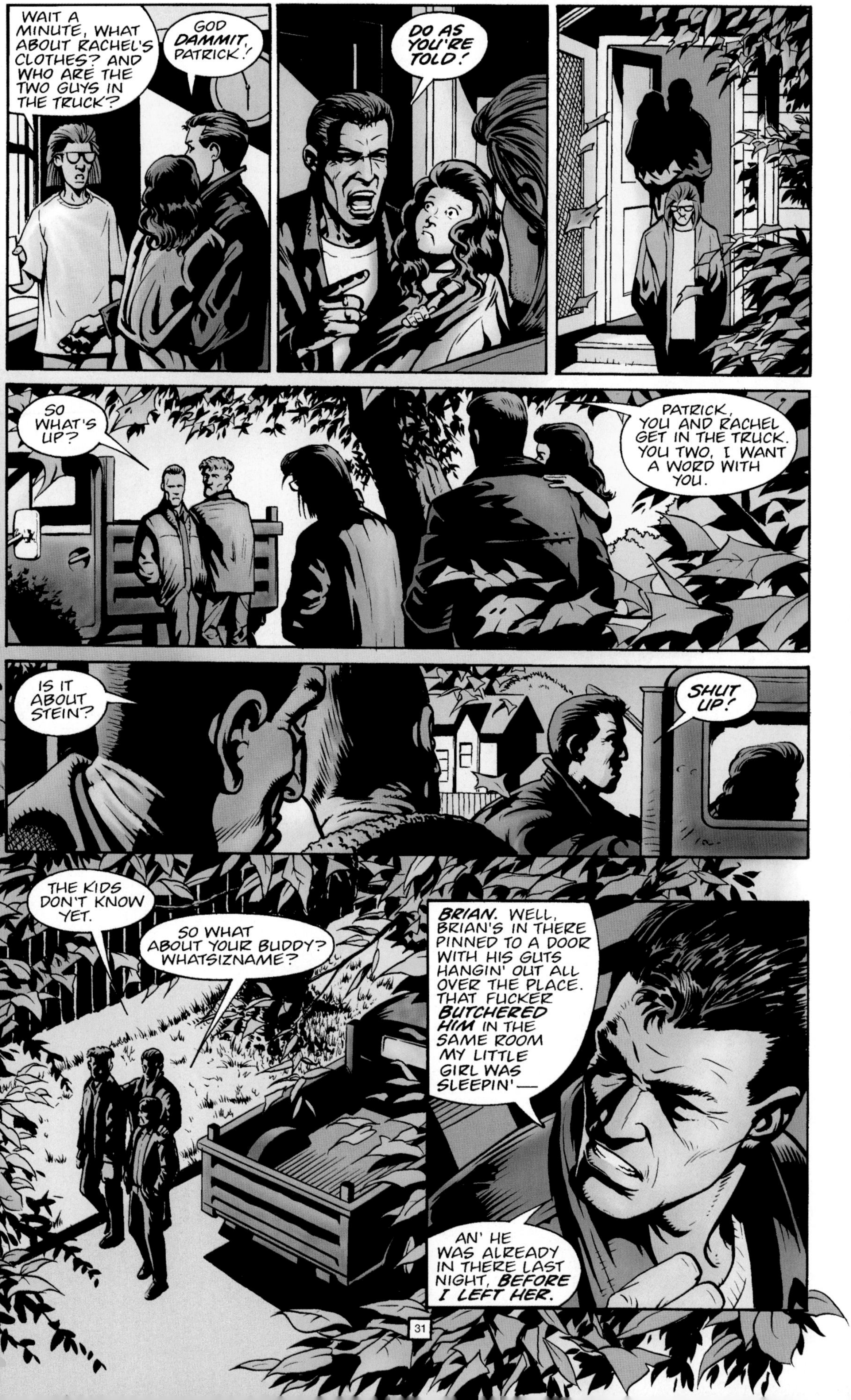
WAIT A MINUTE, WHAT ABOUT RACHEL'S CLOTHES? AND WHO ARE THE TWO GUYS IN THE TRUCK?
GOD DAMMIT, PATRICK!
DO AS YOU'RE TOLD!
SO WHAT'S UP?
PATRICK, YOU AND RACHEL GET IN THE TRUCK. YOU TWO, I WANT A WORD WITH YOU.
IS IT ABOUT STEIN?
SHUT UP!
THE KIDS DON'T KNOW YET.
SO WHAT ABOUT YOUR BUDDY? WHATSIZNAME?
BRIAN. WELL, BRIAN'S IN THERE PINNED TO A DOOR WITH HIS GUTS HANGIN' OUT ALL OVER THE PLACE. THAT FUCKER BUTCHERED HIM IN THE SAME ROOM MY LITTLE GIRL WAS SLEEPIN'—
AN' HE WAS ALREADY IN THERE LAST NIGHT, BEFORE I LEFT HER.

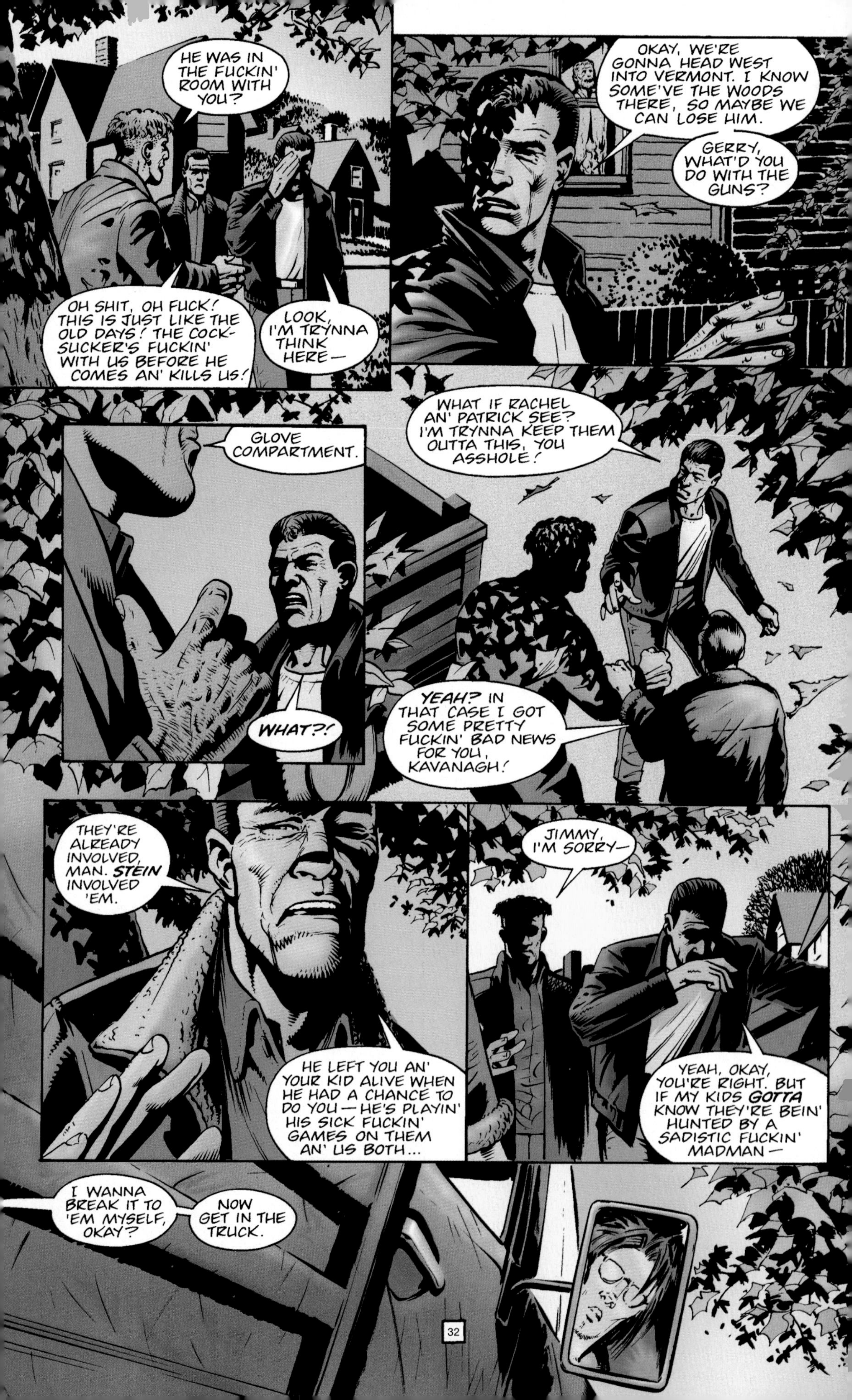
HE WAS IN THE FUCKIN' ROOM WITH YOU?
OH SHIT, OH FUCK! THIS IS JUST LIKE THE OLD DAYS! THE COCK-SUCKER'S FUCKIN' WITH US BEFORE HE COMES AN' KILLS US!
LOOK, I'M TRYNNA THINK HERE—
OKAY, WE'RE GONNA HEAD WEST INTO VERMONT. I KNOW SOME'VE THE WOODS THERE, SO MAYBE WE CAN LOSE HIM.
GERRY, WHAT'D YOU DO WITH THE GUNS?
GLOVE COMPARTMENT.
WHAT?!
WHAT IF RACHEL AN' PATRICK SEE? I'M TRYNNA KEEP THEM OUTTA THIS, YOU ASSHOLE!
YEAH? IN THAT CASE I GOT SOME PRETTY FUCKIN' BAD NEWS FOR YOU, KAVANAGH!
THEY'RE ALREADY INVOLVED, MAN. STEIN INVOLVED 'EM.
HE LEFT YOU AN' YOUR KID ALIVE WHEN HE HAD A CHANCE TO DO YOU—HE'S PLAYIN' HIS SICK FUCKIN' GAMES ON THEM AN' US BOTH...
JIMMY, I'M SORRY—
YEAH, OKAY, YOU'RE RIGHT. BUT IF MY KIDS GOTTA KNOW THEY'RE BEIN' HUNTED BY A SADISTIC FUCKIN' MADMAN—
I WANNA BREAK IT TO 'EM MYSELF, OKAY?
NOW GET IN THE TRUCK.

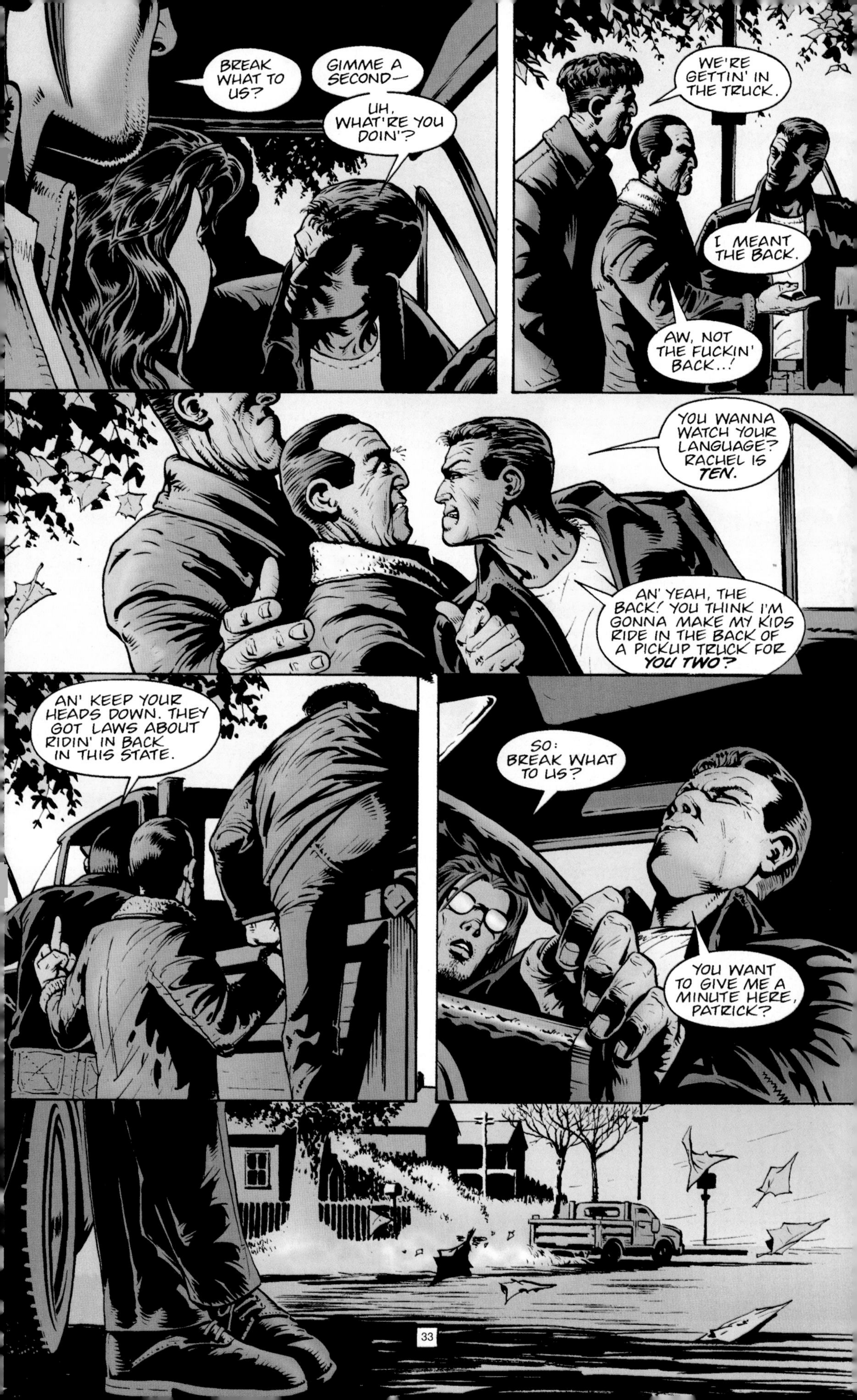
BREAK WHAT TO US?
GIMME A SECOND—
UH, WHAT'RE YOU DOIN'?
WE'RE GETTIN' IN THE TRUCK.
I MEANT THE BACK.
AW, NOT THE FUCKIN' BACK...!
YOU WANNA WATCH YOUR LANGUAGE? RACHEL IS TEN.
AN' YEAH, THE BACK! YOU THINK I'M GONNA MAKE MY KIDS RIDE IN THE BACK OF A PICKUP TRUCK FOR YOU TWO?
AN' KEEP YOUR HEADS DOWN. THEY GOT LAWS ABOUT RIDIN' IN BACK IN THIS STATE.
SO: BREAK WHAT TO US?
YOU WANT TO GIVE ME A MINUTE HERE, PATRICK?

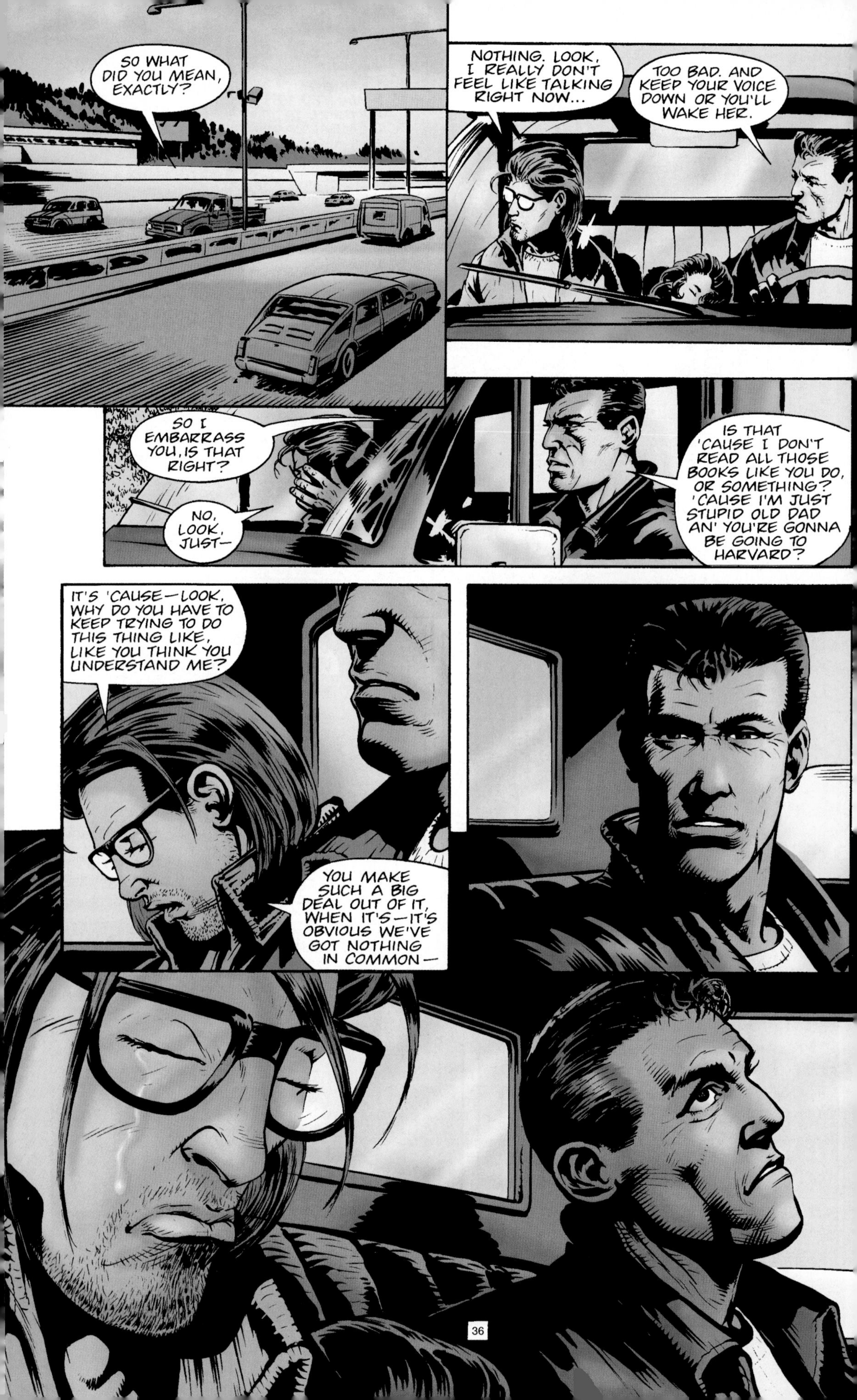
SO WHAT DID YOU MEAN, EXACTLY?
NOTHING. LOOK, I REALLY DON'T FEEL LIKE TALKING RIGHT NOW...
TOO BAD. AND KEEP YOUR VOICE DOWN OR YOU'LL WAKE HER.
SO I EMBARRASS YOU, IS THAT RIGHT?
NO, LOOK, JUST—
IS THAT 'CAUSE I DON'T READ ALL THOSE BOOKS LIKE YOU DO, OR SOMETHING? 'CAUSE I'M JUST STUPID OLD DAD AN' YOU'RE GONNA BE GOING TO HARVARD?
IT'S 'CAUSE—LOOK, WHY DO YOU HAVE TO KEEP TRYING TO DO THIS THING LIKE, LIKE YOU THINK YOU UNDERSTAND ME?
YOU MAKE SUCH A BIG DEAL OUT OF IT, WHEN IT'S—IT'S OBVIOUS WE'VE GOT NOTHING IN COMMON—

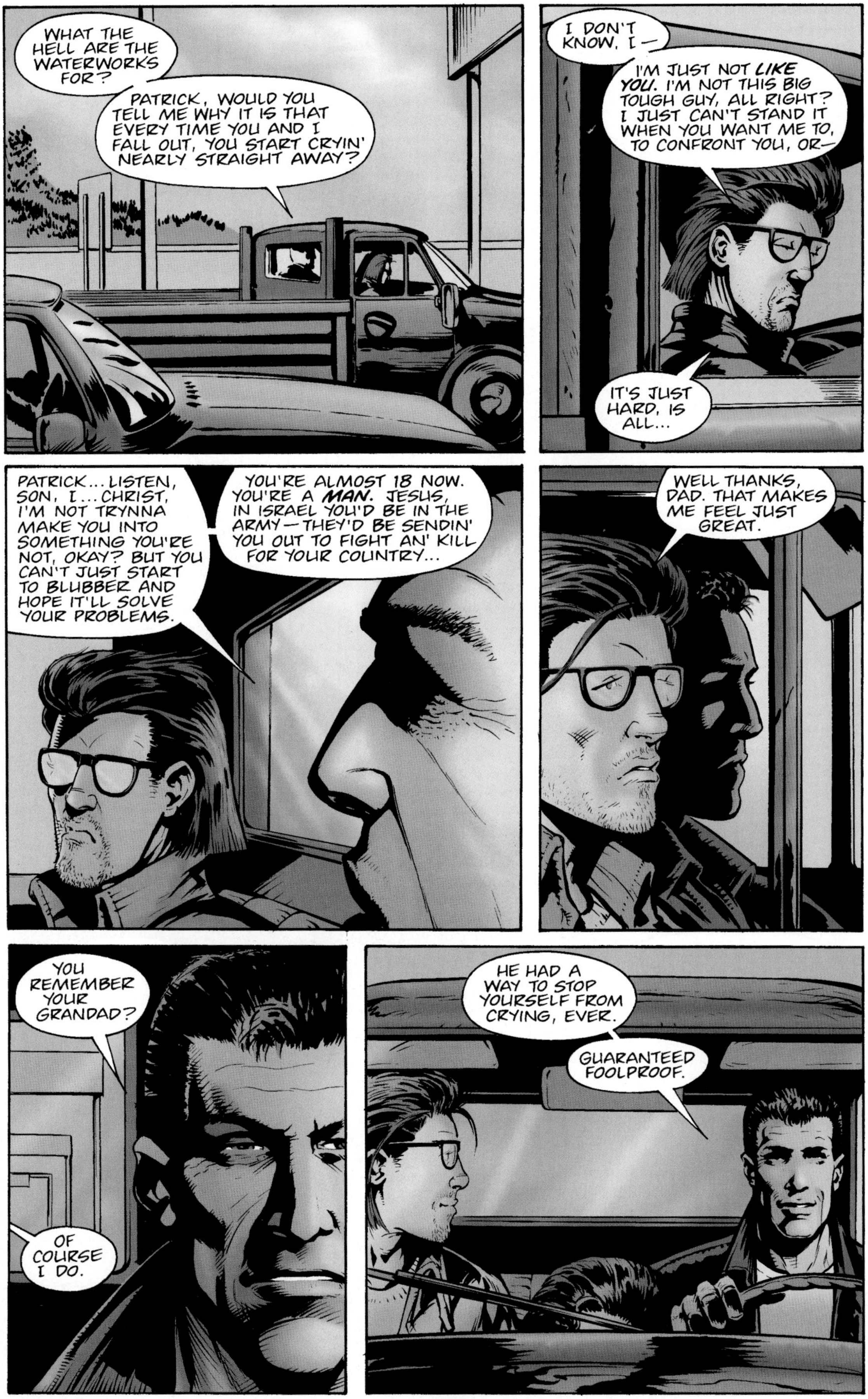
WHAT THE HELL ARE THE WATERWORKS FOR?
PATRICK, WOULD YOU TELL ME WHY IT IS THAT EVERY TIME YOU AND I FALL OUT, YOU START CRYIN' NEARLY STRAIGHT AWAY?
I DON'T KNOW. I—
I'M JUST NOT LIKE YOU. I'M NOT THIS BIG TOUGH GUY, ALL RIGHT? I JUST CAN'T STAND IT WHEN YOU WANT ME TO, TO CONFRONT YOU, OR—
IT'S JUST HARD, IS ALL...
PATRICK... LISTEN, SON, I... CHRIST, I'M NOT TRYNNA MAKE YOU INTO SOMETHING YOU'RE NOT, OKAY? BUT YOU CAN'T JUST START TO BLUBBER AND HOPE IT'LL SOLVE YOUR PROBLEMS.
YOU'RE ALMOST 18 NOW. YOU'RE A MAN. JESUS, IN ISRAEL YOU'D BE IN THE ARMY—THEY'D BE SENDIN' YOU OUT TO FIGHT AN' KILL FOR YOUR COUNTRY...
WELL THANKS, DAD. THAT MAKES ME FEEL JUST GREAT.
YOU REMEMBER YOUR GRANDAD?
OF COURSE I DO.
HE HAD A WAY TO STOP YOURSELF FROM CRYING, EVER.
GUARANTEED FOOLPROOF.

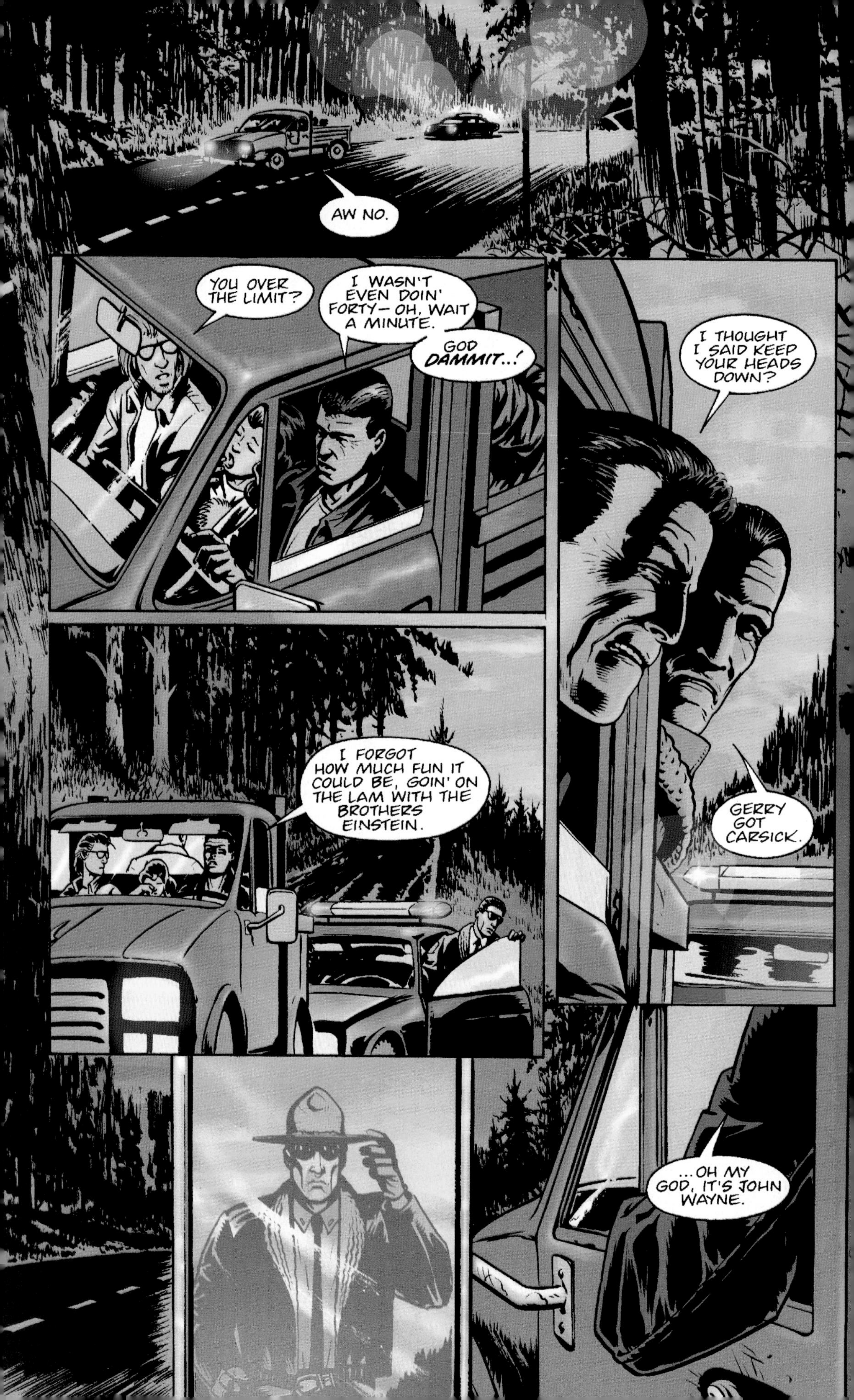
AW NO.
YOU OVER THE LIMIT?
I WASN'T EVEN DOIN' FORTY— OH, WAIT A MINUTE.
GOD DAMMIT..!
I THOUGHT I SAID KEEP YOUR HEADS DOWN?
GERRY GOT CARSICK.
I FORGOT HOW MUCH FUN IT COULD BE, GOIN' ON THE LAM WITH THE BROTHERS EINSTEIN.
...OH MY GOD, IT'S JOHN WAYNE.

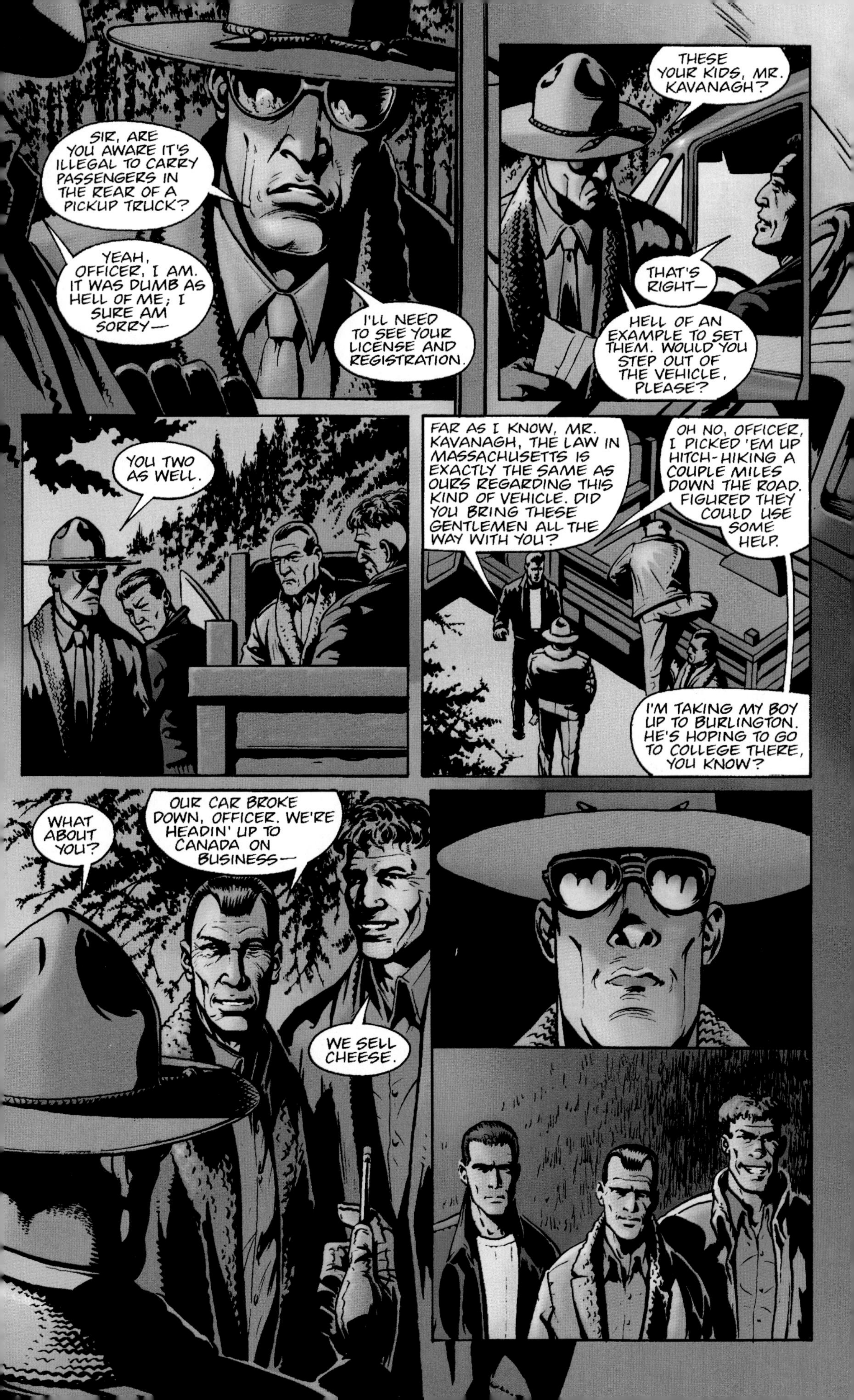
SIR, ARE YOU AWARE IT'S ILLEGAL TO CARRY PASSENGERS IN THE REAR OF A PICKUP TRUCK?
YEAH, OFFICER, I AM. IT WAS DUMB AS HELL OF ME; I SURE AM SORRY—
I'LL NEED TO SEE YOUR LICENSE AND REGISTRATION.
THESE YOUR KIDS, MR. KAVANAGH?
THAT'S RIGHT—
HELL OF AN EXAMPLE TO SET THEM. WOULD YOU STEP OUT OF THE VEHICLE, PLEASE?
YOU TWO AS WELL.
FAR AS I KNOW, MR. KAVANAGH, THE LAW IN MASSACHUSETTS IS EXACTLY THE SAME AS OURS REGARDING THIS KIND OF VEHICLE. DID YOU BRING THESE GENTLEMEN ALL THE WAY WITH YOU?
OH NO, OFFICER, I PICKED 'EM UP HITCH-HIKING A COUPLE MILES DOWN THE ROAD. FIGURED THEY COULD USE SOME HELP.
I'M TAKING MY BOY UP TO BURLINGTON. HE'S HOPING TO GO TO COLLEGE THERE, YOU KNOW?
WHAT ABOUT YOU?
OUR CAR BROKE DOWN, OFFICER. WE'RE HEADIN' UP TO CANADA ON BUSINESS—
WE SELL CHEESE.

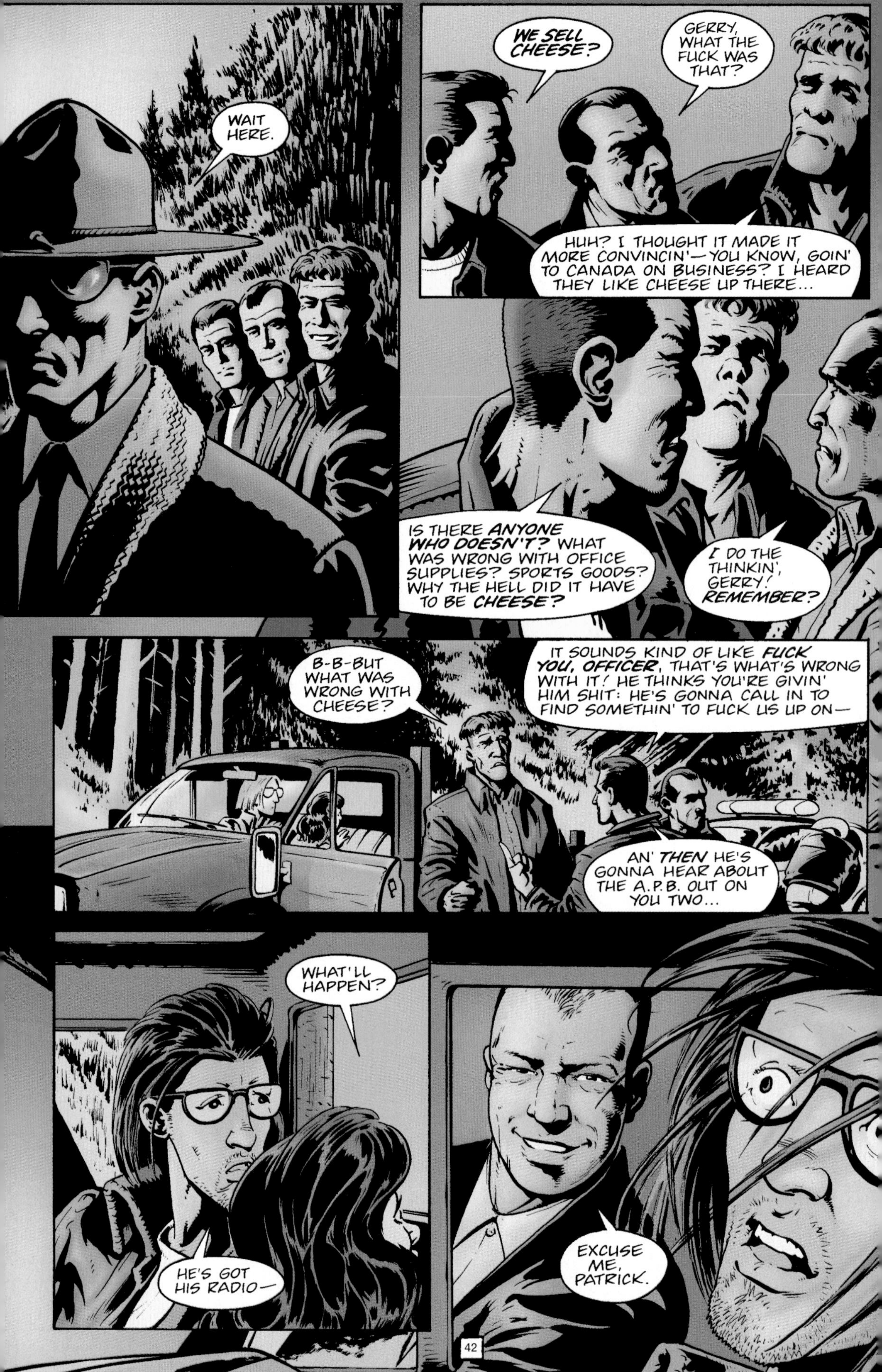
WAIT HERE.
WE SELL CHEESE?
GERRY, WHAT THE FUCK WAS THAT?
HUH? I THOUGHT IT MADE IT MORE CONVINCIN'—YOU KNOW, GOIN' TO CANADA ON BUSINESS? I HEARD THEY LIKE CHEESE UP THERE...
IS THERE ANYONE WHO DOESN'T? WHAT WAS WRONG WITH OFFICE SUPPLIES? SPORTS GOODS? WHY THE HELL DID IT HAVE TO BE CHEESE?
I DO THE THINKIN', GERRY! REMEMBER?
B-B-BUT WHAT WAS WRONG WITH CHEESE?
IT SOUNDS KIND OF LIKE FUCK YOU, OFFICER, THAT'S WHAT'S WRONG WITH IT! HE THINKS YOU'RE GIVIN' HIM SHIT: HE'S GONNA CALL IN TO FIND SOMETHIN' TO FUCK US UP ON—
AN' THEN HE'S GONNA HEAR ABOUT THE A.P.B. OUT ON YOU TWO...
WHAT'LL HAPPEN?
HE'S GOT HIS RADIO—
EXCUSE ME, PATRICK.

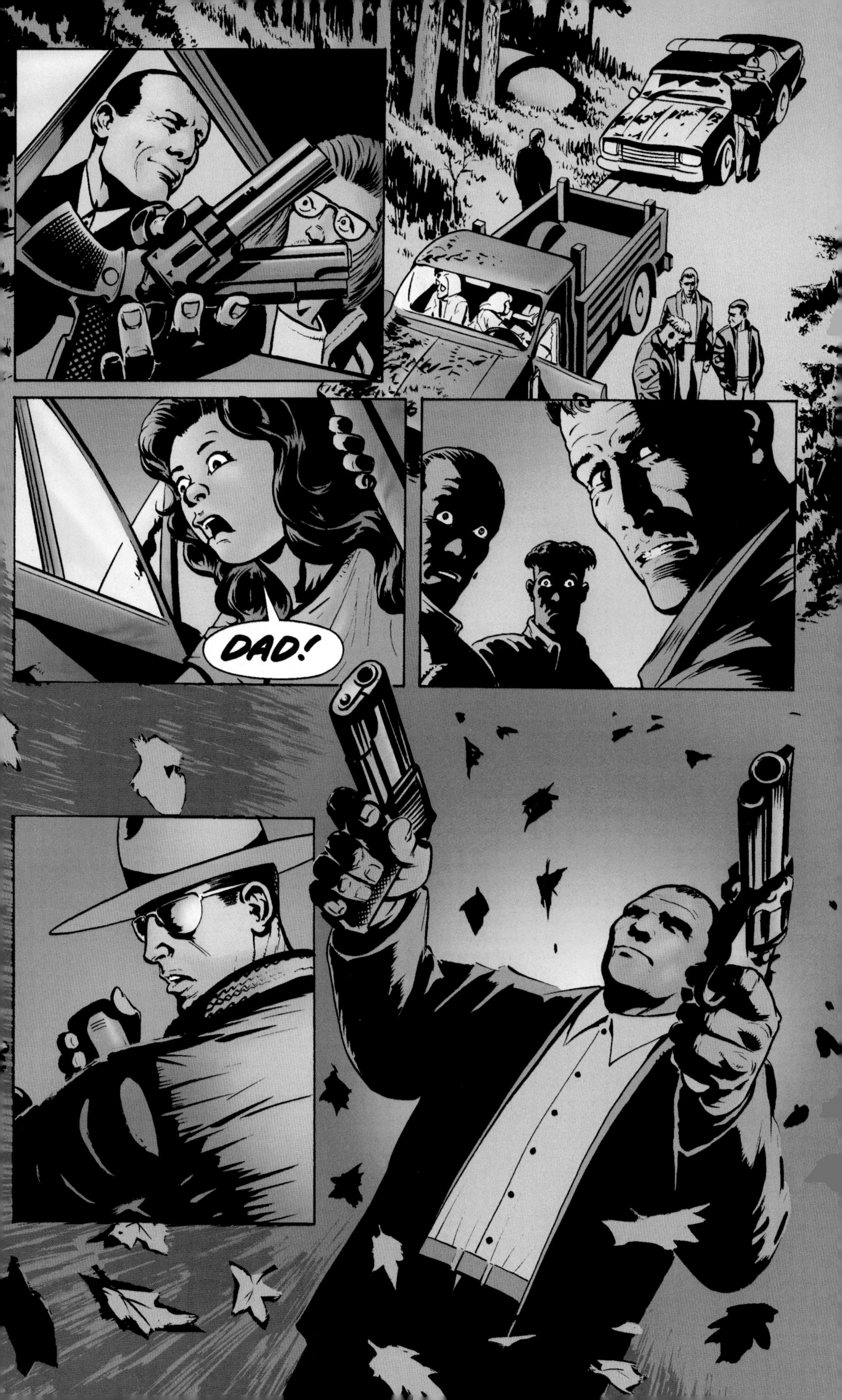
DAD!

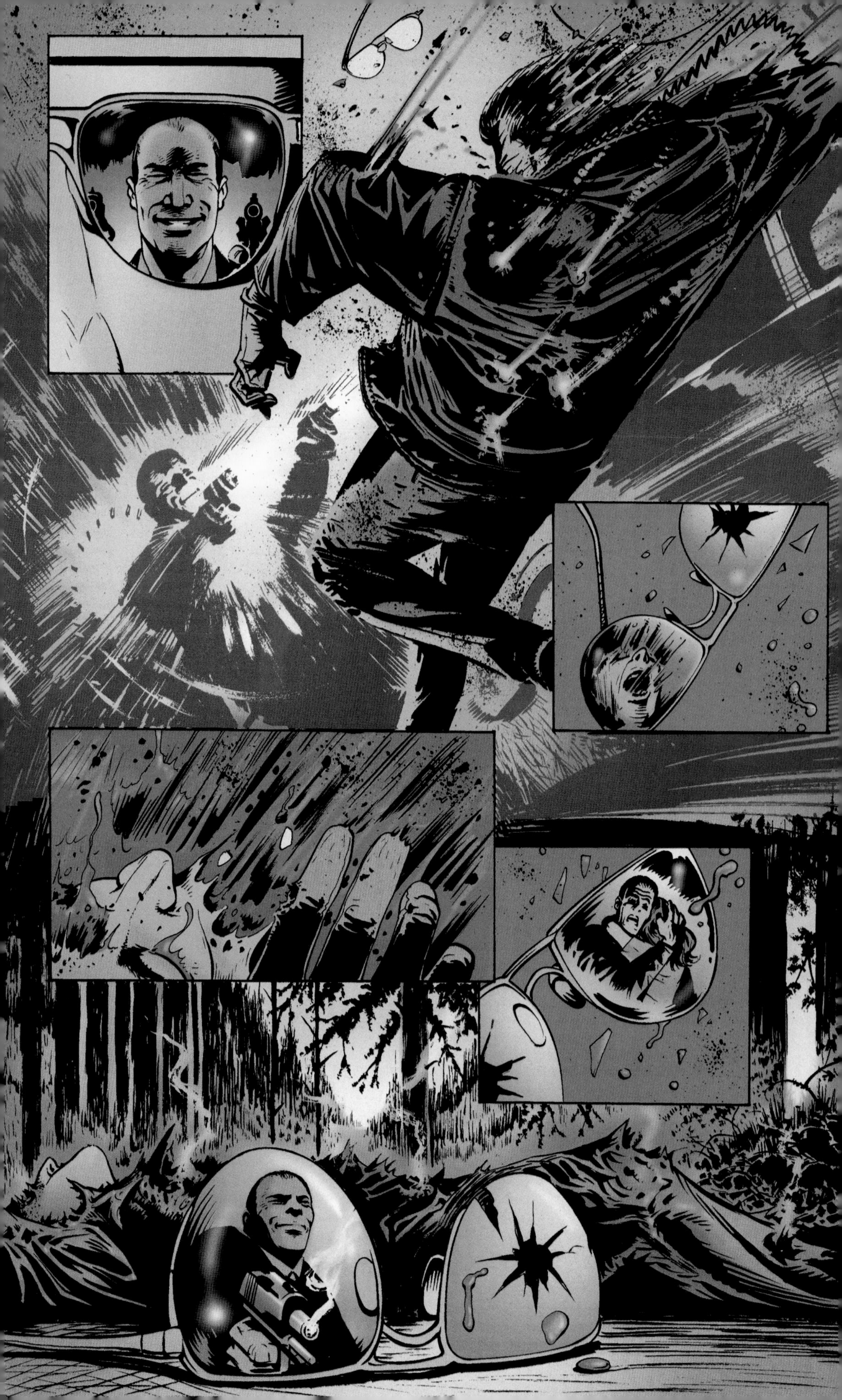

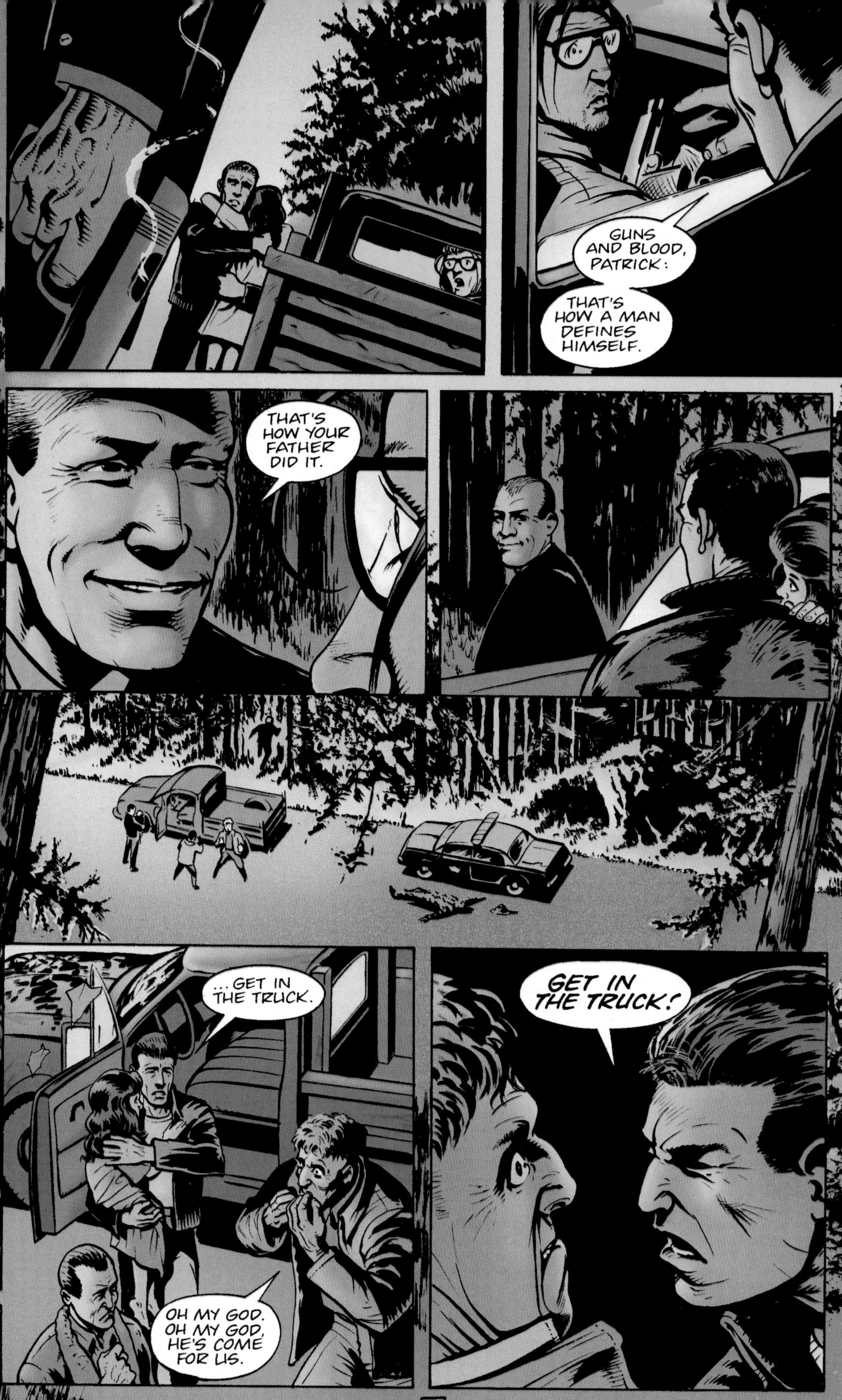
GUNS AND BLOOD, PATRICK:
THAT'S HOW A MAN DEFINES HIMSELF.
THAT'S HOW YOUR FATHER DID IT.
...GET IN THE TRUCK.
OH MY GOD. OH MY GOD, HE'S COME FOR US.
GET IN THE TRUCK!

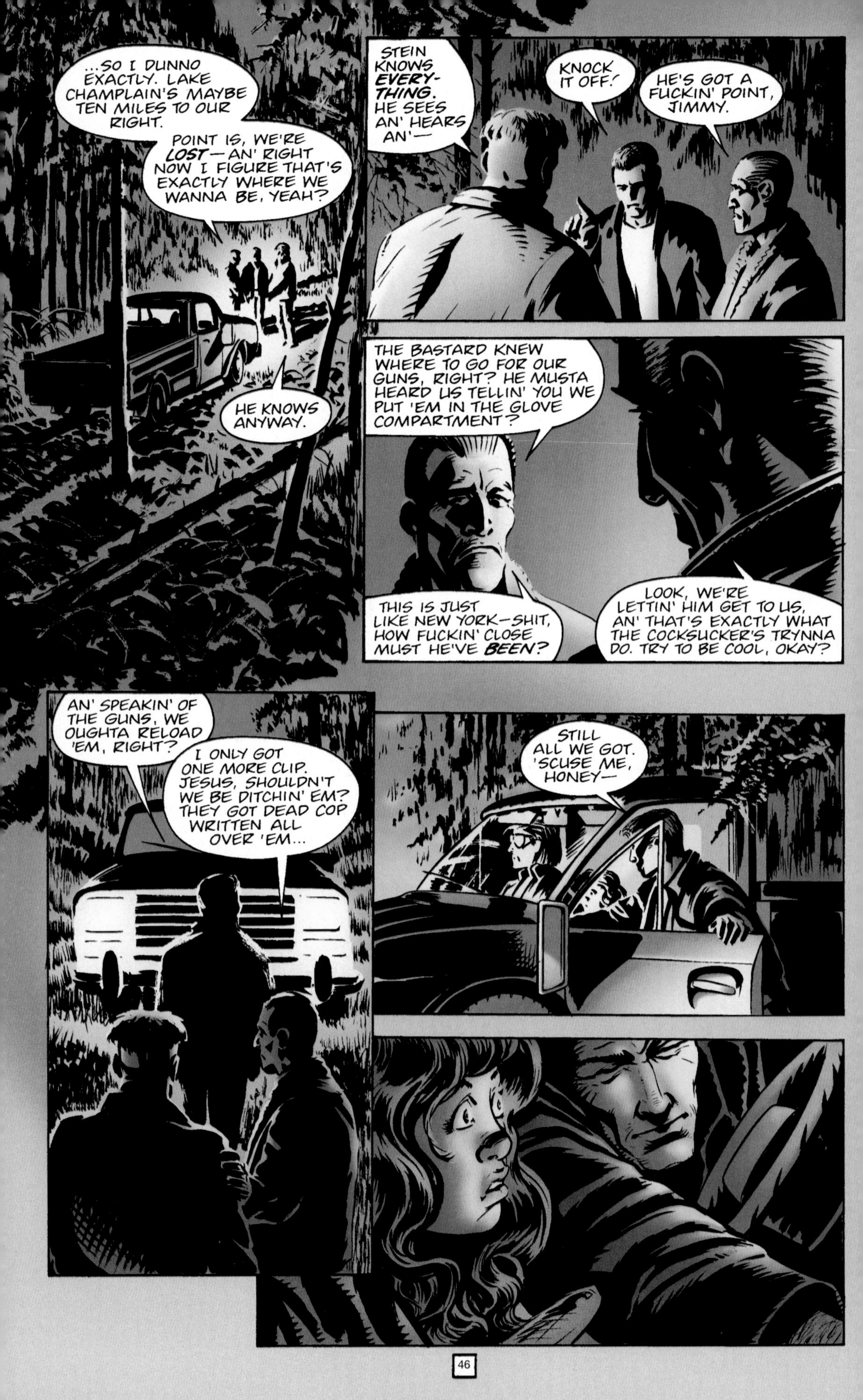
...SO I DUNNO EXACTLY. LAKE CHAMPLAIN'S MAYBE TEN MILES TO OUR RIGHT.
POINT IS, WE'RE LOST— AN' RIGHT NOW I FIGURE THAT'S EXACTLY WHERE WE WANNA BE, YEAH?
HE KNOWS ANYWAY.
STEIN KNOWS EVERYTHING. HE SEES AN' HEARS AN'—
KNOCK IT OFF!
HE'S GOT A FUCKIN' POINT, JIMMY.
THE BASTARD KNEW WHERE TO GO FOR OUR GUNS, RIGHT? HE MUSTA HEARD US TELLIN' YOU WE PUT 'EM IN THE GLOVE COMPARTMENT?
THIS IS JUST LIKE NEW YORK—SHIT, HOW FUCKIN' CLOSE MUST HE'VE BEEN?
LOOK, WE'RE LETTIN' HIM GET TO US, AN' THAT'S EXACTLY WHAT THE COCKSUCKER'S TRYNNA DO. TRY TO BE COOL, OKAY?
AN' SPEAKIN' OF THE GUNS, WE OUGHTA RELOAD 'EM, RIGHT?
I ONLY GOT ONE MORE CLIP. JESUS, SHOULDN'T WE BE DITCHIN' EM? THEY GOT DEAD COP WRITTEN ALL OVER 'EM...
STILL ALL WE GOT. 'SCUSE ME, HONEY—

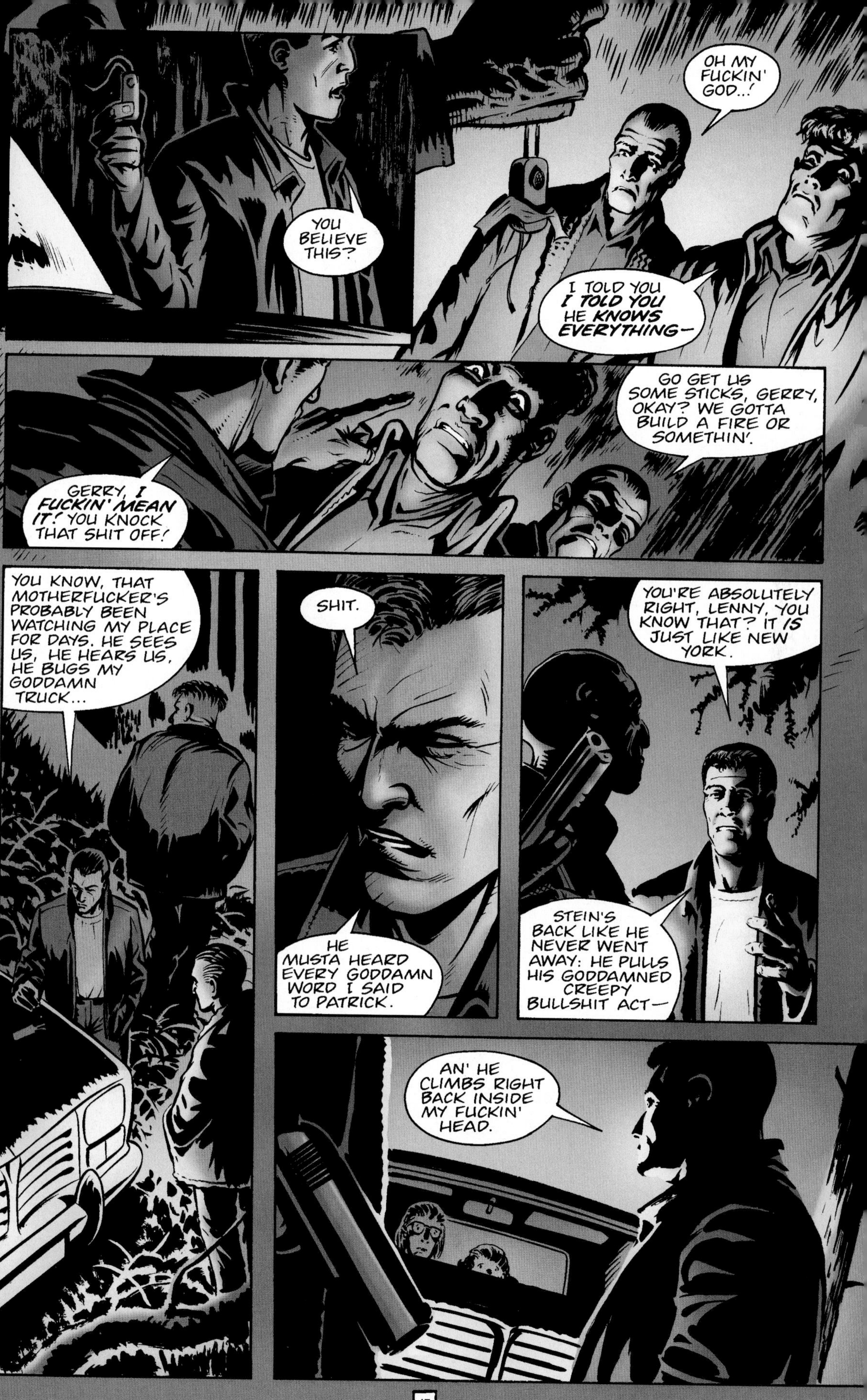

YOU BELIEVE THIS?
OH MY FUCKIN' GOD...!
I TOLD YOU I TOLD YOU HE KNOWS EVERYTHING—
GO GET US SOME STICKS, GERRY, OKAY? WE GOTTA BUILD A FIRE OR SOMETHIN'.
GERRY, I FUCKIN' MEAN IT! YOU KNOCK THAT SHIT OFF!
YOU KNOW, THAT MOTHERFUCKER'S PROBABLY BEEN WATCHING MY PLACE FOR DAYS. HE SEES US, HE HEARS US, HE BUGS MY GODDAMN TRUCK...
SHIT.
HE MUSTA HEARD EVERY GODDAMN WORD I SAID TO PATRICK.
YOU'RE ABSOLUTELY RIGHT, LENNY, YOU KNOW THAT? IT IS JUST LIKE NEW YORK.
STEIN'S BACK LIKE HE NEVER WENT AWAY: HE PULLS HIS GODDAMNED CREEPY BULLSHIT ACT—
AN' HE CLIMBS RIGHT BACK INSIDE MY FUCKIN' HEAD.

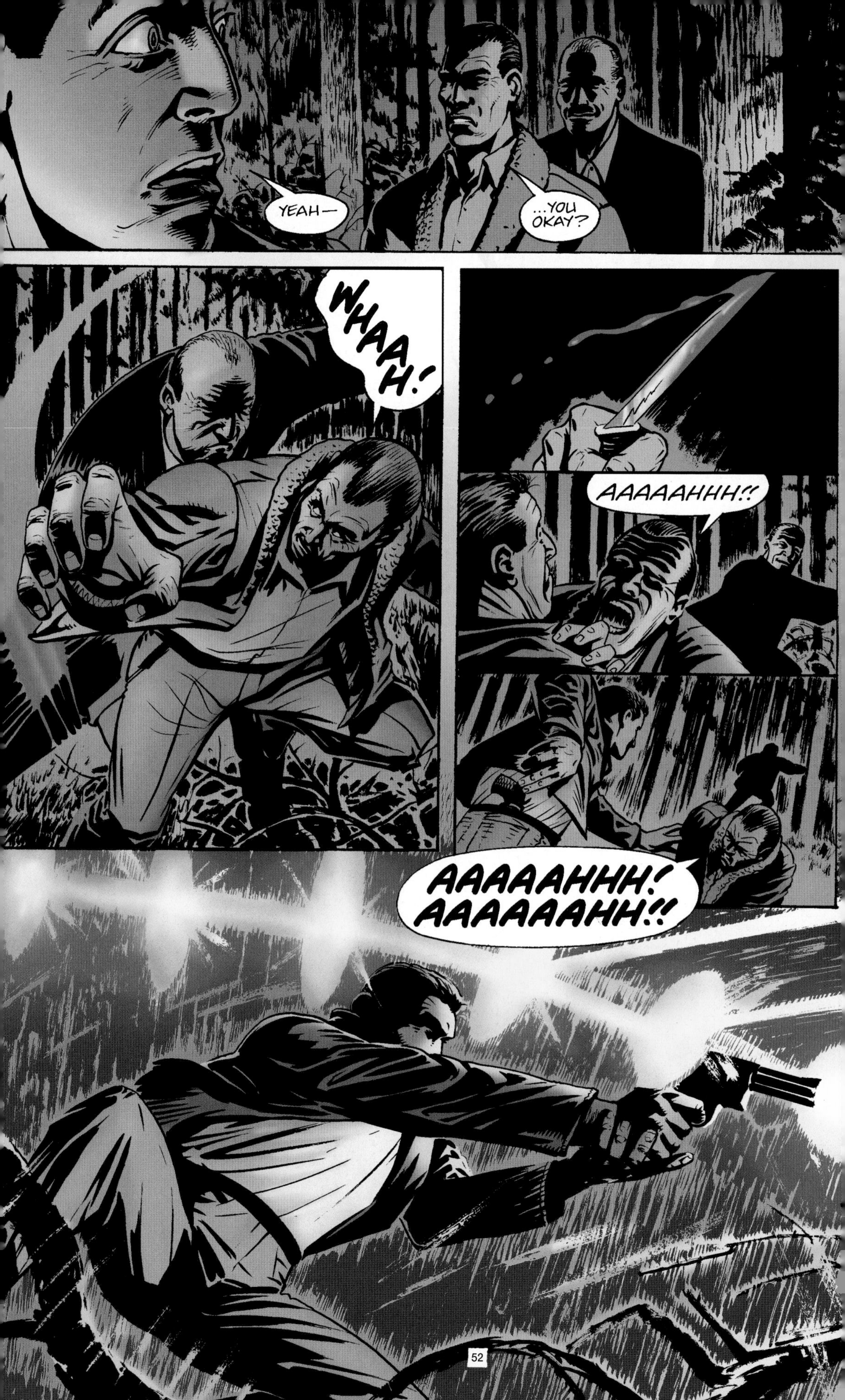
YEAH—
...YOU OKAY?
WHAAAH!
AAAAAHHH!?!
AAAAAHHH!
AAAAAAHH!?!

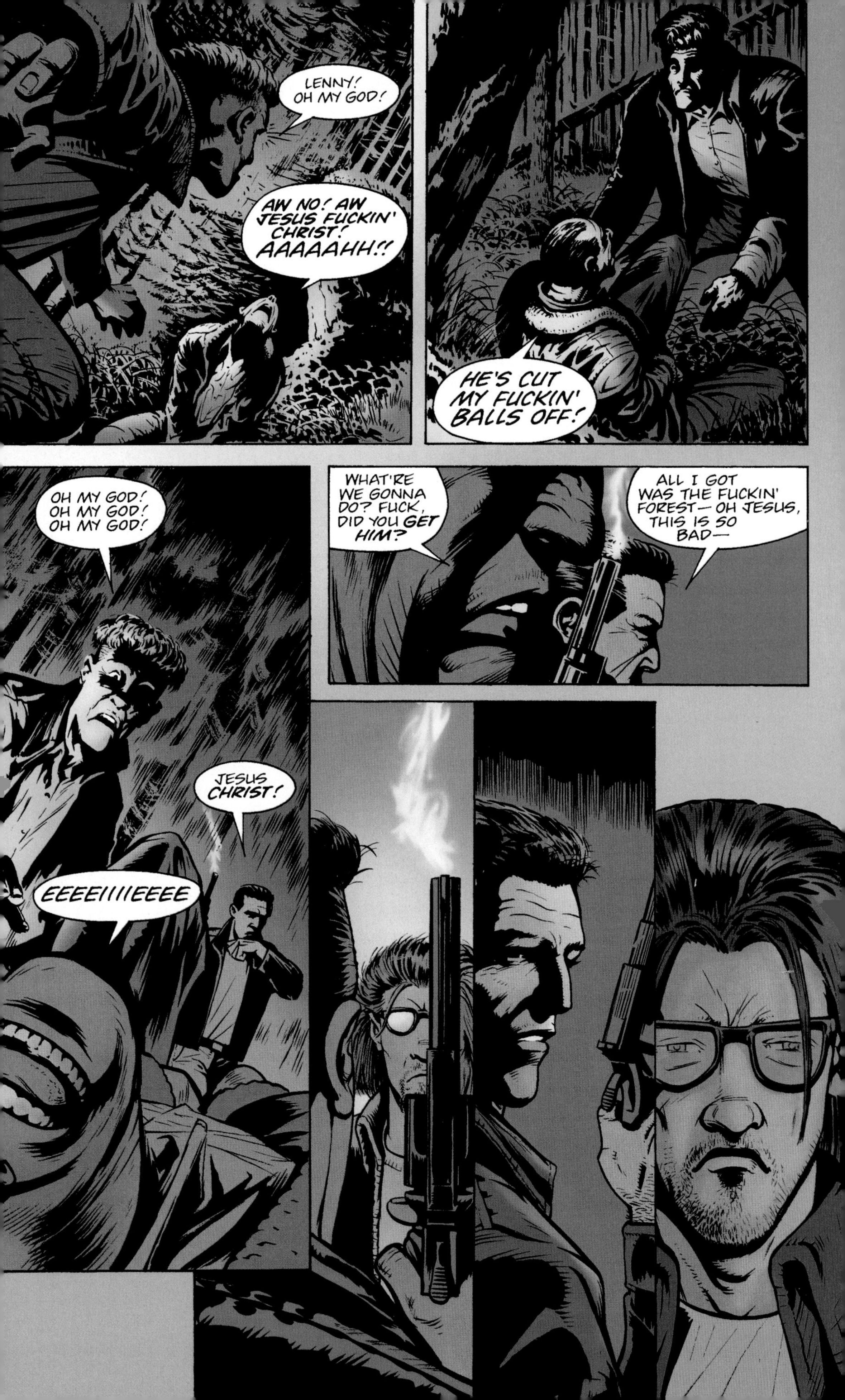
LENNY! OH MY GOD!
AW NO! AW JESUS FUCKIN' CHRIST! AAAAAHH!!
HE'S CUT MY FUCKIN' BALLS OFF!
OH MY GOD! OH MY GOD! OH MY GOD!
JESUS CHRIST!
EEEEIIIIEEEE
WHAT'RE WE GONNA DO? FUCK, DID YOU GET HIM?
ALL I GOT WAS THE FUCKIN' FOREST— OH JESUS, THIS IS SO BAD—

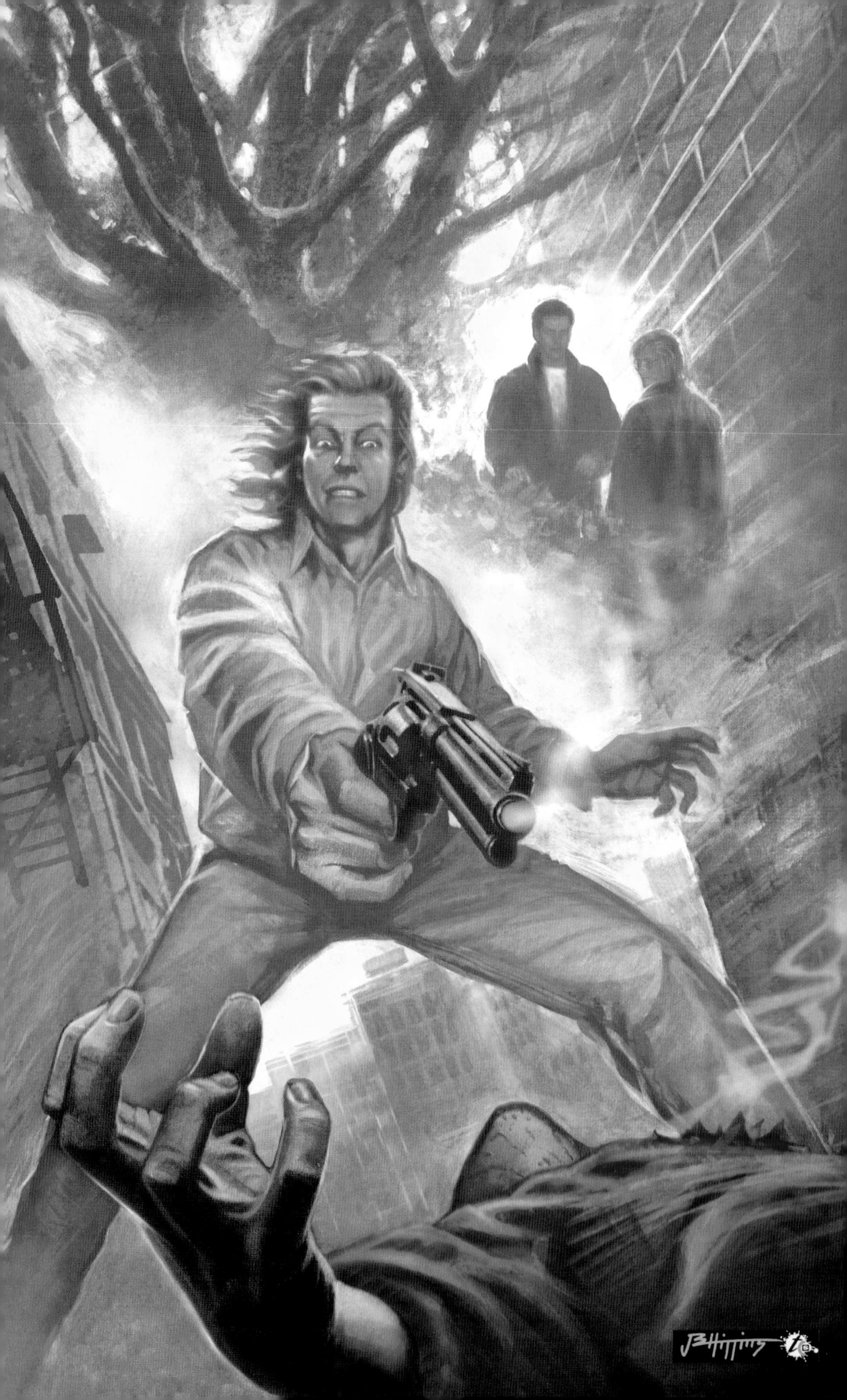

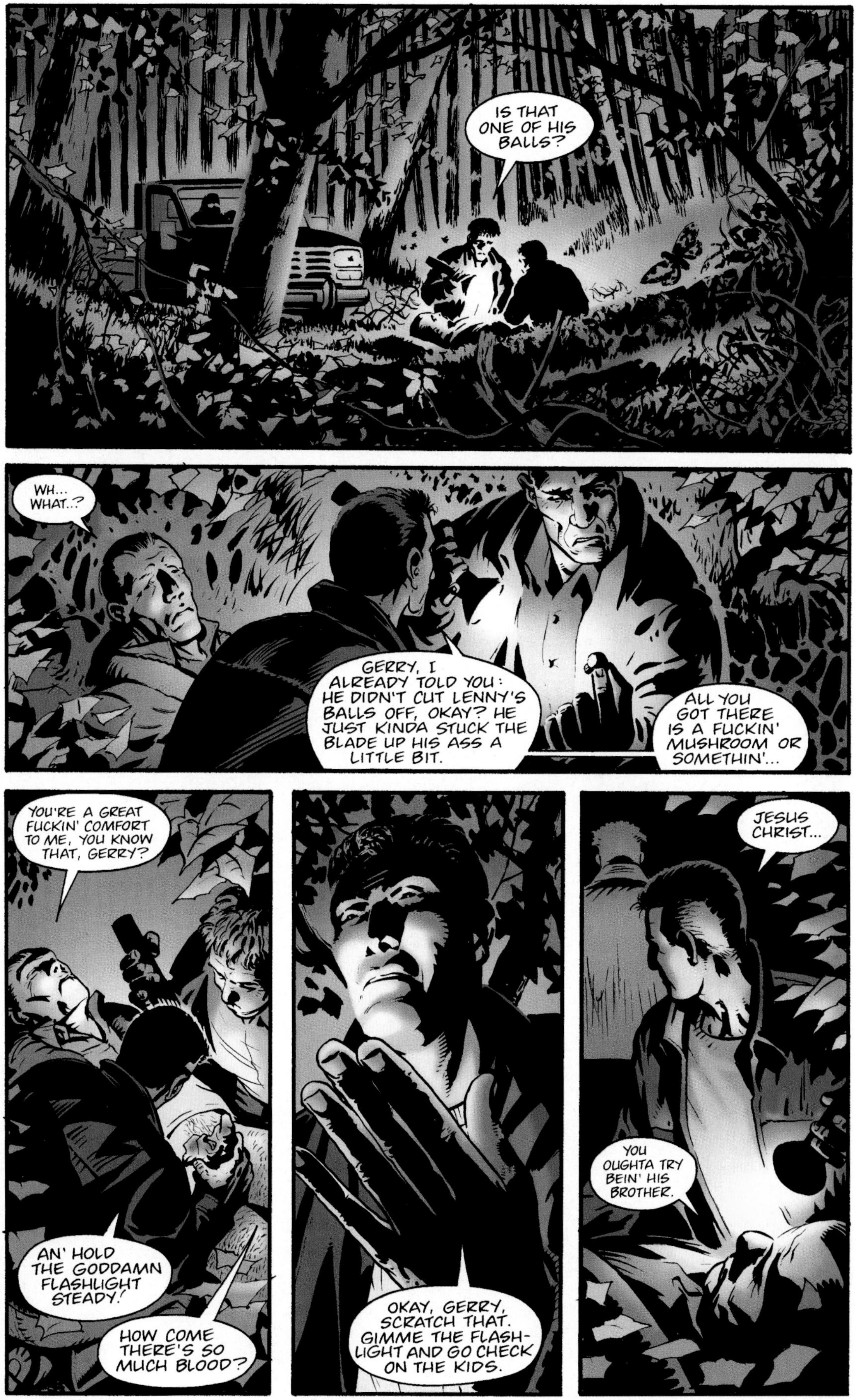
IS THAT ONE OF HIS BALLS?
WH... WHAT..?
GERRY, I ALREADY TOLD YOU: HE DIDN'T CUT LENNY'S BALLS OFF, OKAY? HE JUST KINDA STUCK THE BLADE UP HIS ASS A LITTLE BIT.
ALL YOU GOT THERE IS A FUCKIN' MUSHROOM OR SOMETHIN'...
YOU'RE A GREAT FUCKIN' COMFORT TO ME, YOU KNOW THAT, GERRY?
AN' HOLD THE GODDAMN FLASHLIGHT STEADY!
HOW COME THERE'S SO MUCH BLOOD?
OKAY, GERRY, SCRATCH THAT. GIMME THE FLASH-LIGHT AND GO CHECK ON THE KIDS.
JESUS CHRIST...
YOU OUGHTA TRY BEIN' HIS BROTHER.

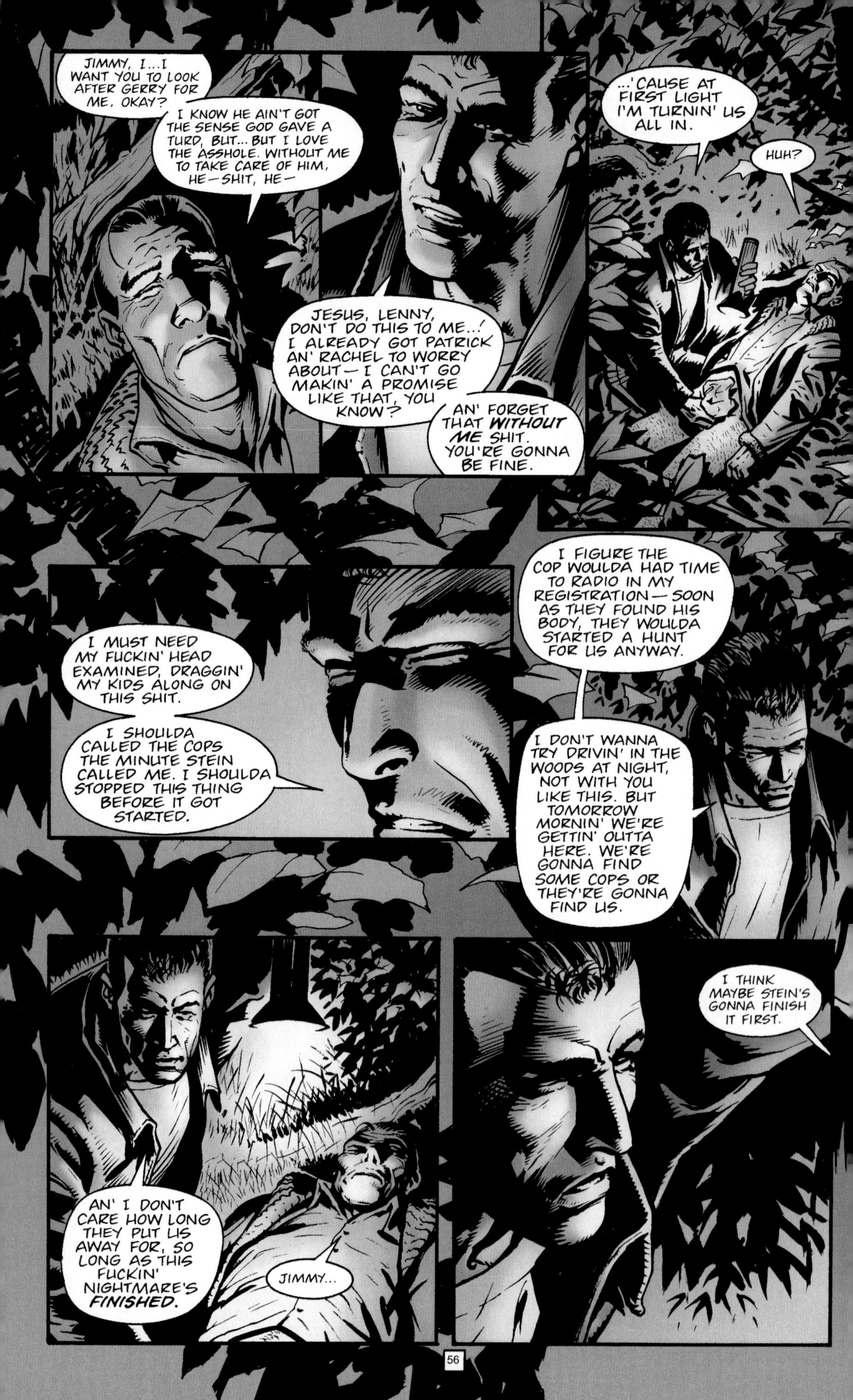
JIMMY, I...I WANT YOU TO LOOK AFTER GERRY FOR ME, OKAY?
I KNOW HE AIN'T GOT THE SENSE GOD GAVE A TURD, BUT... BUT I LOVE THE ASSHOLE. WITHOUT ME TO TAKE CARE OF HIM, HE—SHIT, HE—
JESUS, LENNY, DON'T DO THIS TO ME...! I ALREADY GOT PATRICK AN' RACHEL TO WORRY ABOUT— I CAN'T GO MAKIN' A PROMISE LIKE THAT, YOU KNOW?
AN' FORGET THAT WITHOUT ME SHIT. YOU'RE GONNA BE FINE.
...'CAUSE AT FIRST LIGHT I'M TURNIN' US ALL IN.
HUH?
I MUST NEED MY FUCKIN' HEAD EXAMINED, DRAGGIN' MY KIDS ALONG ON THIS SHIT.
I SHOULDA CALLED THE COPS THE MINUTE STEIN CALLED ME. I SHOULDA STOPPED THIS THING BEFORE IT GOT STARTED.
I FIGURE THE COP WOULDA HAD TIME TO RADIO IN MY REGISTRATION— SOON AS THEY FOUND HIS BODY, THEY WOULDA STARTED A HUNT FOR US ANYWAY.
I DON'T WANNA TRY DRIVIN' IN THE WOODS AT NIGHT, NOT WITH YOU LIKE THIS. BUT TOMORROW MORNIN' WE'RE GETTIN' OUTTA HERE. WE'RE GONNA FIND SOME COPS OR THEY'RE GONNA FIND US.
AN' I DON'T CARE HOW LONG THEY PUT US AWAY FOR, SO LONG AS THIS FUCKIN' NIGHTMARE'S FINISHED.
JIMMY...
I THINK MAYBE STEIN'S GONNA FINISH IT FIRST.

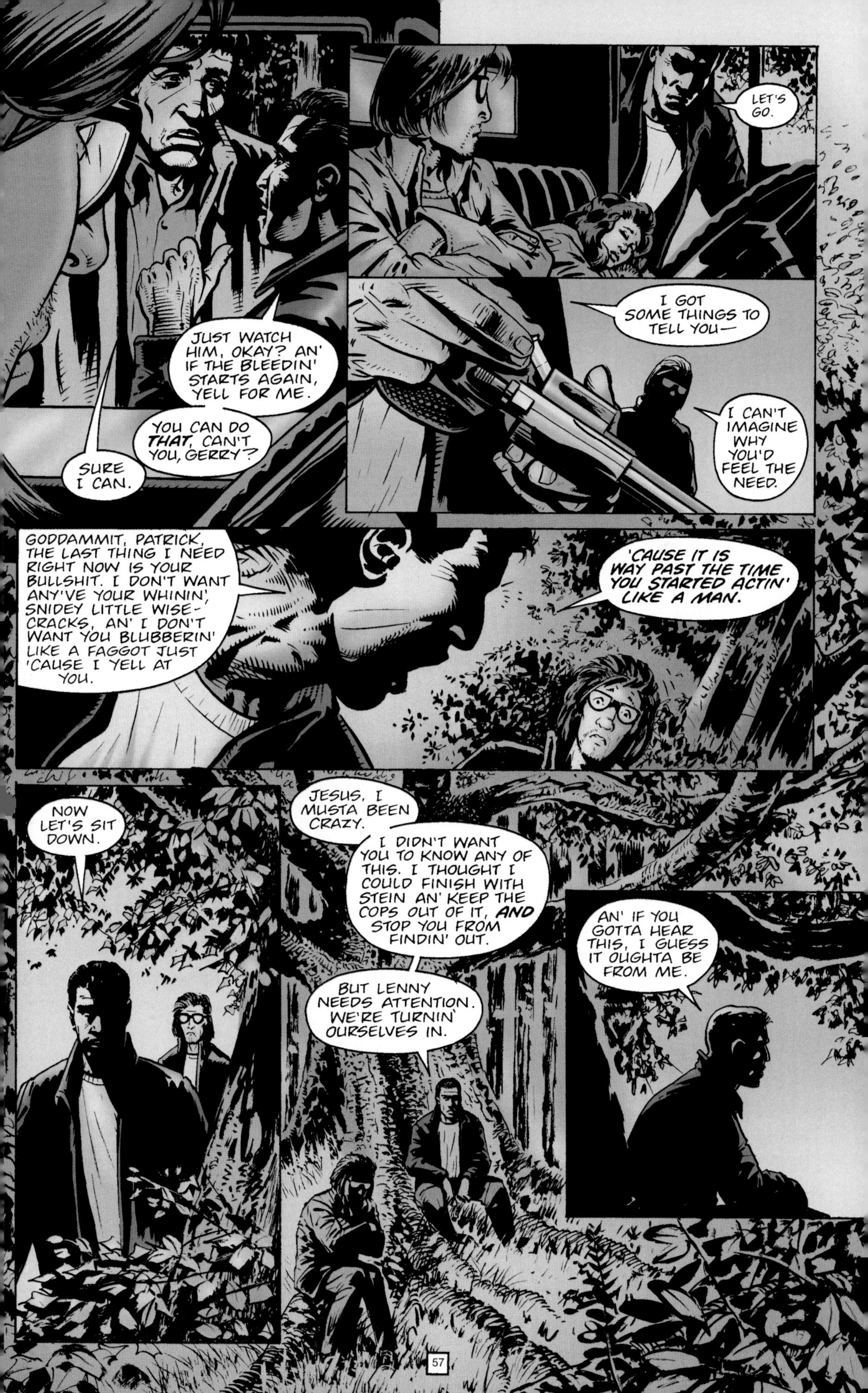
JUST WATCH HIM, OKAY? AN' IF THE BLEEDIN' STARTS AGAIN, YELL FOR ME.
YOU CAN DO THAT, CAN'T YOU, GERRY?
SURE I CAN.
LET'S GO.
I GOT SOME THINGS TO TELL YOU—
I CAN'T IMAGINE WHY YOU'D FEEL THE NEED.
GODDAMMIT, PATRICK, THE LAST THING I NEED RIGHT NOW IS YOUR BULLSHIT. I DON'T WANT ANY'VE YOUR WHININ', SNIDEY LITTLE WISE-CRACKS, AN' I DON'T WANT YOU BLUBBERIN' LIKE A FAGGOT JUST 'CAUSE I YELL AT YOU.
'CAUSE IT IS WAY PAST THE TIME YOU STARTED ACTIN' LIKE A MAN.
NOW LET'S SIT DOWN.
JESUS, I MUSTA BEEN CRAZY.
I DIDN'T WANT YOU TO KNOW ANY OF THIS. I THOUGHT I COULD FINISH WITH STEIN AN' KEEP THE COPS OUT OF IT, AND STOP YOU FROM FINDIN' OUT.
BUT LENNY NEEDS ATTENTION. WE'RE TURNIN' OURSELVES IN.
AN' IF YOU GOTTA HEAR THIS, I GUESS IT OUGHTA BE FROM ME.

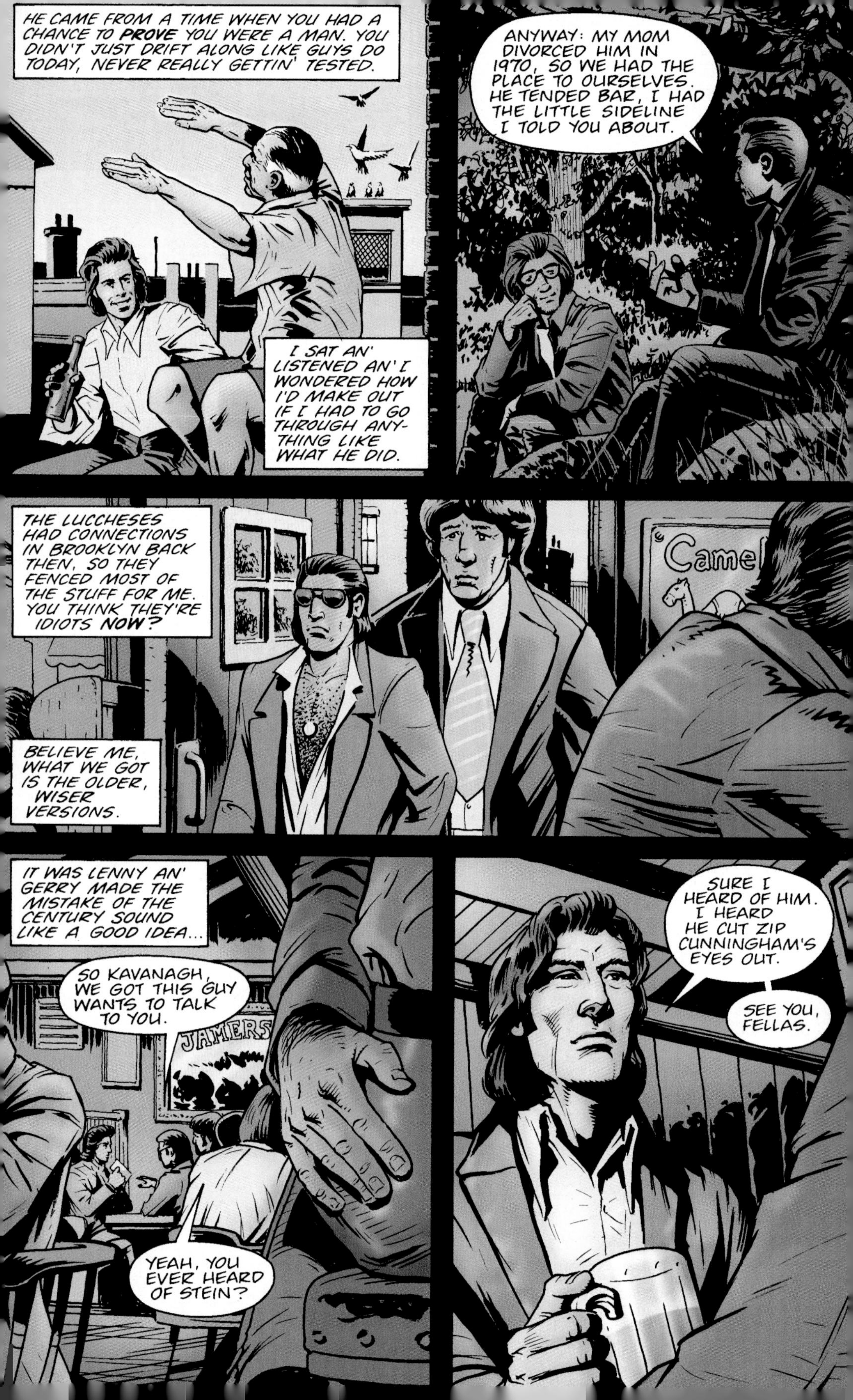
HE CAME FROM A TIME WHEN YOU HAD A CHANCE TO **PROVE** YOU WERE A MAN. YOU DIDN'T JUST DRIFT ALONG LIKE GUYS DO TODAY, NEVER REALLY GETTIN' TESTED.
I SAT AN' LISTENED AN' I WONDERED HOW I'D MAKE OUT IF I HAD TO GO THROUGH ANYTHING LIKE WHAT HE DID.
ANYWAY: MY MOM DIVORCED HIM IN 1970, SO WE HAD THE PLACE TO OURSELVES. HE TENDED BAR, I HAD THE LITTLE SIDELINE I TOLD YOU ABOUT.
THE LUCCHESES HAD CONNECTIONS IN BROOKLYN BACK THEN, SO THEY FENCED MOST OF THE STUFF FOR ME. YOU THINK THEY'RE IDIOTS **NOW**?
Camel
BELIEVE ME, WHAT WE GOT IS THE OLDER, WISER VERSIONS.
IT WAS LENNY AN' GERRY MADE THE MISTAKE OF THE CENTURY SOUND LIKE A GOOD IDEA...
SO KAVANAGH, WE GOT THIS GUY WANTS TO TALK TO YOU.
JAMERS
YEAH, YOU EVER HEARD OF STEIN?
SURE I HEARD OF HIM. I HEARD HE CUT ZIP CUNNINGHAM'S EYES OUT.
SEE YOU, FELLAS.

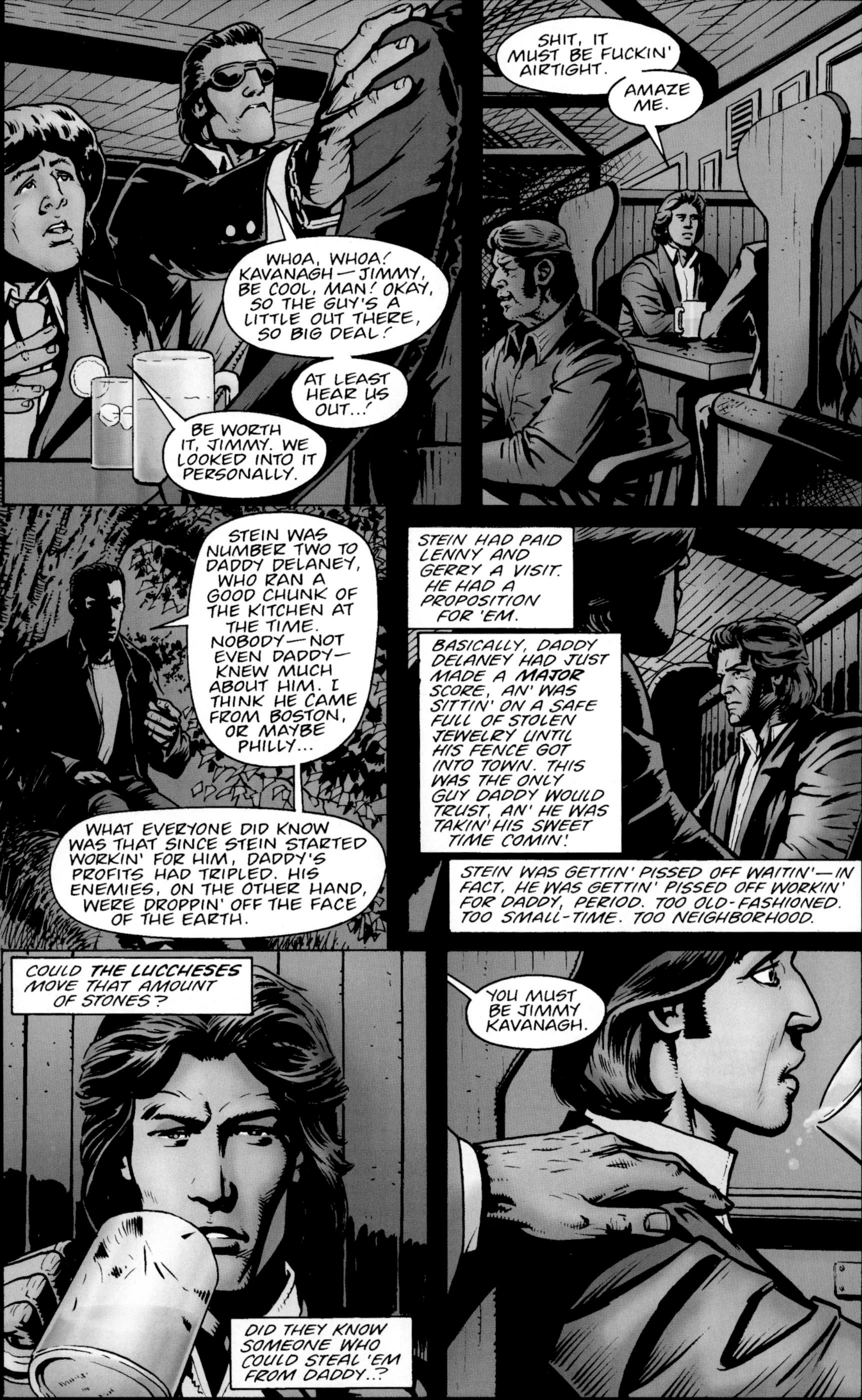
WHOA, WHOA! KAVANAGH—JIMMY, BE COOL, MAN! OKAY, SO THE GUY'S A LITTLE OUT THERE, SO BIG DEAL!
AT LEAST HEAR US OUT...!
BE WORTH IT, JIMMY. WE LOOKED INTO IT PERSONALLY.
SHIT, IT MUST BE FUCKIN' AIRTIGHT.
AMAZE ME.
STEIN WAS NUMBER TWO TO DADDY DELANEY, WHO RAN A GOOD CHUNK OF THE KITCHEN AT THE TIME. NOBODY—NOT EVEN DADDY—KNEW MUCH ABOUT HIM. I THINK HE CAME FROM BOSTON, OR MAYBE PHILLY...
WHAT EVERYONE DID KNOW WAS THAT SINCE STEIN STARTED WORKIN' FOR HIM, DADDY'S PROFITS HAD TRIPLED. HIS ENEMIES, ON THE OTHER HAND, WERE DROPPIN' OFF THE FACE OF THE EARTH.
STEIN HAD PAID LENNY AND GERRY A VISIT. HE HAD A PROPOSITION FOR 'EM.
BASICALLY, DADDY DELANEY HAD JUST MADE A MAJOR SCORE, AN' WAS SITTIN' ON A SAFE FULL OF STOLEN JEWELRY UNTIL HIS FENCE GOT INTO TOWN. THIS WAS THE ONLY GUY DADDY WOULD TRUST, AN' HE WAS TAKIN' HIS SWEET TIME COMIN'.
STEIN WAS GETTIN' PISSED OFF WAITIN'—IN FACT, HE WAS GETTIN' PISSED OFF WORKIN' FOR DADDY, PERIOD. TOO OLD-FASHIONED. TOO SMALL-TIME. TOO NEIGHBORHOOD.
COULD THE LUCCHESES MOVE THAT AMOUNT OF STONES?
DID THEY KNOW SOMEONE WHO COULD STEAL 'EM FROM DADDY..?
YOU MUST BE JIMMY KAVANAGH.

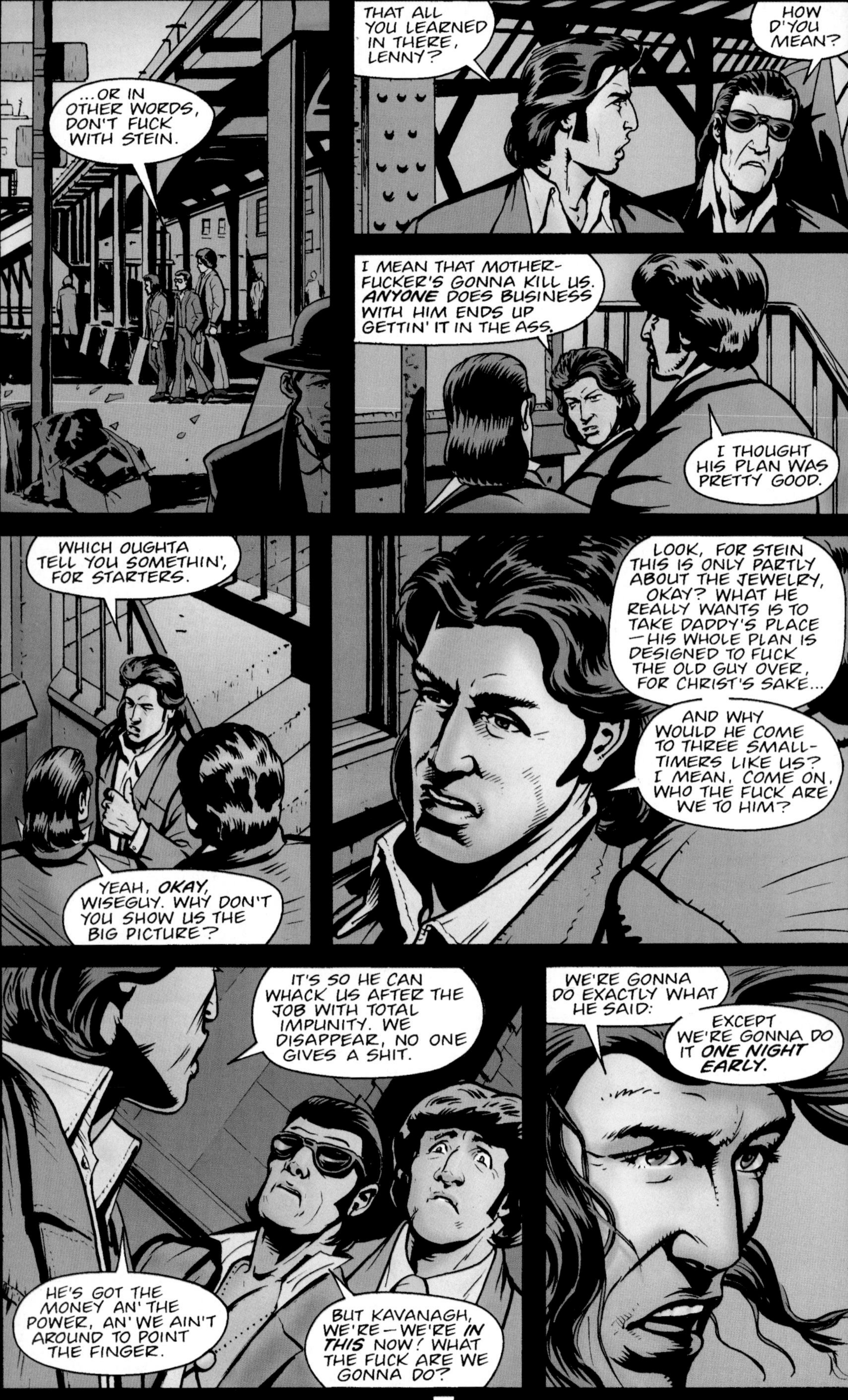

...OR IN OTHER WORDS, DON'T FUCK WITH STEIN.
THAT ALL YOU LEARNED IN THERE, LENNY?
HOW D'YOU MEAN?
I MEAN THAT MOTHER-FUCKER'S GONNA KILL US. ANYONE DOES BUSINESS WITH HIM ENDS UP GETTIN' IT IN THE ASS.
I THOUGHT HIS PLAN WAS PRETTY GOOD.
WHICH OUGHTA TELL YOU SOMETHIN', FOR STARTERS.
YEAH, OKAY, WISEGUY. WHY DON'T YOU SHOW US THE BIG PICTURE?
LOOK, FOR STEIN THIS IS ONLY PARTLY ABOUT THE JEWELRY, OKAY? WHAT HE REALLY WANTS IS TO TAKE DADDY'S PLACE —HIS WHOLE PLAN IS DESIGNED TO FUCK THE OLD GUY OVER, FOR CHRIST'S SAKE...
AND WHY WOULD HE COME TO THREE SMALL-TIMERS LIKE US? I MEAN, COME ON, WHO THE FUCK ARE WE TO HIM?
IT'S SO HE CAN WHACK US AFTER THE JOB WITH TOTAL IMPUNITY. WE DISAPPEAR, NO ONE GIVES A SHIT.
HE'S GOT THE MONEY AN' THE POWER, AN' WE AIN'T AROUND TO POINT THE FINGER.
BUT KAVANAGH, WE'RE—WE'RE IN THIS NOW! WHAT THE FUCK ARE WE GONNA DO?
WE'RE GONNA DO EXACTLY WHAT HE SAID:
EXCEPT WE'RE GONNA DO IT ONE NIGHT EARLY.

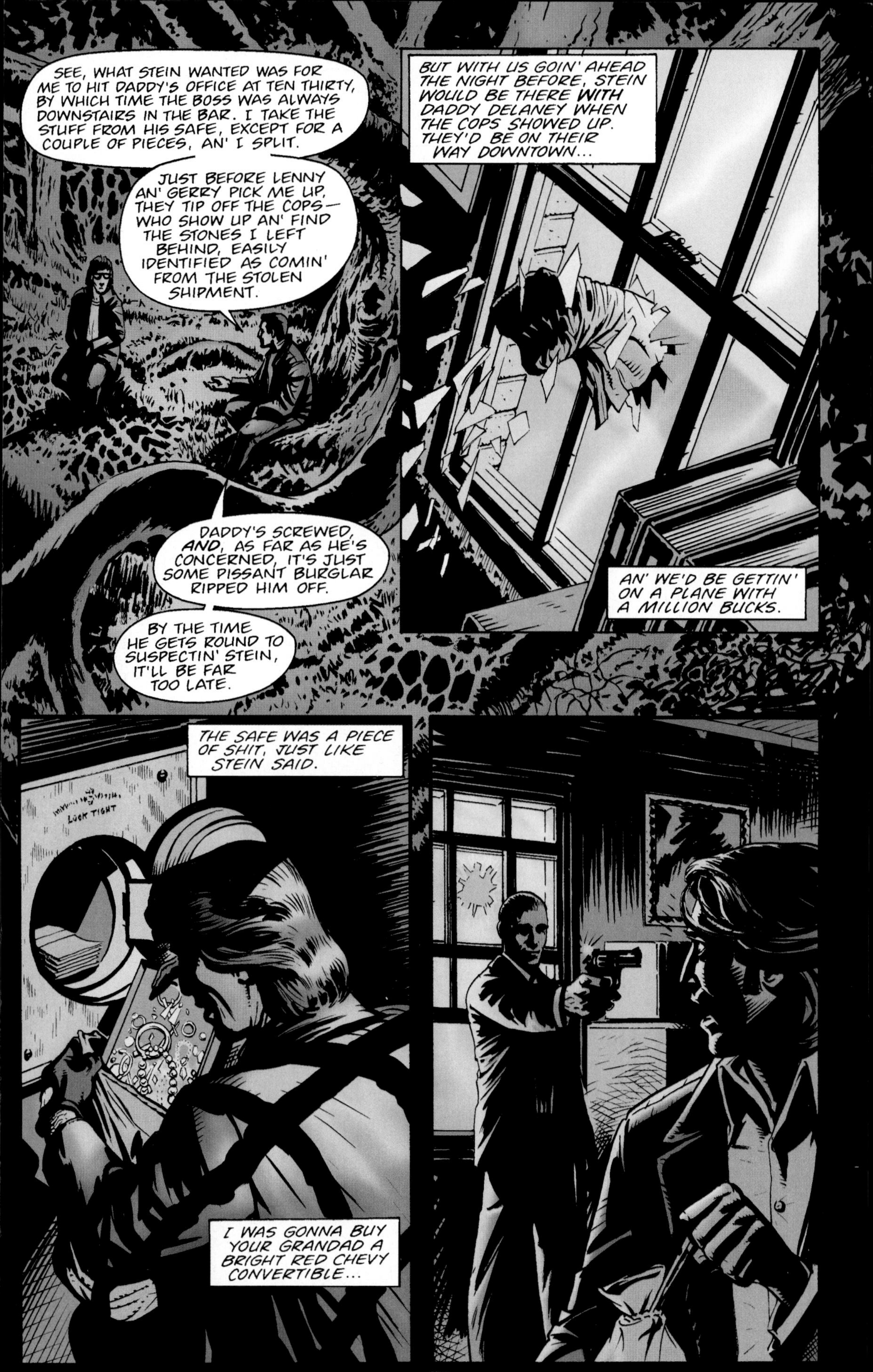
SEE, WHAT STEIN WANTED WAS FOR ME TO HIT DADDY'S OFFICE AT TEN THIRTY, BY WHICH TIME THE BOSS WAS ALWAYS DOWNSTAIRS IN THE BAR. I TAKE THE STUFF FROM HIS SAFE, EXCEPT FOR A COUPLE OF PIECES, AN' I SPLIT.
JUST BEFORE LENNY AN' GERRY PICK ME UP, THEY TIP OFF THE COPS— WHO SHOW UP AN' FIND THE STONES I LEFT BEHIND, EASILY IDENTIFIED AS COMIN' FROM THE STOLEN SHIPMENT.
DADDY'S SCREWED, AND, AS FAR AS HE'S CONCERNED, IT'S JUST SOME PISSANT BURGLAR RIPPED HIM OFF.
BY THE TIME HE GETS ROUND TO SUSPECTIN' STEIN, IT'LL BE FAR TOO LATE.
BUT WITH US GOIN' AHEAD THE NIGHT BEFORE, STEIN WOULD BE THERE WITH DADDY DELANEY WHEN THE COPS SHOWED UP. THEY'D BE ON THEIR WAY DOWNTOWN...
AN' WE'D BE GETTIN' ON A PLANE WITH A MILLION BUCKS.
THE SAFE WAS A PIECE OF SHIT, JUST LIKE STEIN SAID.
LOCK TIGHT
I WAS GONNA BUY YOUR GRANDAD A BRIGHT RED CHEVY CONVERTIBLE...

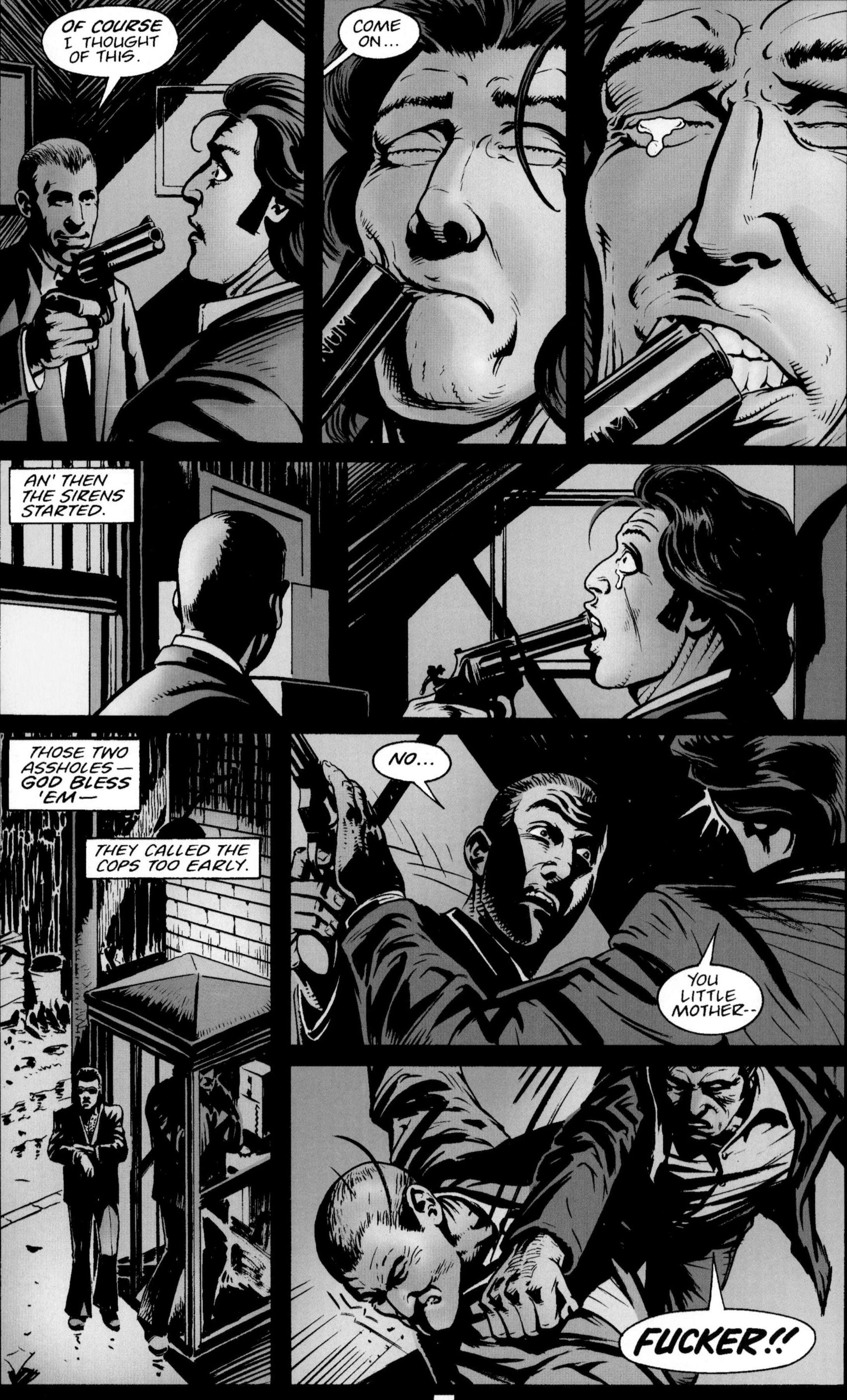
OF COURSE I THOUGHT OF THIS.
COME ON...
AN' THEN THE SIRENS STARTED.
THOSE TWO ASSHOLES — GOD BLESS 'EM —
THEY CALLED THE COPS TOO EARLY.
NO...
YOU LITTLE MOTHER--
FUCKER!!

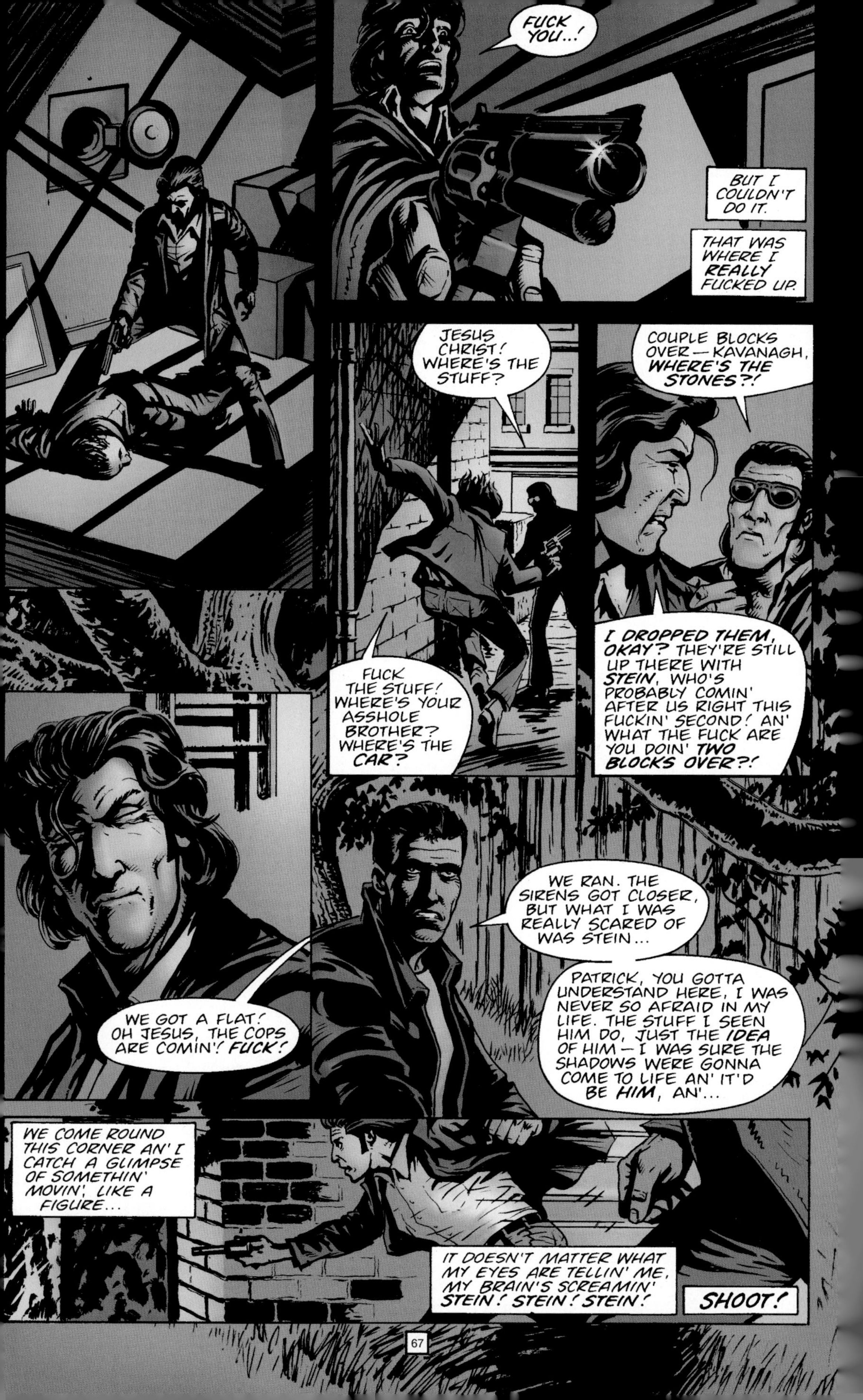
FUCK YOU...!
BUT I COULDN'T DO IT.
THAT WAS WHERE I REALLY FUCKED UP.
JESUS CHRIST! WHERE'S THE STUFF?
COUPLE BLOCKS OVER—KAVANAGH, WHERE'S THE STONES?!
FUCK THE STUFF! WHERE'S YOUR ASSHOLE BROTHER? WHERE'S THE CAR?
I DROPPED THEM, OKAY? THEY'RE STILL UP THERE WITH STEIN, WHO'S PROBABLY COMIN' AFTER US RIGHT THIS FUCKIN' SECOND! AN' WHAT THE FUCK ARE YOU DOIN' TWO BLOCKS OVER?!
WE GOT A FLAT! OH JESUS, THE COPS ARE COMIN'! FUCK!
WE RAN. THE SIRENS GOT CLOSER, BUT WHAT I WAS REALLY SCARED OF WAS STEIN...
PATRICK, YOU GOTTA UNDERSTAND HERE, I WAS NEVER SO AFRAID IN MY LIFE. THE STUFF I SEEN HIM DO, JUST THE IDEA OF HIM—I WAS SURE THE SHADOWS WERE GONNA COME TO LIFE AN' IT'D BE HIM, AN'...
WE COME ROUND THIS CORNER AN' I CATCH A GLIMPSE OF SOMETHIN' MOVIN', LIKE A FIGURE...
IT DOESN'T MATTER WHAT MY EYES ARE TELLIN' ME, MY BRAIN'S SCREAMIN' STEIN! STEIN! STEIN!
SHOOT!

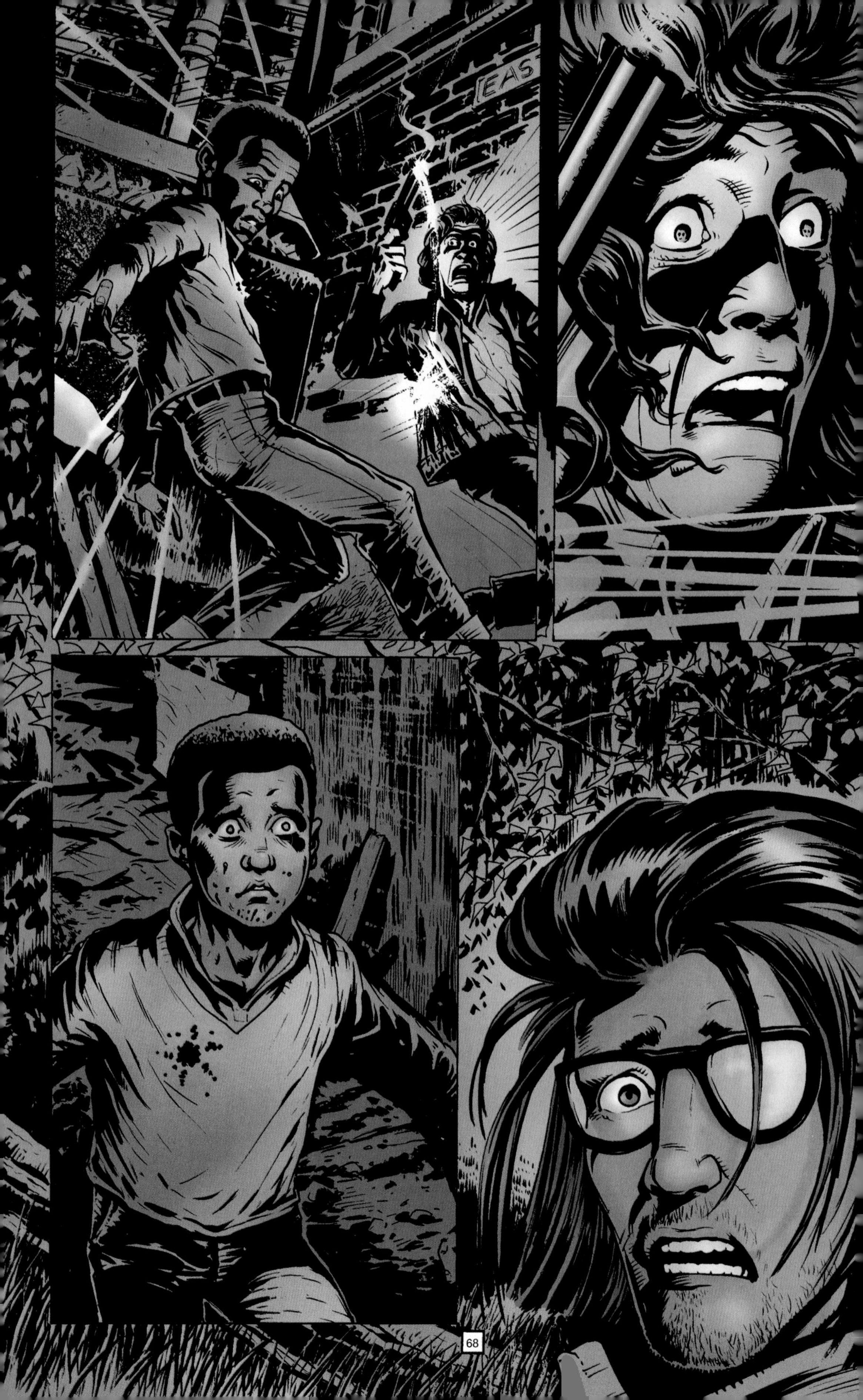
EAS

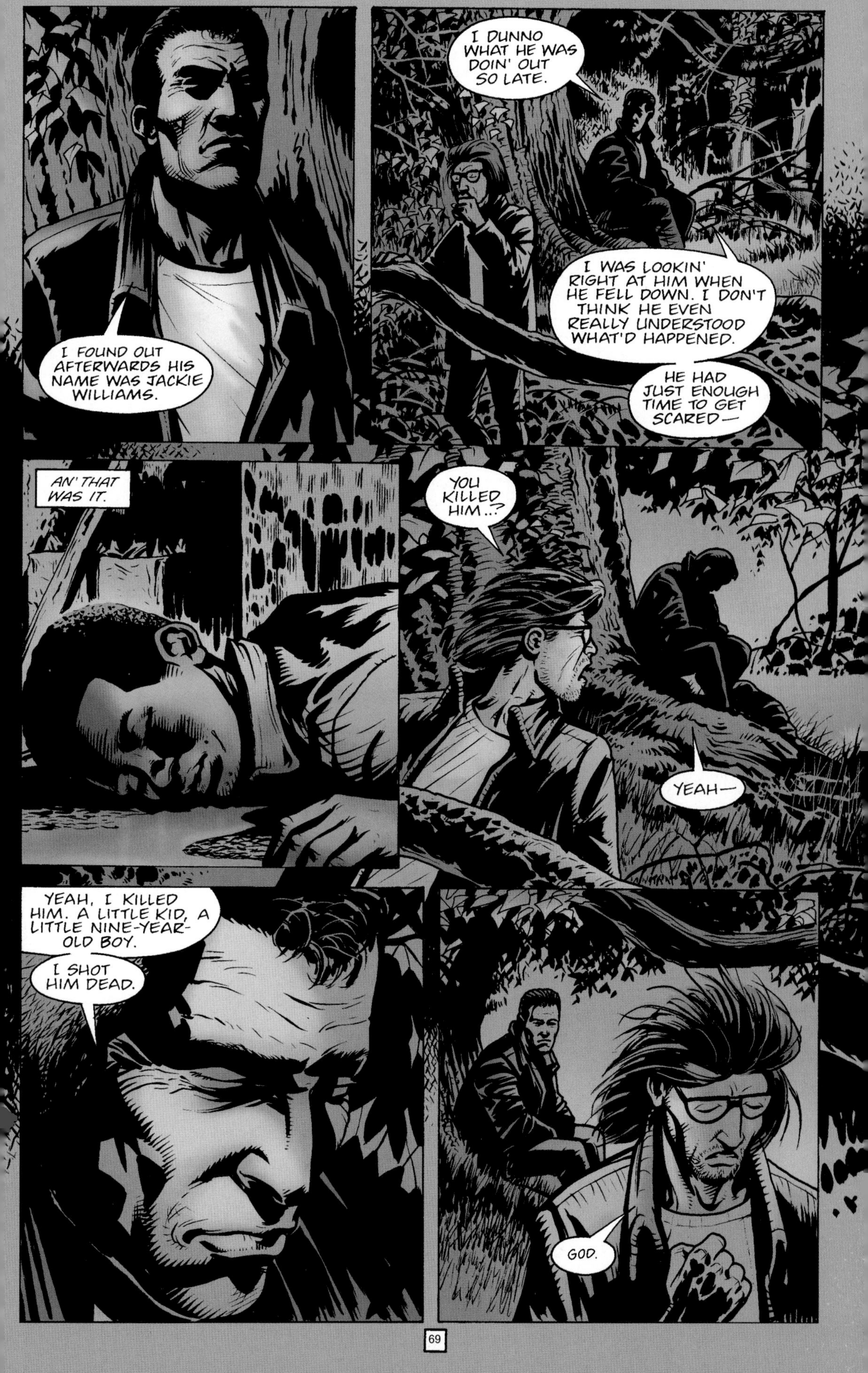
I FOUND OUT AFTERWARDS HIS NAME WAS JACKIE WILLIAMS.
I DUNNO WHAT HE WAS DOIN' OUT SO LATE.
I WAS LOOKIN' RIGHT AT HIM WHEN HE FELL DOWN. I DON'T THINK HE EVEN REALLY UNDERSTOOD WHAT'D HAPPENED.
HE HAD JUST ENOUGH TIME TO GET SCARED—
AN' THAT WAS IT.
YOU KILLED HIM...?
YEAH—
YEAH, I KILLED HIM. A LITTLE KID, A LITTLE NINE-YEAR-OLD BOY.
I SHOT HIM DEAD.
GOD.

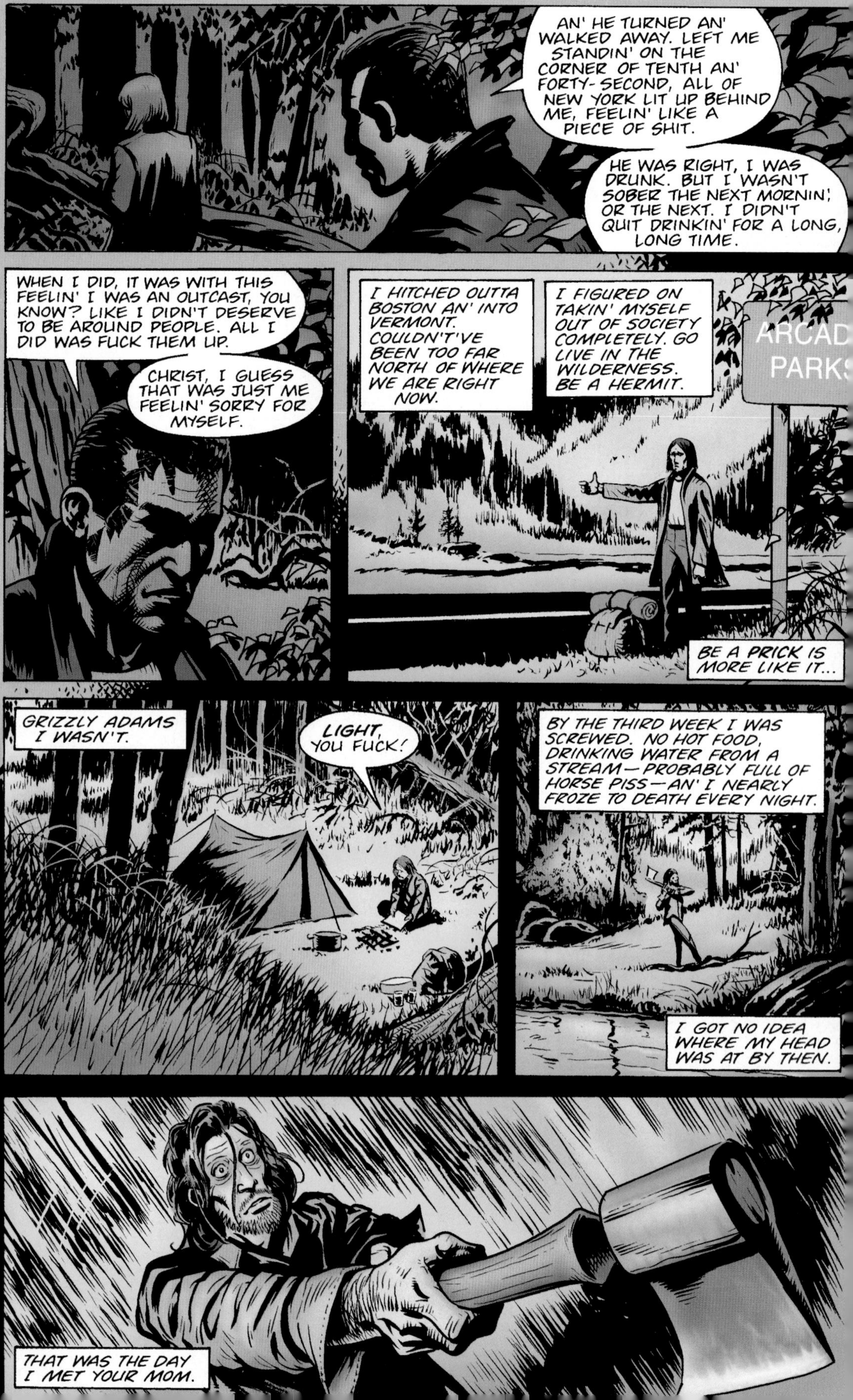
AN' HE TURNED AN' WALKED AWAY. LEFT ME STANDIN' ON THE CORNER OF TENTH AN' FORTY-SECOND, ALL OF NEW YORK LIT UP BEHIND ME, FEELIN' LIKE A PIECE OF SHIT.
HE WAS RIGHT, I WAS DRUNK. BUT I WASN'T SOBER THE NEXT MORNIN', OR THE NEXT. I DIDN'T QUIT DRINKIN' FOR A LONG, LONG TIME.
WHEN I DID, IT WAS WITH THIS FEELIN' I WAS AN OUTCAST, YOU KNOW? LIKE I DIDN'T DESERVE TO BE AROUND PEOPLE. ALL I DID WAS FUCK THEM UP.
CHRIST, I GUESS THAT WAS JUST ME FEELIN' SORRY FOR MYSELF.
I HITCHED OUTTA BOSTON AN' INTO VERMONT. COULDN'T'VE BEEN TOO FAR NORTH OF WHERE WE ARE RIGHT NOW.
I FIGURED ON TAKIN' MYSELF OUT OF SOCIETY COMPLETELY. GO LIVE IN THE WILDERNESS. BE A HERMIT.
ARCAD
PARKS
BE A PRICK IS MORE LIKE IT...
GRIZZLY ADAMS I WASN'T.
LIGHT, YOU FUCK!
BY THE THIRD WEEK I WAS SCREWED. NO HOT FOOD, DRINKING WATER FROM A STREAM—PROBABLY FULL OF HORSE PISS—AN' I NEARLY FROZE TO DEATH EVERY NIGHT.
I GOT NO IDEA WHERE MY HEAD WAS AT BY THEN.
THAT WAS THE DAY I MET YOUR MOM.

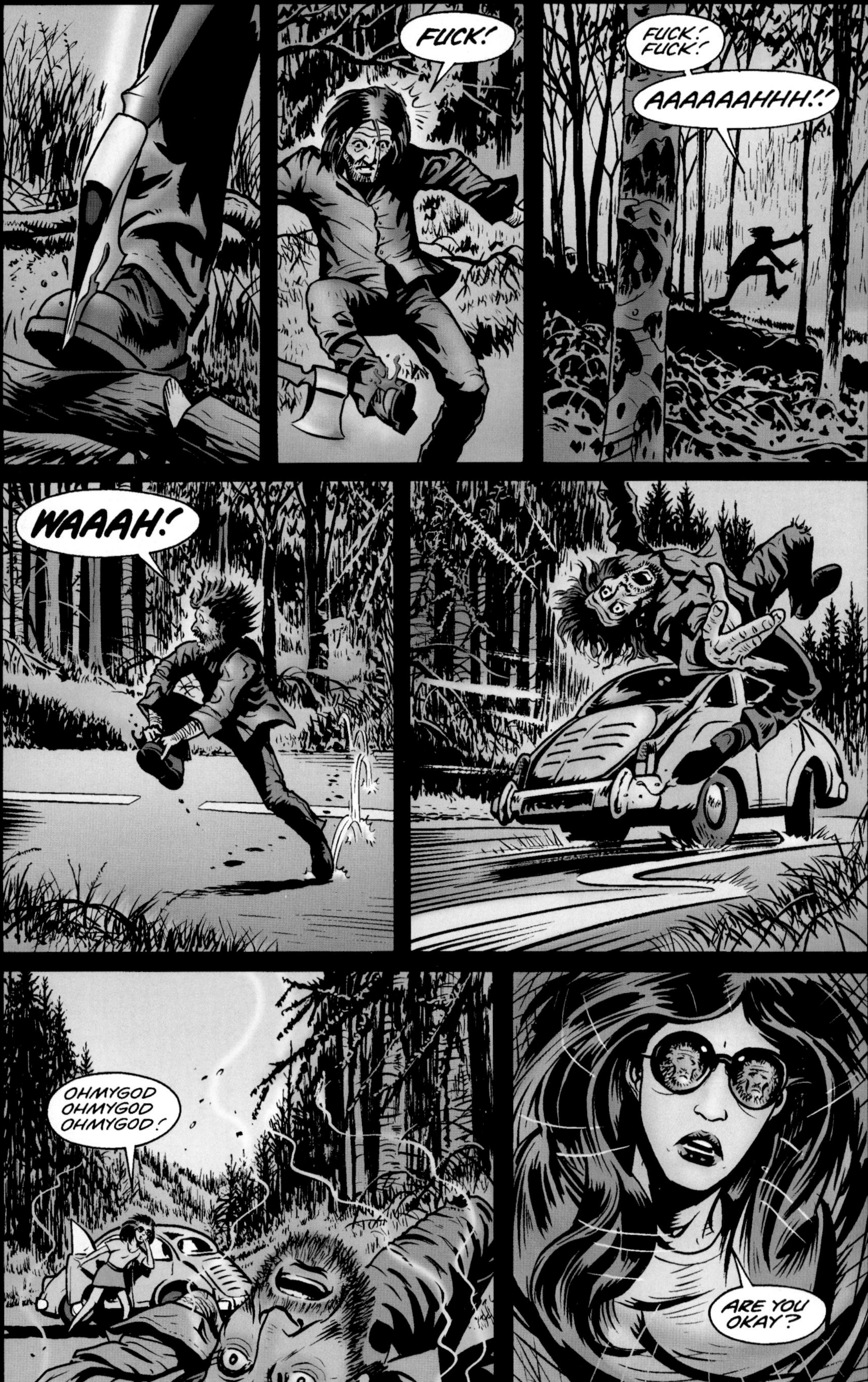
FUCK!
FUCK! FUCK!
AAAAAAHHH!!
WAAAH!
OHMYGOD OHMYGOD OHMYGOD!
ARE YOU OKAY?

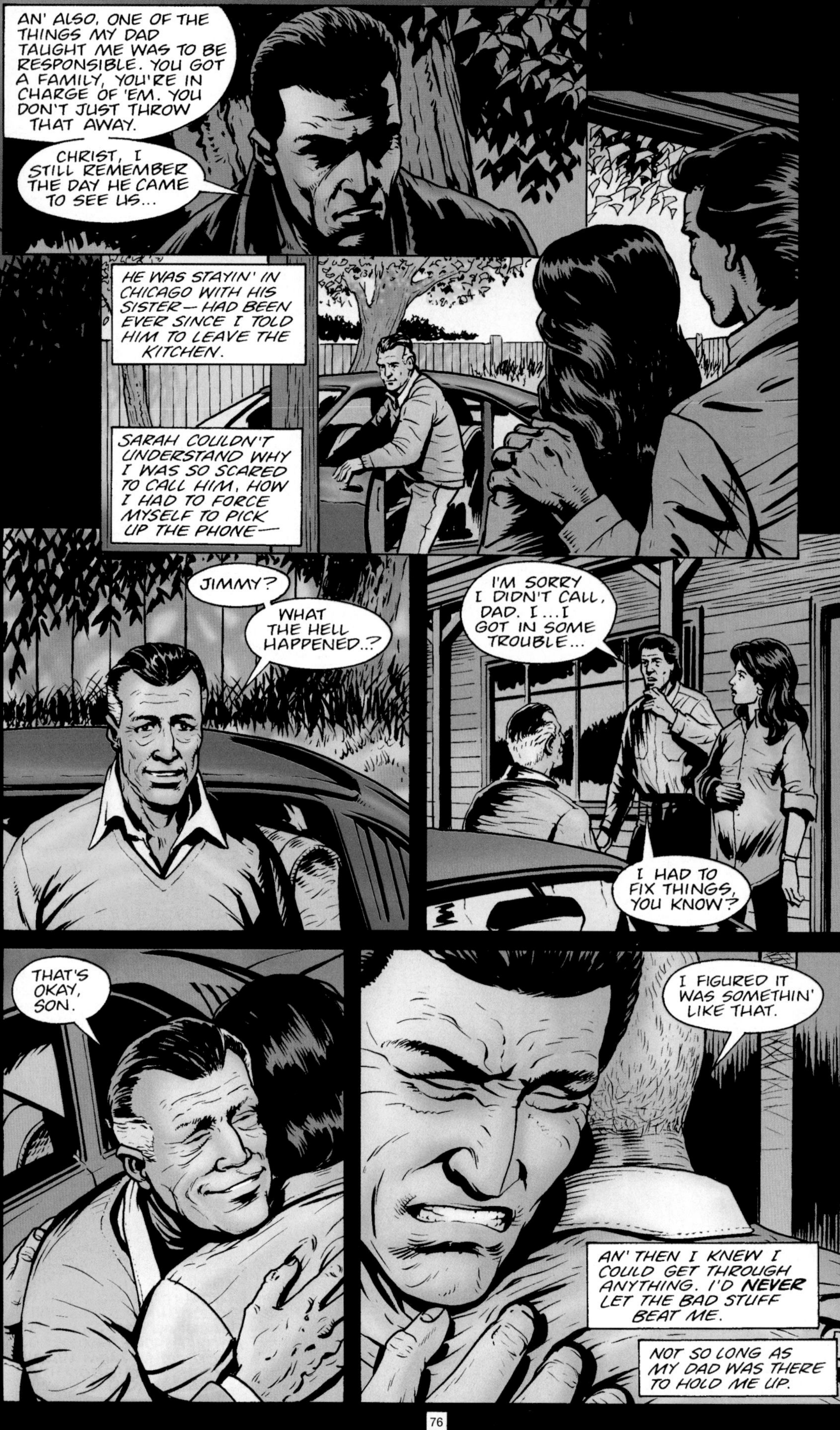
AN' ALSO, ONE OF THE THINGS MY DAD TAUGHT ME WAS TO BE RESPONSIBLE. YOU GOT A FAMILY, YOU'RE IN CHARGE OF 'EM. YOU DON'T JUST THROW THAT AWAY.
CHRIST, I STILL REMEMBER THE DAY HE CAME TO SEE US...
HE WAS STAYIN' IN CHICAGO WITH HIS SISTER— HAD BEEN EVER SINCE I TOLD HIM TO LEAVE THE KITCHEN.
SARAH COULDN'T UNDERSTAND WHY I WAS SO SCARED TO CALL HIM. HOW I HAD TO FORCE MYSELF TO PICK UP THE PHONE—
JIMMY?
WHAT THE HELL HAPPENED..?
I'M SORRY I DIDN'T CALL, DAD. I...I GOT IN SOME TROUBLE...
I HAD TO FIX THINGS, YOU KNOW?
THAT'S OKAY, SON.
I FIGURED IT WAS SOMETHIN' LIKE THAT.
AN' THEN I KNEW I COULD GET THROUGH ANYTHING. I'D **NEVER** LET THE BAD STUFF BEAT ME.
NOT SO LONG AS MY DAD WAS THERE TO HOLD ME UP.

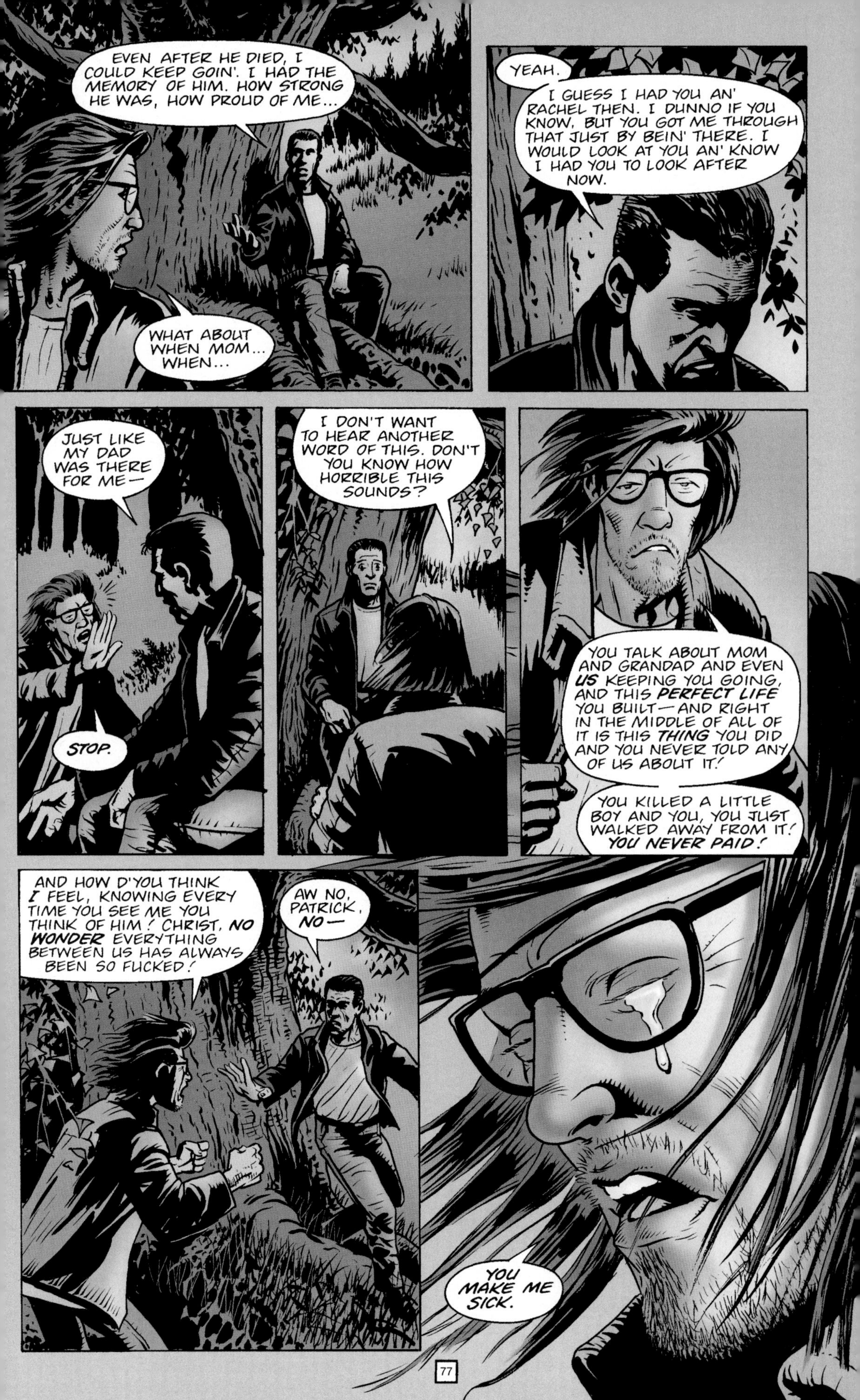
EVEN AFTER HE DIED, I COULD KEEP GOIN'. I HAD THE MEMORY OF HIM. HOW STRONG HE WAS, HOW PROUD OF ME...
WHAT ABOUT WHEN MOM... WHEN...
YEAH.
I GUESS I HAD YOU AN' RACHEL THEN. I DUNNO IF YOU KNOW, BUT YOU GOT ME THROUGH THAT JUST BY BEIN' THERE. I WOULD LOOK AT YOU AN' KNOW I HAD YOU TO LOOK AFTER NOW.
JUST LIKE MY DAD WAS THERE FOR ME—
STOP.
I DON'T WANT TO HEAR ANOTHER WORD OF THIS. DON'T YOU KNOW HOW HORRIBLE THIS SOUNDS?
YOU TALK ABOUT MOM AND GRANDAD AND EVEN US KEEPING YOU GOING, AND THIS PERFECT LIFE YOU BUILT—AND RIGHT IN THE MIDDLE OF ALL OF IT IS THIS THING YOU DID AND YOU NEVER TOLD ANY OF US ABOUT IT!
YOU KILLED A LITTLE BOY AND YOU, YOU JUST WALKED AWAY FROM IT! YOU NEVER PAID!
AND HOW D'YOU THINK I FEEL, KNOWING EVERY TIME YOU SEE ME YOU THINK OF HIM! CHRIST, NO WONDER EVERYTHING BETWEEN US HAS ALWAYS BEEN SO FUCKED!
AW NO, PATRICK, NO—
YOU MAKE ME SICK.

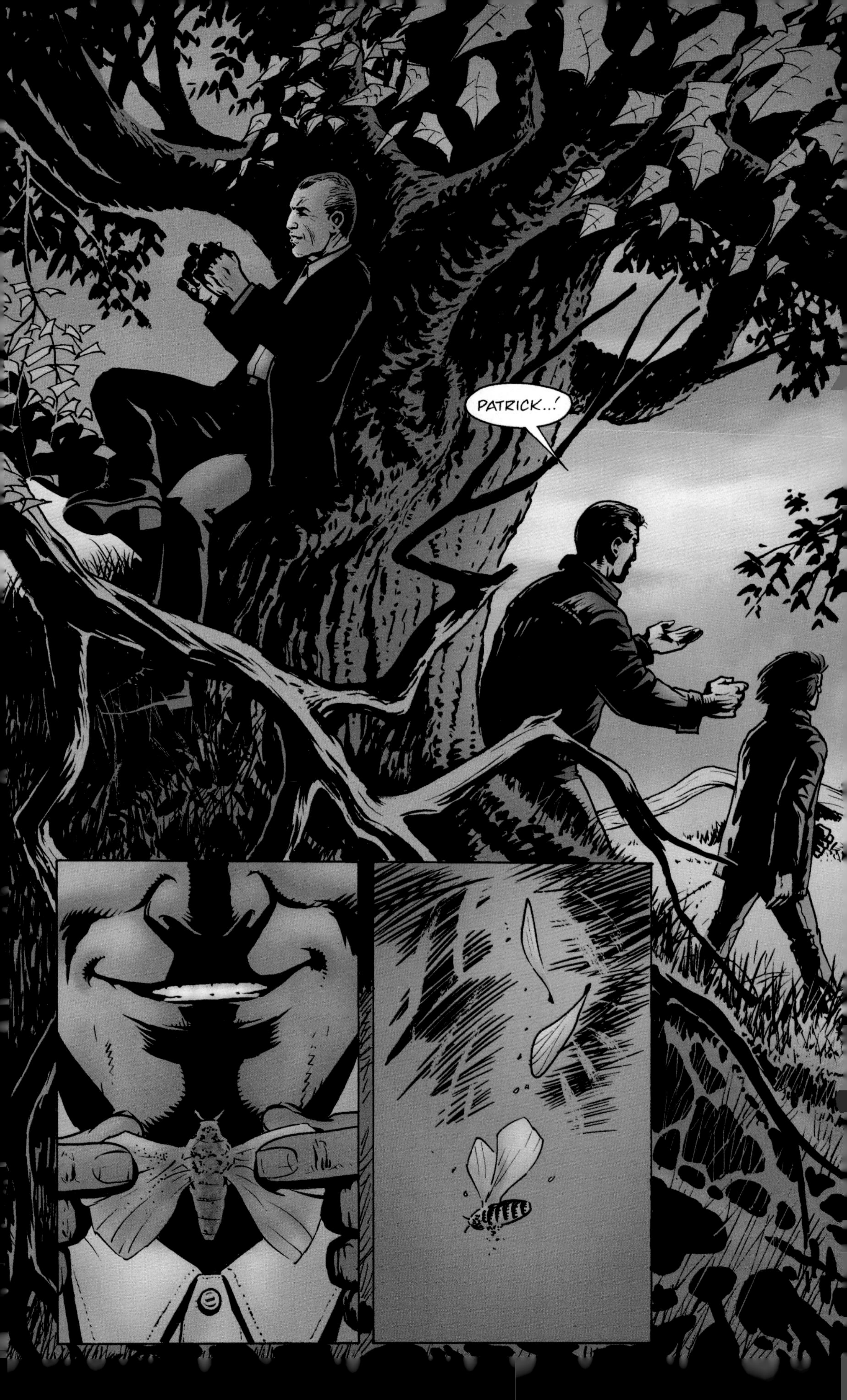
PATRICK...!

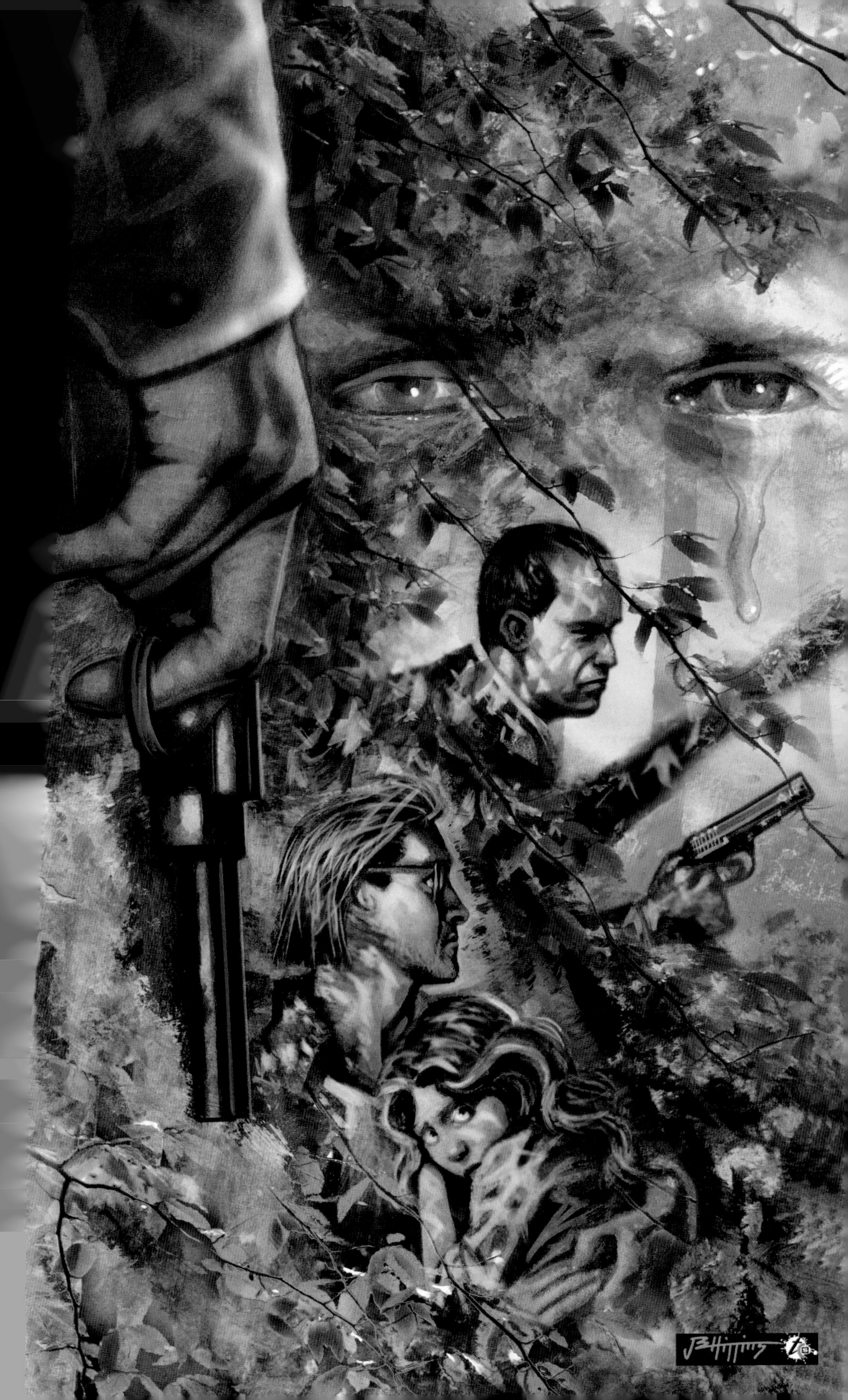

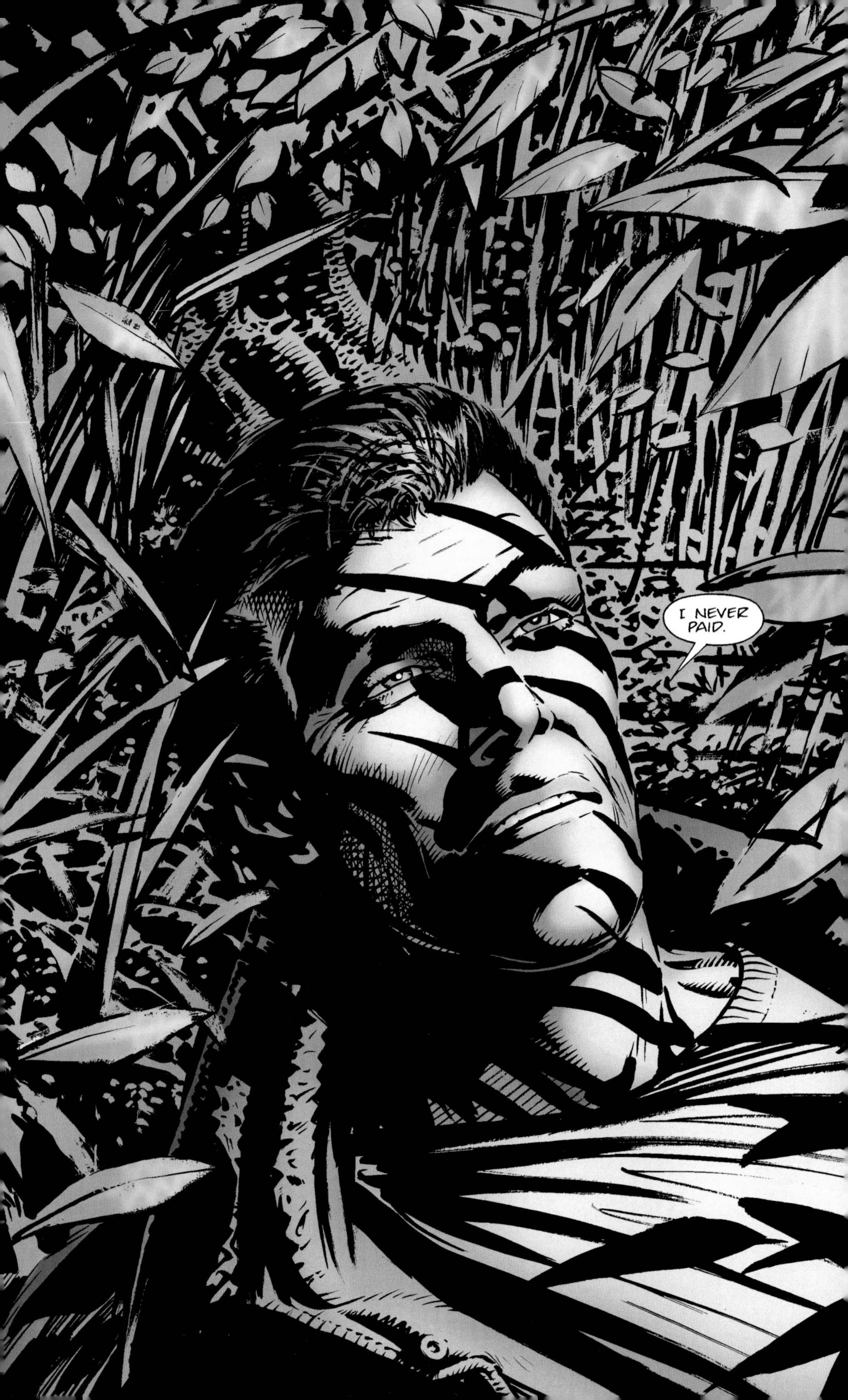
I NEVER PAID.

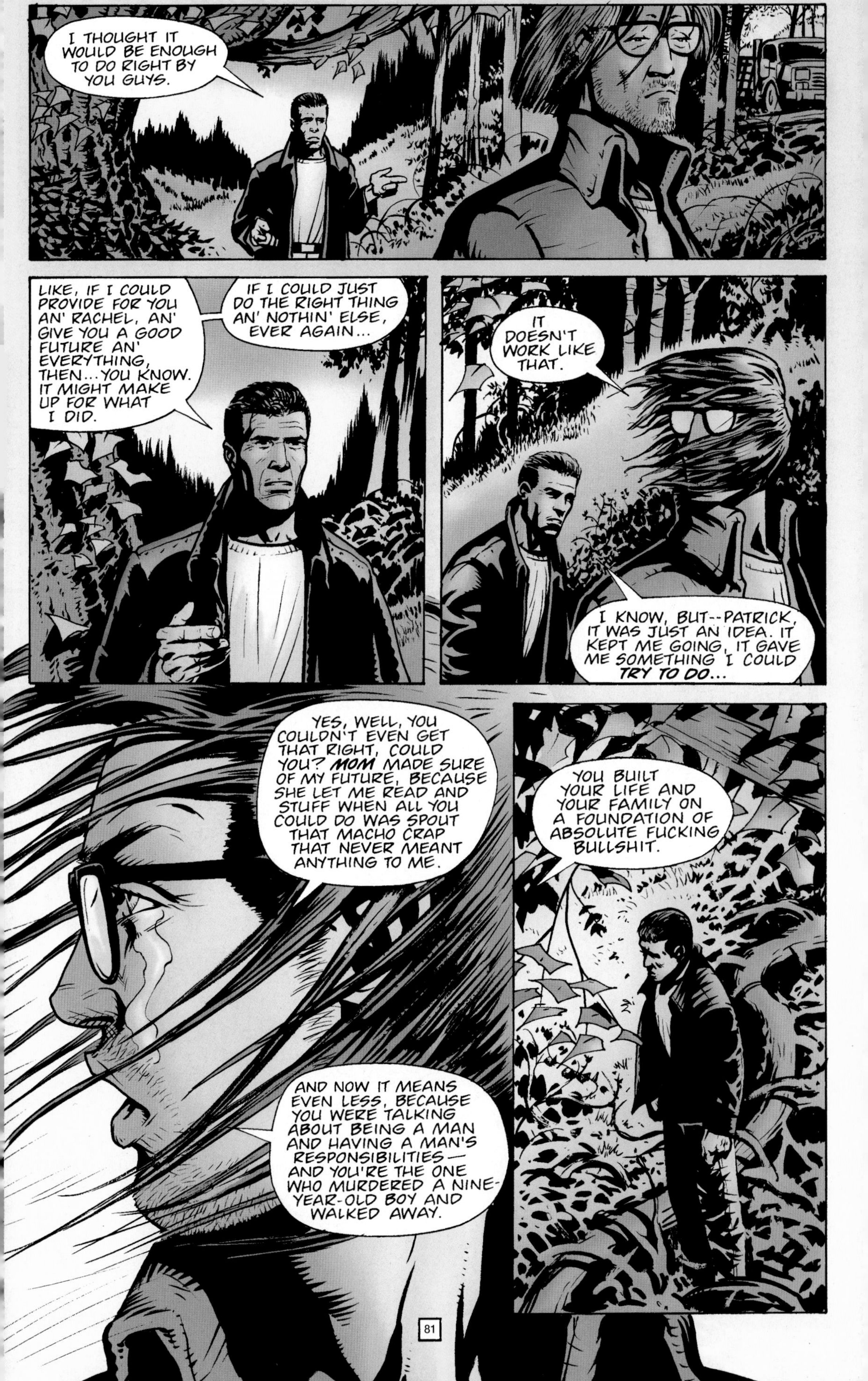

I THOUGHT IT WOULD BE ENOUGH TO DO RIGHT BY YOU GUYS.
LIKE, IF I COULD PROVIDE FOR YOU AN' RACHEL, AN' GIVE YOU A GOOD FUTURE AN' EVERYTHING, THEN... YOU KNOW. IT MIGHT MAKE UP FOR WHAT I DID.
IF I COULD JUST DO THE RIGHT THING AN' NOTHIN' ELSE, EVER AGAIN...
IT DOESN'T WORK LIKE THAT.
I KNOW, BUT--PATRICK, IT WAS JUST AN IDEA. IT KEPT ME GOING, IT GAVE ME SOMETHING I COULD TRY TO DO...
YES, WELL, YOU COULDN'T EVEN GET THAT RIGHT, COULD YOU? MOM MADE SURE OF MY FUTURE, BECAUSE SHE LET ME READ AND STUFF WHEN ALL YOU COULD DO WAS SPOUT THAT MACHO CRAP THAT NEVER MEANT ANYTHING TO ME.
AND NOW IT MEANS EVEN LESS, BECAUSE YOU WERE TALKING ABOUT BEING A MAN AND HAVING A MAN'S RESPONSIBILITIES— AND YOU'RE THE ONE WHO MURDERED A NINE-YEAR-OLD BOY AND WALKED AWAY.
YOU BUILT YOUR LIFE AND YOUR FAMILY ON A FOUNDATION OF ABSOLUTE FUCKING BULLSHIT.

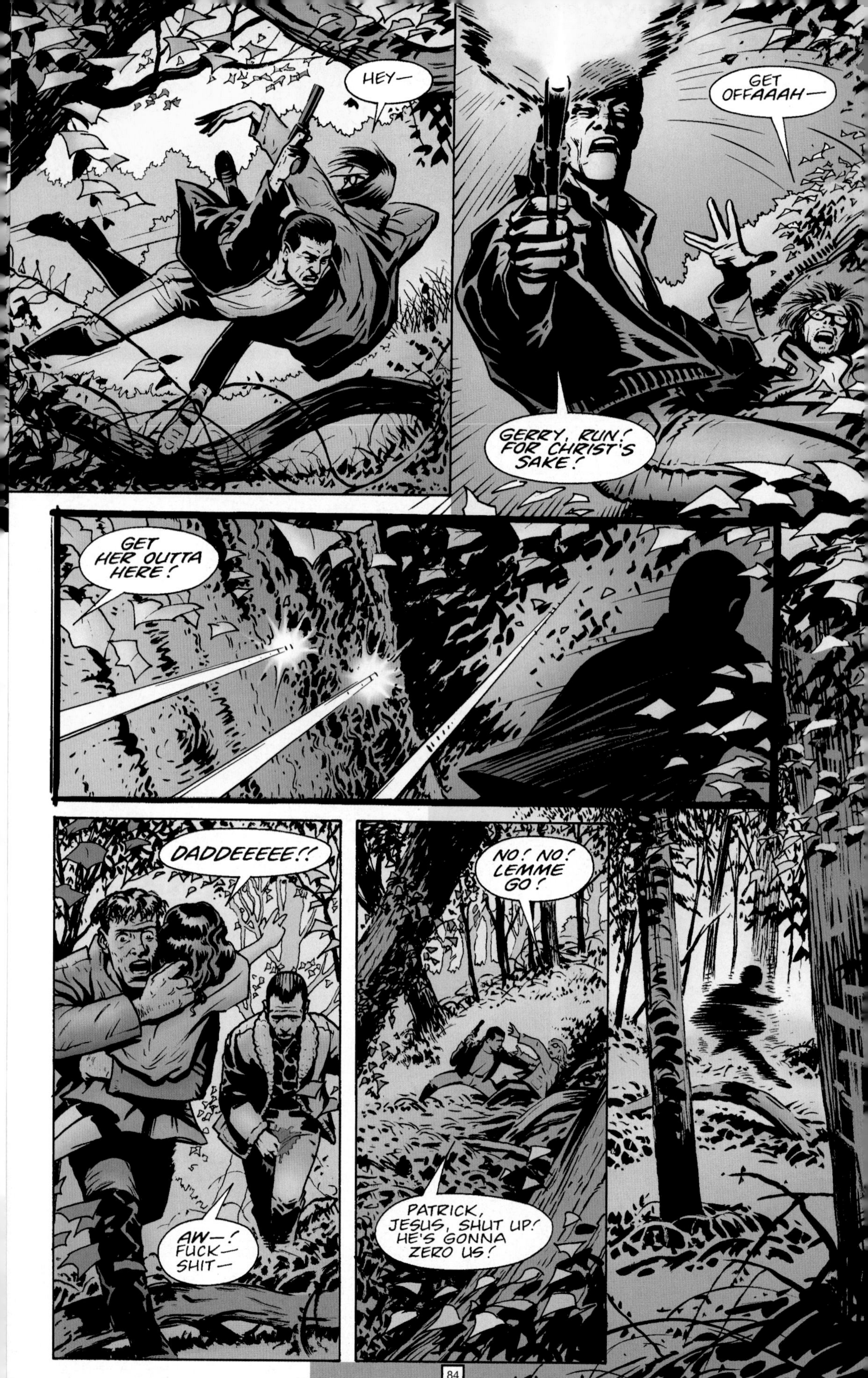
HEY—
GET OFFAAAH—
GERRY, RUN! FOR CHRIST'S SAKE!
GET HER OUTTA HERE!
DADDEEEEE!!
AW—! FUCK— SHIT—
NO! NO! LEMME GO!
PATRICK, JESUS, SHUT UP! HE'S GONNA ZERO US!

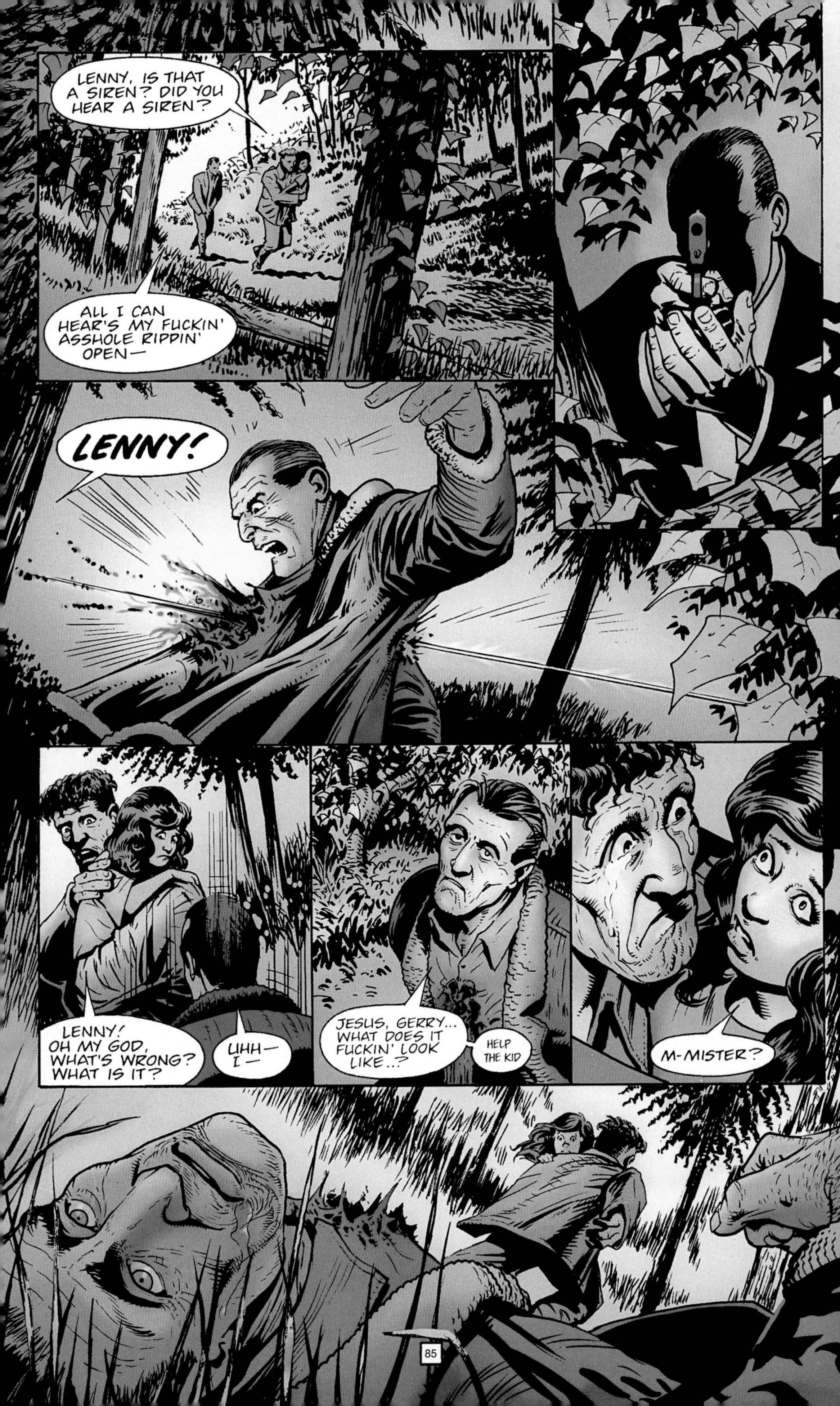
LENNY, IS THAT A SIREN? DID YOU HEAR A SIREN?
ALL I CAN HEAR'S MY FUCKIN' ASSHOLE RIPPIN' OPEN—
LENNY!
LENNY! OH MY GOD, WHAT'S WRONG? WHAT IS IT?
UHH— I—
JESUS, GERRY... WHAT DOES IT FUCKIN' LOOK LIKE..?
HELP THE KID
M-MISTER?

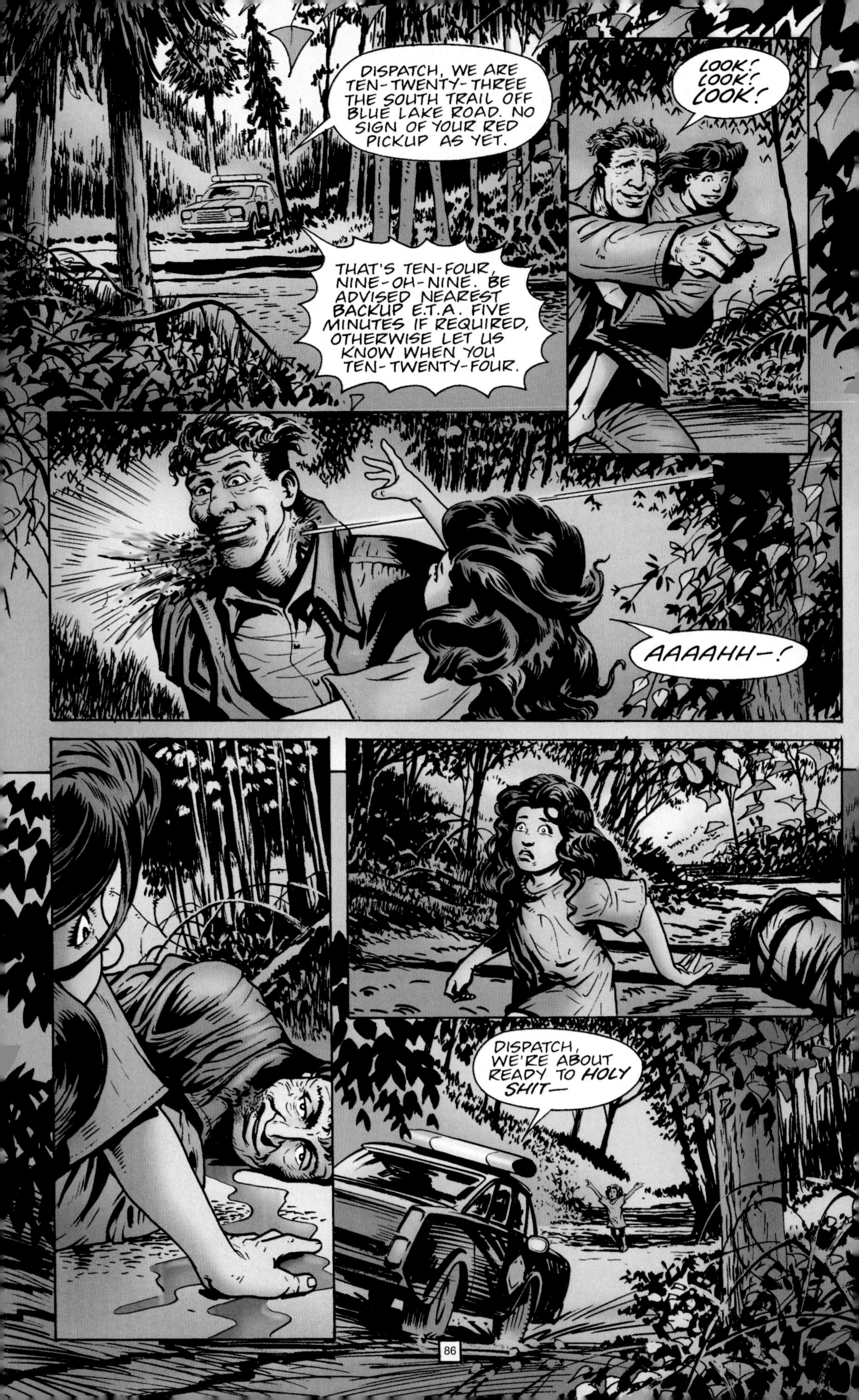
DISPATCH, WE ARE TEN-TWENTY-THREE THE SOUTH TRAIL OFF BLUE LAKE ROAD. NO SIGN OF YOUR RED PICKUP AS YET.
THAT'S TEN-FOUR, NINE-OH-NINE. BE ADVISED NEAREST BACKUP E.T.A. FIVE MINUTES IF REQUIRED, OTHERWISE LET US KNOW WHEN YOU TEN-TWENTY-FOUR.
LOOK! LOOK! LOOK!
AAAAHH-!
DISPATCH, WE'RE ABOUT READY TO HOLY SHIT—

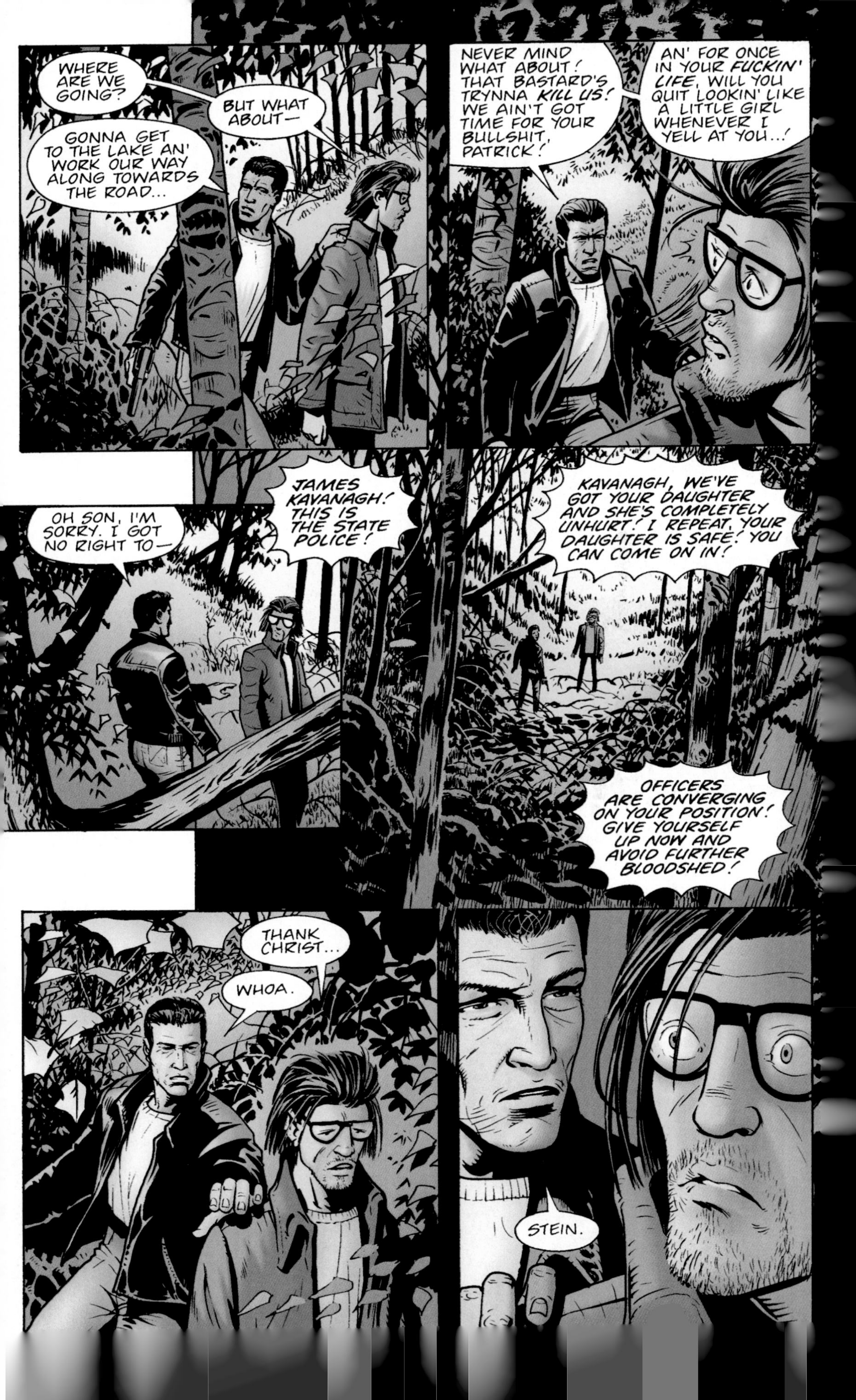
WHERE ARE WE GOING?
BUT WHAT ABOUT—
GONNA GET TO THE LAKE AN' WORK OUR WAY ALONG TOWARDS THE ROAD...
NEVER MIND WHAT ABOUT! THAT BASTARD'S TRYNNA KILL US! WE AIN'T GOT TIME FOR YOUR BULLSHIT, PATRICK!
AN' FOR ONCE IN YOUR FUCKIN' LIFE, WILL YOU QUIT LOOKIN' LIKE A LITTLE GIRL WHENEVER I YELL AT YOU...!
OH SON, I'M SORRY. I GOT NO RIGHT TO—
JAMES KAVANAGH! THIS IS THE STATE POLICE!
KAVANAGH, WE'VE GOT YOUR DAUGHTER AND SHE'S COMPLETELY UNHURT! I REPEAT, YOUR DAUGHTER IS SAFE! YOU CAN COME ON IN!
OFFICERS ARE CONVERGING ON YOUR POSITION! GIVE YOURSELF UP NOW AND AVOID FURTHER BLOODSHED!
THANK CHRIST...
WHOA.
STEIN.

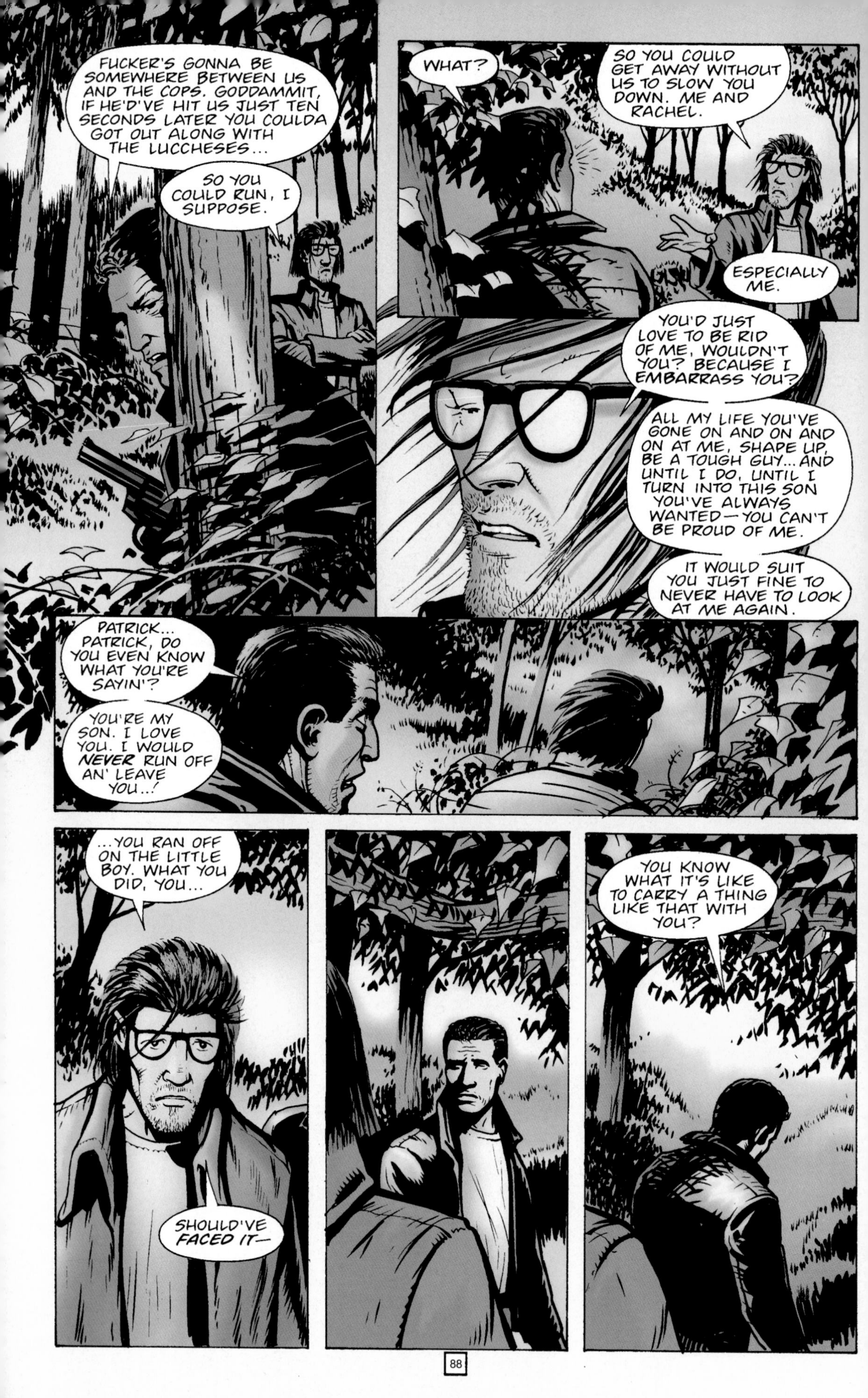
FUCKER'S GONNA BE SOMEWHERE BETWEEN US AND THE COPS. GODDAMMIT, IF HE'D'VE HIT US JUST TEN SECONDS LATER YOU COULDA GOT OUT ALONG WITH THE LUCCHESES...
SO YOU COULD RUN, I SUPPOSE.
WHAT?
SO YOU COULD GET AWAY WITHOUT US TO SLOW YOU DOWN. ME AND RACHEL.
ESPECIALLY ME.
YOU'D JUST LOVE TO BE RID OF ME, WOULDN'T YOU? BECAUSE I EMBARRASS YOU?
ALL MY LIFE YOU'VE GONE ON AND ON AND ON AT ME, SHAPE UP, BE A TOUGH GUY... AND UNTIL I DO, UNTIL I TURN INTO THIS SON YOU'VE ALWAYS WANTED—YOU CAN'T BE PROUD OF ME.
IT WOULD SUIT YOU JUST FINE TO NEVER HAVE TO LOOK AT ME AGAIN.
PATRICK... PATRICK, DO YOU EVEN KNOW WHAT YOU'RE SAYIN'?
YOU'RE MY SON. I LOVE YOU. I WOULD NEVER RUN OFF AN' LEAVE YOU...!
...YOU RAN OFF ON THE LITTLE BOY. WHAT YOU DID, YOU...
SHOULD'VE FACED IT—
YOU KNOW WHAT IT'S LIKE TO CARRY A THING LIKE THAT WITH YOU?

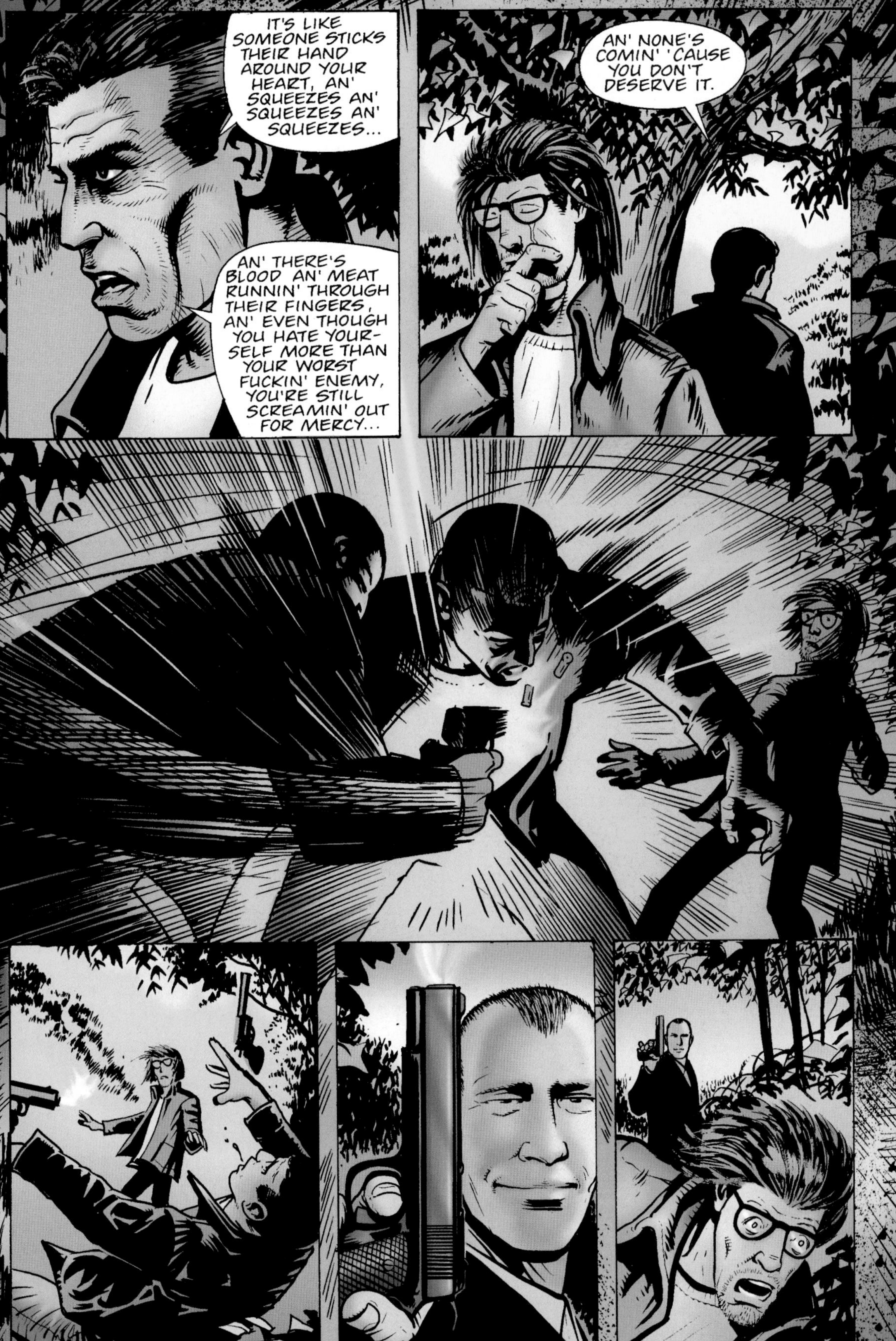
IT'S LIKE SOMEONE STICKS THEIR HAND AROUND YOUR HEART, AN' SQUEEZES AN' SQUEEZES AN' SQUEEZES...
AN' THERE'S BLOOD AN' MEAT RUNNIN' THROUGH THEIR FINGERS, AN' EVEN THOUGH YOU HATE YOURSELF MORE THAN YOUR WORST FUCKIN' ENEMY, YOU'RE STILL SCREAMIN' OUT FOR MERCY...
AN' NONE'S COMIN' 'CAUSE YOU DON'T DESERVE IT.

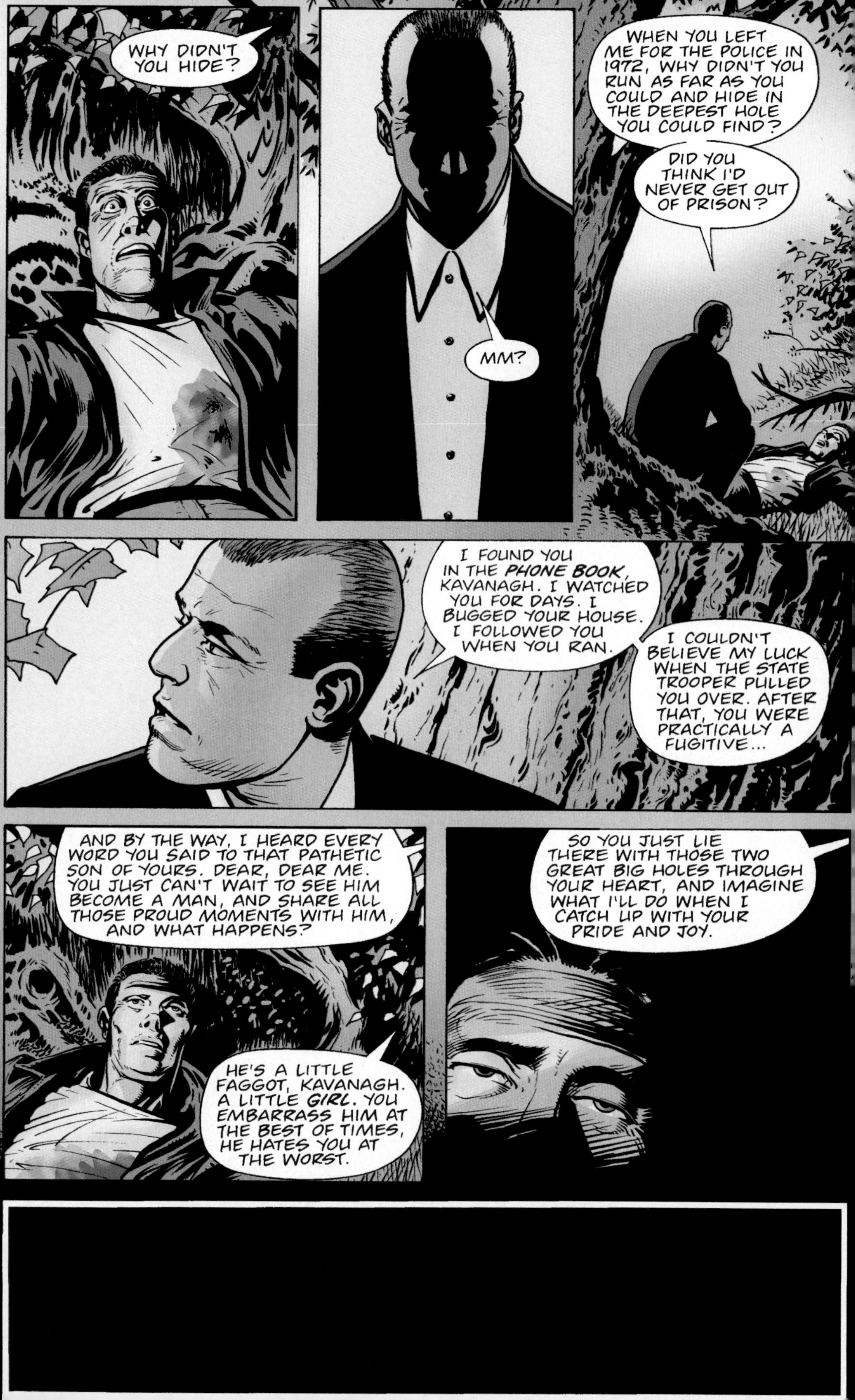
WHY DIDN'T YOU HIDE?
MM?
WHEN YOU LEFT ME FOR THE POLICE IN 1972, WHY DIDN'T YOU RUN AS FAR AS YOU COULD AND HIDE IN THE DEEPEST HOLE YOU COULD FIND?
DID YOU THINK I'D NEVER GET OUT OF PRISON?
I FOUND YOU IN THE PHONE BOOK, KAVANAGH. I WATCHED YOU FOR DAYS. I BUGGED YOUR HOUSE. I FOLLOWED YOU WHEN YOU RAN.
I COULDN'T BELIEVE MY LUCK WHEN THE STATE TROOPER PULLED YOU OVER. AFTER THAT, YOU WERE PRACTICALLY A FUGITIVE...
AND BY THE WAY, I HEARD EVERY WORD YOU SAID TO THAT PATHETIC SON OF YOURS. DEAR, DEAR ME. YOU JUST CAN'T WAIT TO SEE HIM BECOME A MAN, AND SHARE ALL THOSE PROUD MOMENTS WITH HIM, AND WHAT HAPPENS?
HE'S A LITTLE FAGGOT, KAVANAGH. A LITTLE GIRL. YOU EMBARRASS HIM AT THE BEST OF TIMES, HE HATES YOU AT THE WORST.
SO YOU JUST LIE THERE WITH THOSE TWO GREAT BIG HOLES THROUGH YOUR HEART, AND IMAGINE WHAT I'LL DO WHEN I CATCH UP WITH YOUR PRIDE AND JOY.

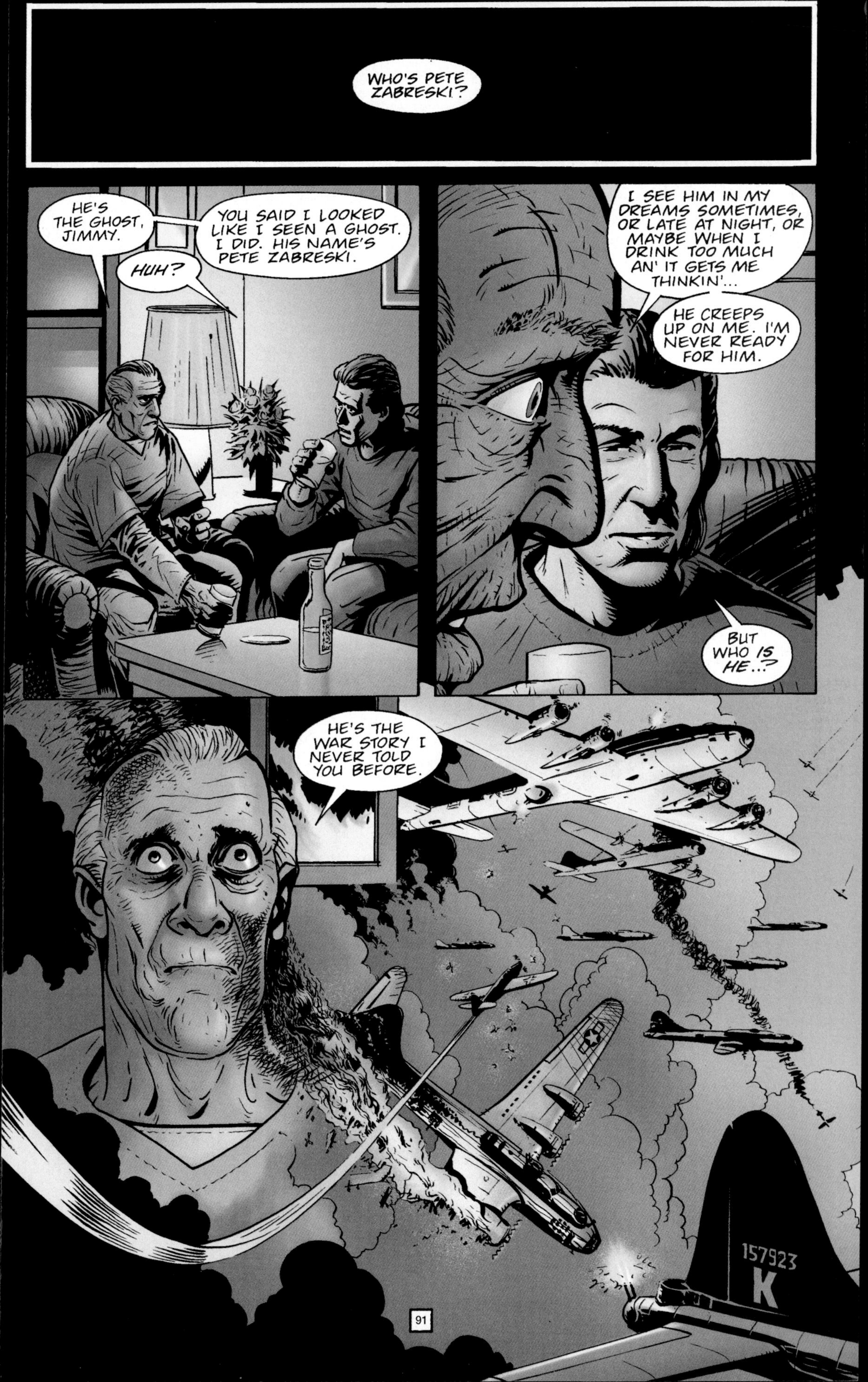
WHO'S PETE ZABRESKI?
HE'S THE GHOST, JIMMY.
YOU SAID I LOOKED LIKE I SEEN A GHOST. I DID. HIS NAME'S PETE ZABRESKI.
HUH?
I SEE HIM IN MY DREAMS SOMETIMES, OR LATE AT NIGHT, OR MAYBE WHEN I DRINK TOO MUCH AN' IT GETS ME THINKIN'...
HE CREEPS UP ON ME. I'M NEVER READY FOR HIM.
BUT WHO *IS* HE..?
HE'S THE WAR STORY I NEVER TOLD YOU BEFORE.
157923
K

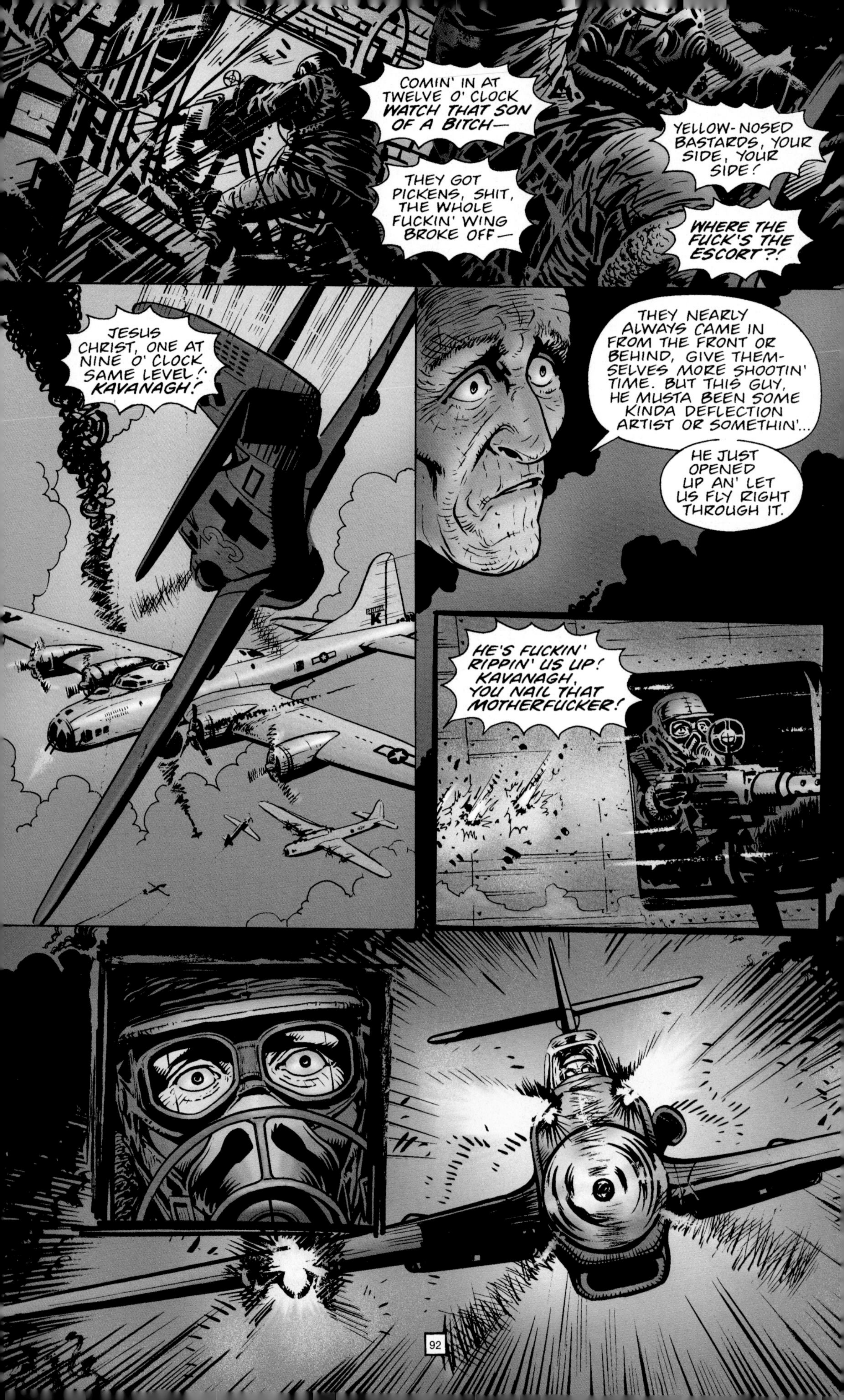
COMIN' IN AT TWELVE O' CLOCK WATCH THAT SON OF A BITCH—
THEY GOT PICKENS, SHIT, THE WHOLE FUCKIN' WING BROKE OFF—
YELLOW-NOSED BASTARDS, YOUR SIDE, YOUR SIDE!
WHERE THE FUCK'S THE ESCORT?!
JESUS CHRIST, ONE AT NINE O' CLOCK SAME LEVEL! KAVANAGH!
THEY NEARLY ALWAYS CAME IN FROM THE FRONT OR BEHIND, GIVE THEMSELVES MORE SHOOTIN' TIME. BUT THIS GUY, HE MUSTA BEEN SOME KINDA DEFLECTION ARTIST OR SOMETHIN'...
HE JUST OPENED UP AN' LET US FLY RIGHT THROUGH IT.
HE'S FUCKIN' RIPPIN' US UP! KAVANAGH, YOU NAIL THAT MOTHERFUCKER!

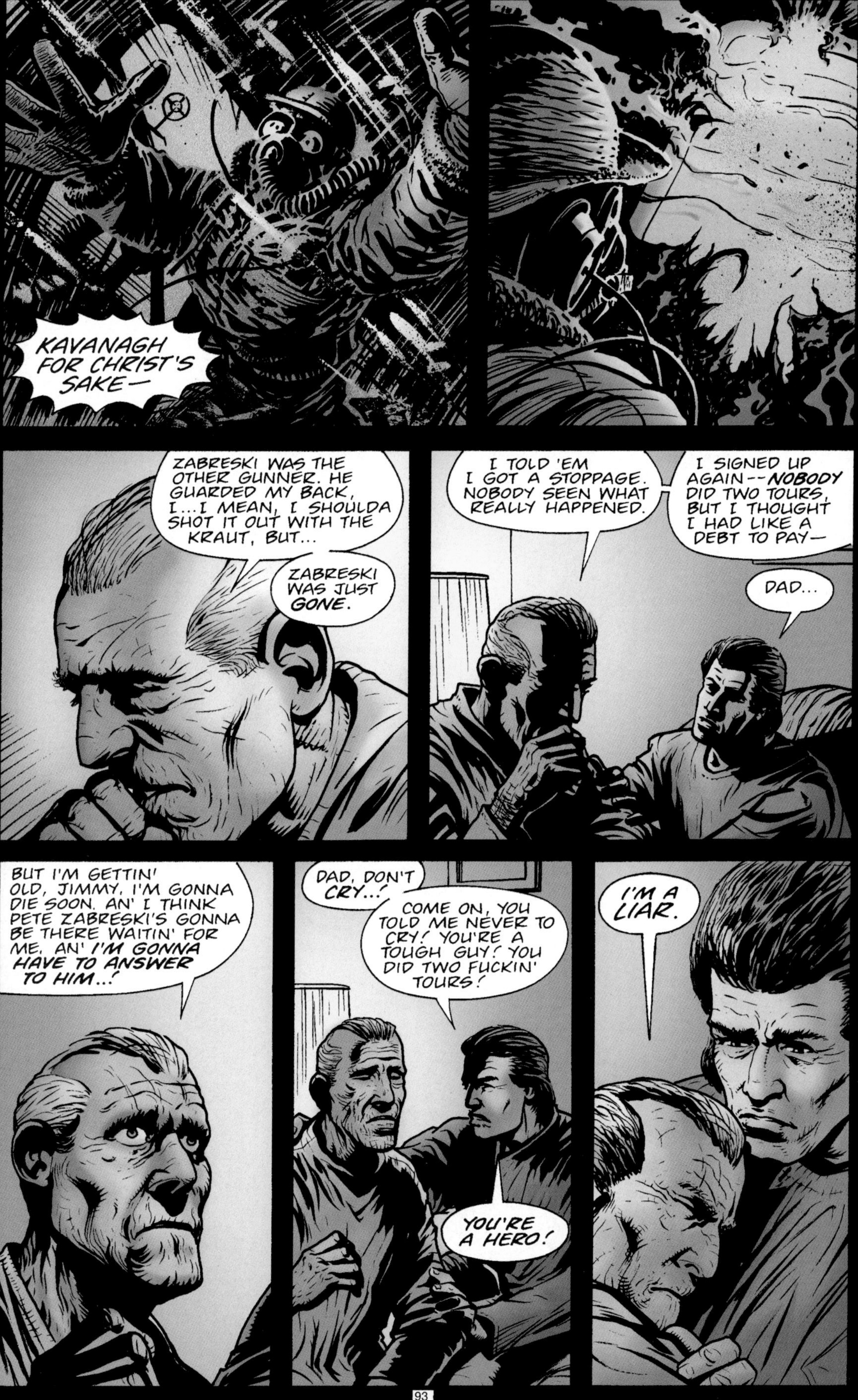
KAVANAGH FOR CHRIST'S SAKE—
ZABRESKI WAS THE OTHER GUNNER. HE GUARDED MY BACK, I...I MEAN, I SHOULDA SHOT IT OUT WITH THE KRAUT, BUT...
ZABRESKI WAS JUST GONE.
I TOLD 'EM I GOT A STOPPAGE. NOBODY SEEN WHAT REALLY HAPPENED.
I SIGNED UP AGAIN--NOBODY DID TWO TOURS, BUT I THOUGHT I HAD LIKE A DEBT TO PAY—
DAD...
BUT I'M GETTIN' OLD, JIMMY. I'M GONNA DIE SOON. AN' I THINK PETE ZABRESKI'S GONNA BE THERE WAITIN' FOR ME. AN' I'M GONNA HAVE TO ANSWER TO HIM...!
DAD, DON'T CRY...!
COME ON, YOU TOLD ME NEVER TO CRY! YOU'RE A TOUGH GUY! YOU DID TWO FUCKIN' TOURS!
YOU'RE A HERO!
I'M A LIAR.

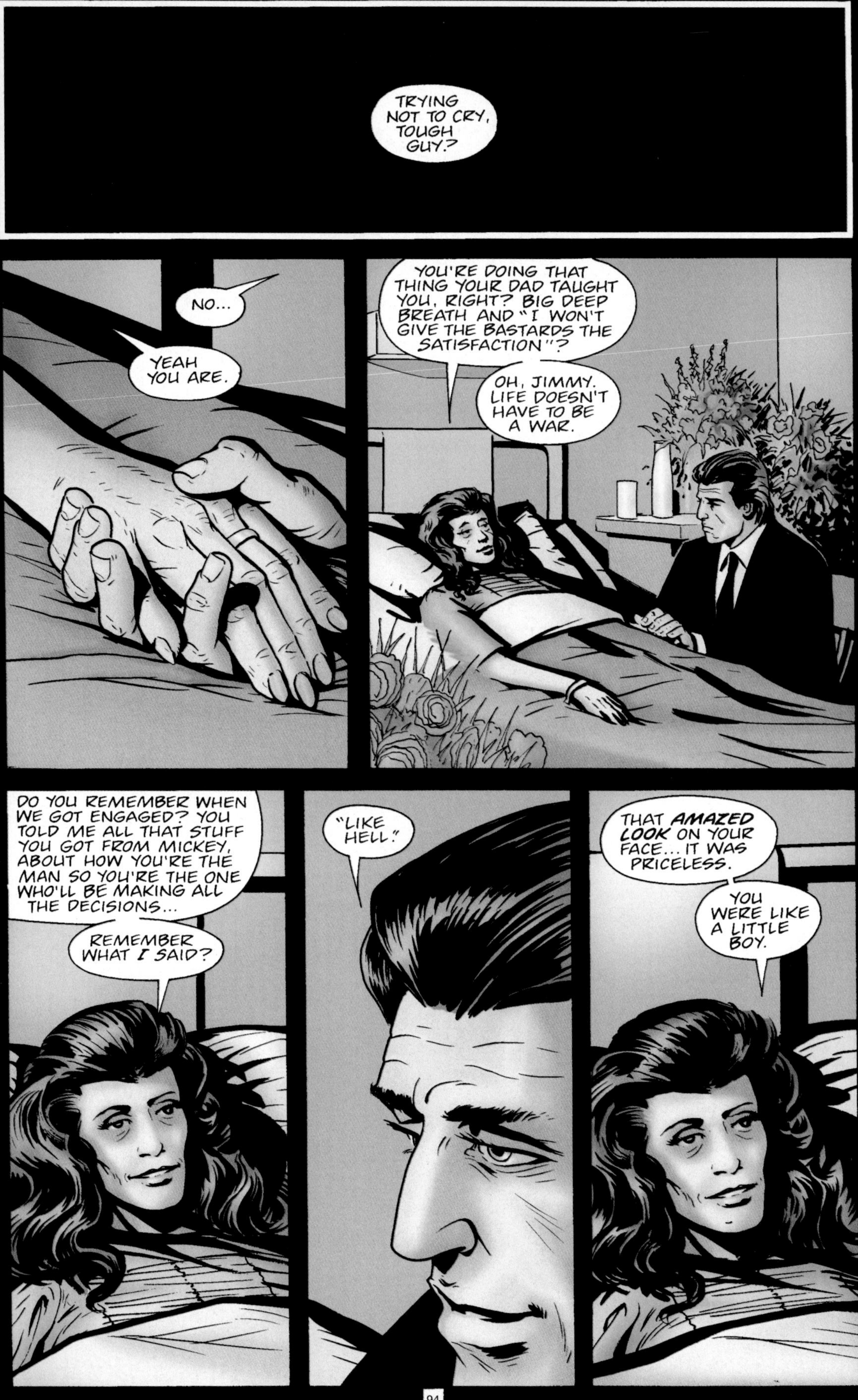
TRYING NOT TO CRY, TOUGH GUY?
NO...
YEAH YOU ARE.
YOU'RE DOING THAT THING YOUR DAD TAUGHT YOU, RIGHT? BIG DEEP BREATH AND "I WON'T GIVE THE BASTARDS THE SATISFACTION"?
OH, JIMMY. LIFE DOESN'T HAVE TO BE A WAR.
DO YOU REMEMBER WHEN WE GOT ENGAGED? YOU TOLD ME ALL THAT STUFF YOU GOT FROM MICKEY, ABOUT HOW YOU'RE THE MAN SO YOU'RE THE ONE WHO'LL BE MAKING ALL THE DECISIONS...
REMEMBER WHAT *I* SAID?
"LIKE HELL."
THAT ***AMAZED LOOK*** ON YOUR FACE... IT WAS PRICELESS.
YOU WERE LIKE A LITTLE BOY.

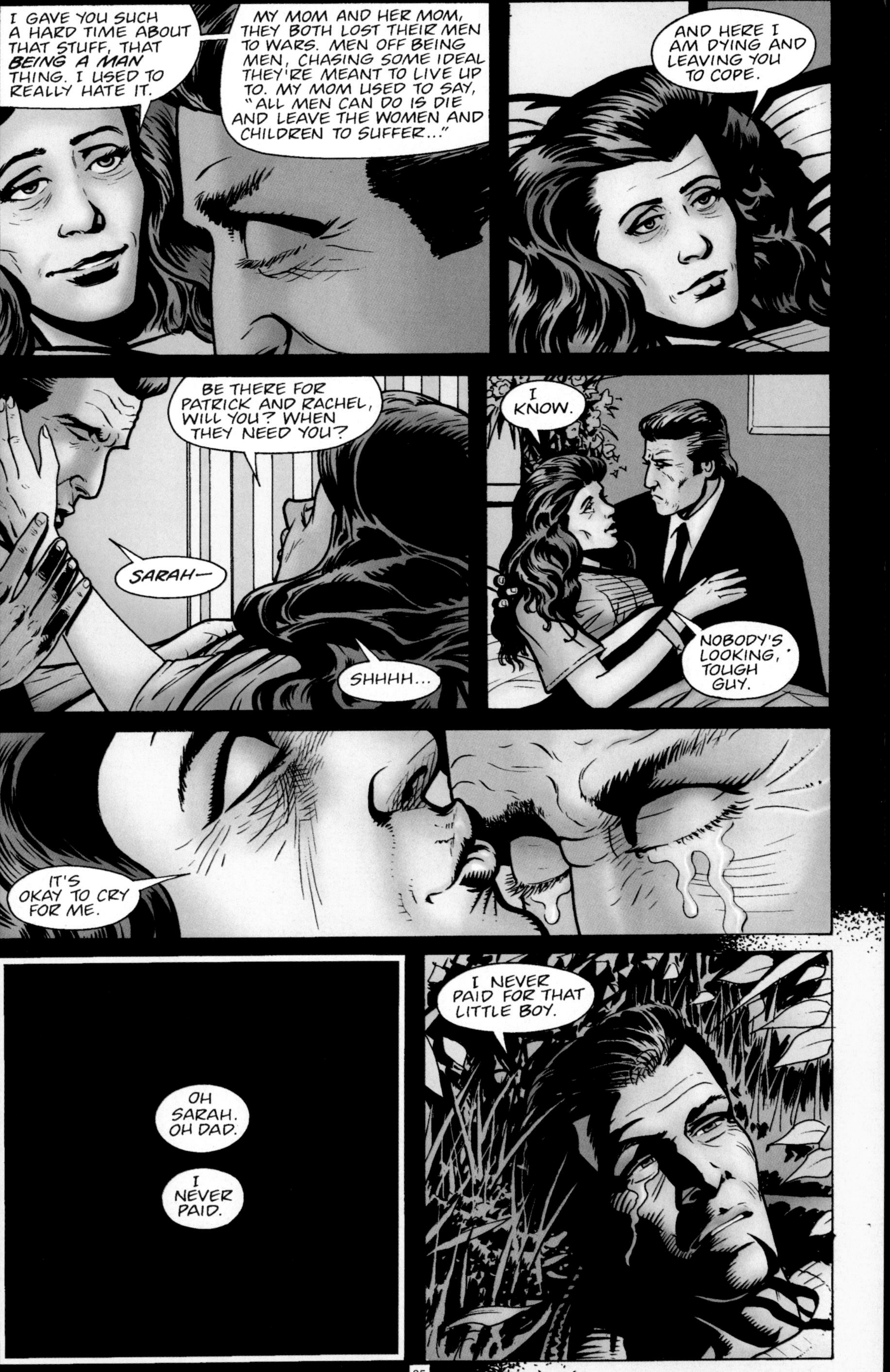
I GAVE YOU SUCH A HARD TIME ABOUT THAT STUFF, THAT BEING A MAN THING. I USED TO REALLY HATE IT.
MY MOM AND HER MOM, THEY BOTH LOST THEIR MEN TO WARS. MEN OFF BEING MEN, CHASING SOME IDEAL THEY'RE MEANT TO LIVE UP TO. MY MOM USED TO SAY, "ALL MEN CAN DO IS DIE AND LEAVE THE WOMEN AND CHILDREN TO SUFFER..."
AND HERE I AM DYING AND LEAVING YOU TO COPE.
BE THERE FOR PATRICK AND RACHEL, WILL YOU? WHEN THEY NEED YOU?
SARAH—
SHHHH...
I KNOW.
NOBODY'S LOOKING, TOUGH GUY.
IT'S OKAY TO CRY FOR ME.
OH SARAH. OH DAD.
I NEVER PAID.
I NEVER PAID FOR THAT LITTLE BOY.

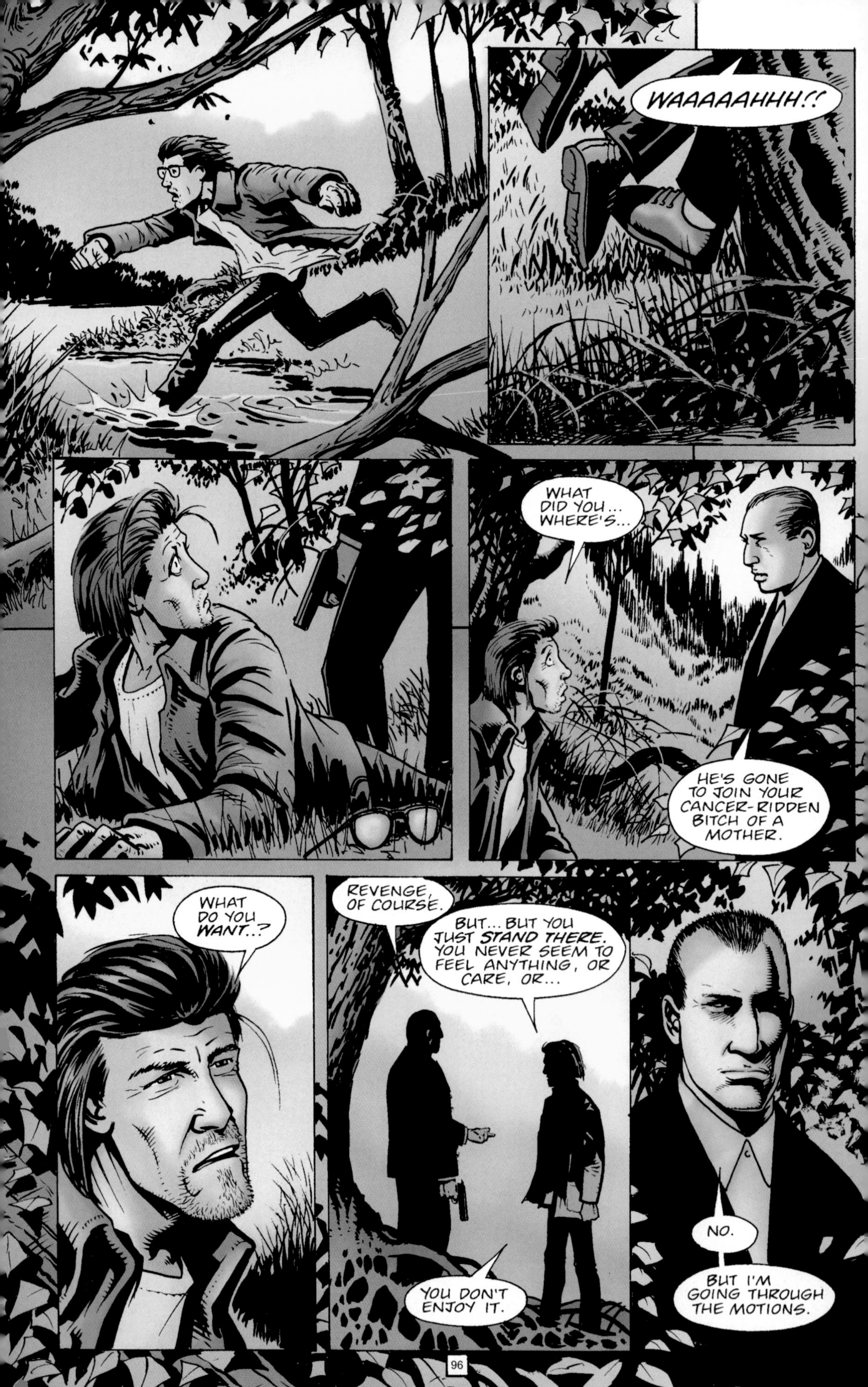
WAAAAAHHH!!
WHAT DID YOU... WHERE'S...
HE'S GONE TO JOIN YOUR CANCER-RIDDEN BITCH OF A MOTHER.
WHAT DO YOU WANT..?
REVENGE, OF COURSE.
BUT... BUT YOU JUST STAND THERE. YOU NEVER SEEM TO FEEL ANYTHING, OR CARE, OR...
YOU DON'T ENJOY IT.
NO.
BUT I'M GOING THROUGH THE MOTIONS.

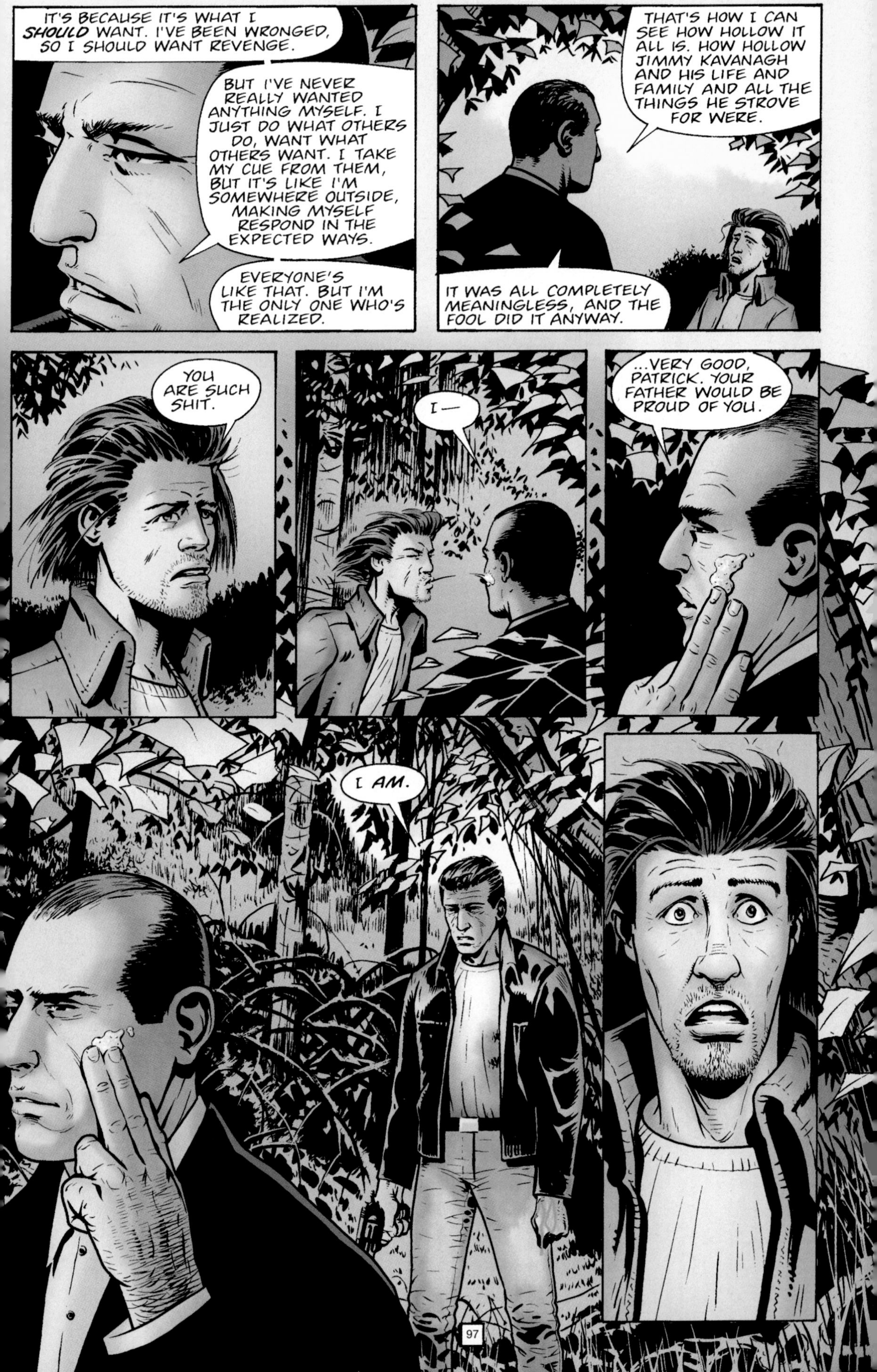
IT'S BECAUSE IT'S WHAT I SHOULD WANT. I'VE BEEN WRONGED, SO I SHOULD WANT REVENGE.
BUT I'VE NEVER REALLY WANTED ANYTHING MYSELF. I JUST DO WHAT OTHERS DO, WANT WHAT OTHERS WANT. I TAKE MY CUE FROM THEM, BUT IT'S LIKE I'M SOMEWHERE OUTSIDE, MAKING MYSELF RESPOND IN THE EXPECTED WAYS.
EVERYONE'S LIKE THAT. BUT I'M THE ONLY ONE WHO'S REALIZED.
THAT'S HOW I CAN SEE HOW HOLLOW IT ALL IS. HOW HOLLOW JIMMY KAVANAGH AND HIS LIFE AND FAMILY AND ALL THE THINGS HE STROVE FOR WERE.
IT WAS ALL COMPLETELY MEANINGLESS, AND THE FOOL DID IT ANYWAY.
YOU ARE SUCH SHIT.
I—
...VERY GOOD, PATRICK. YOUR FATHER WOULD BE PROUD OF YOU.
I AM.

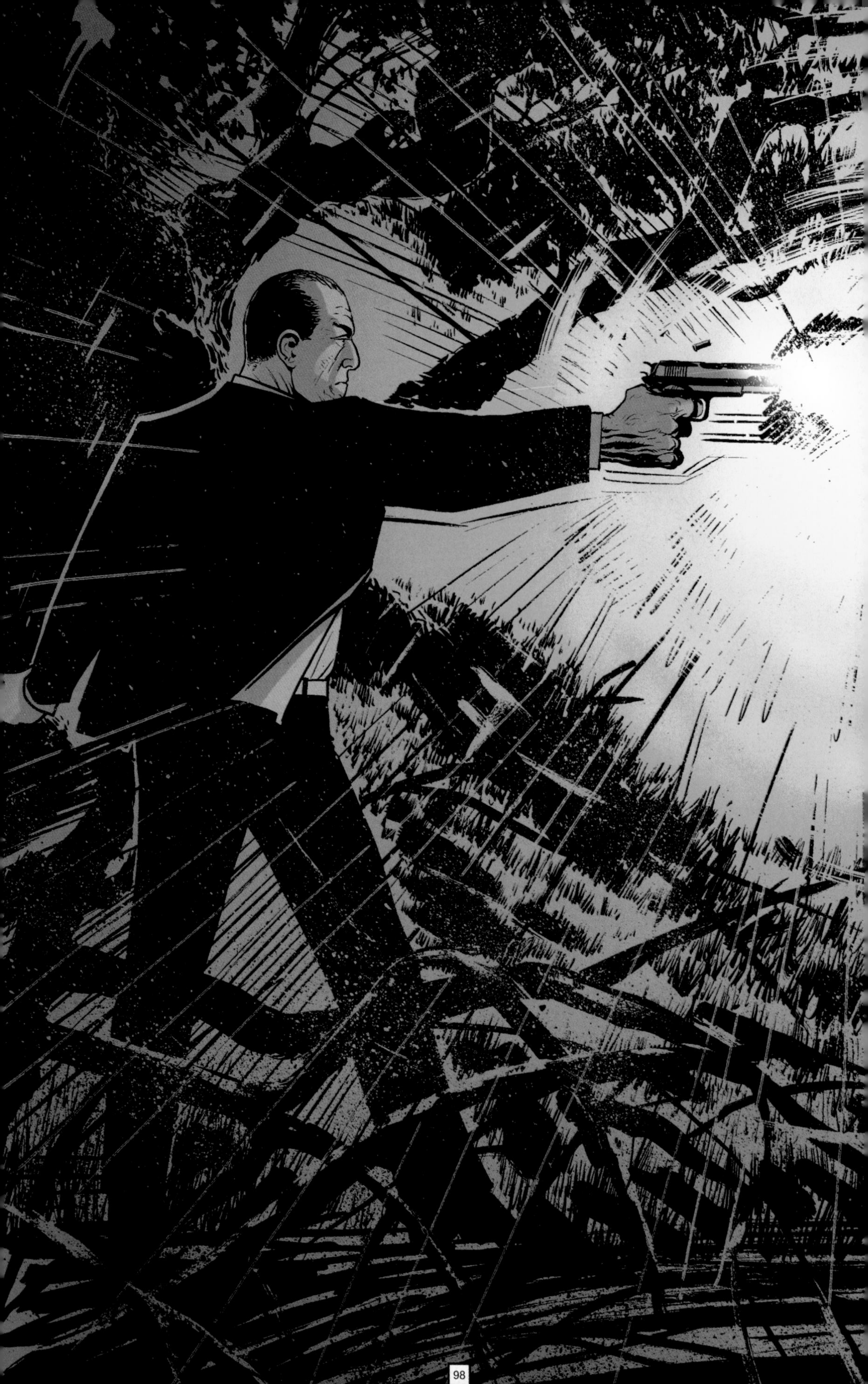

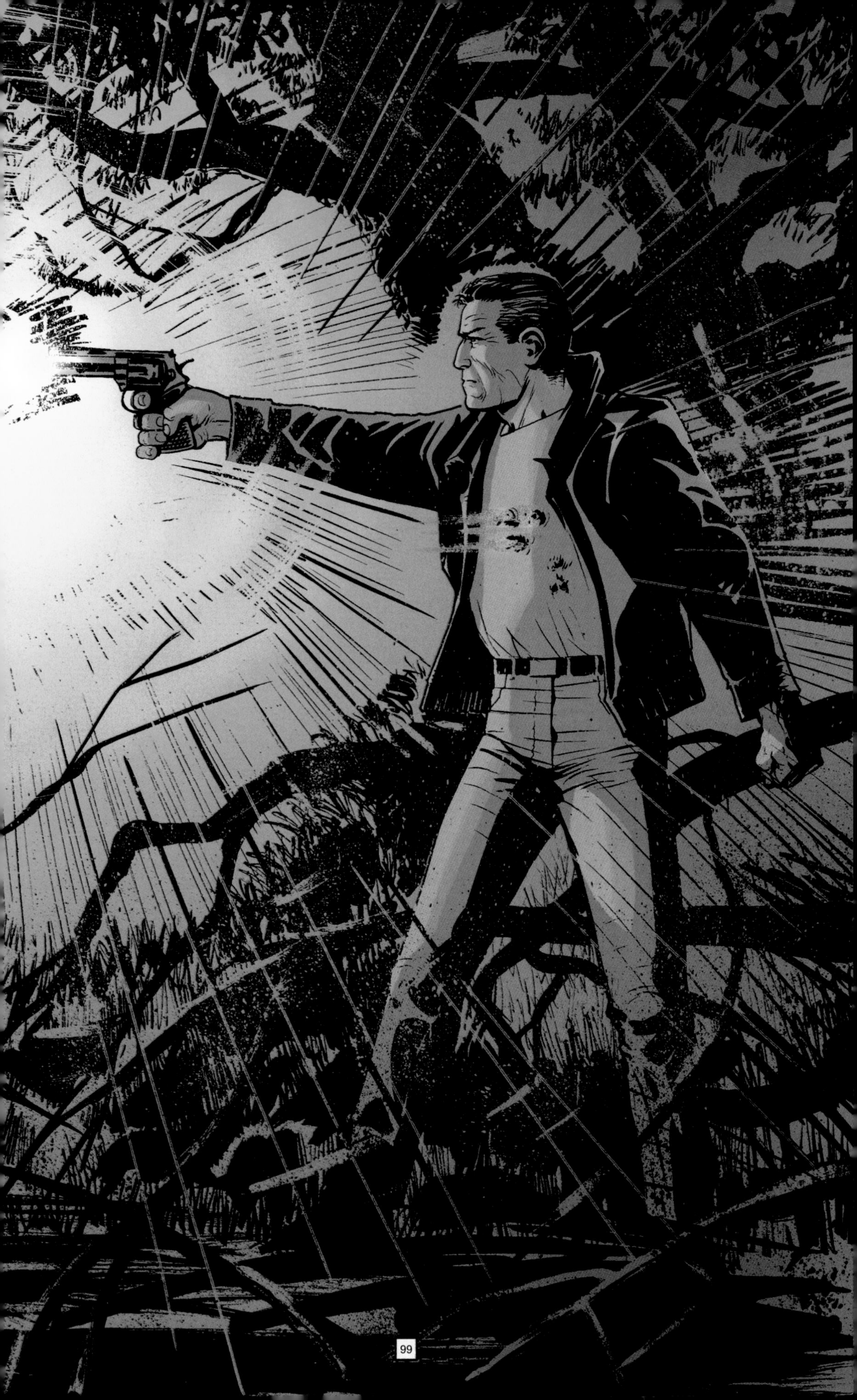

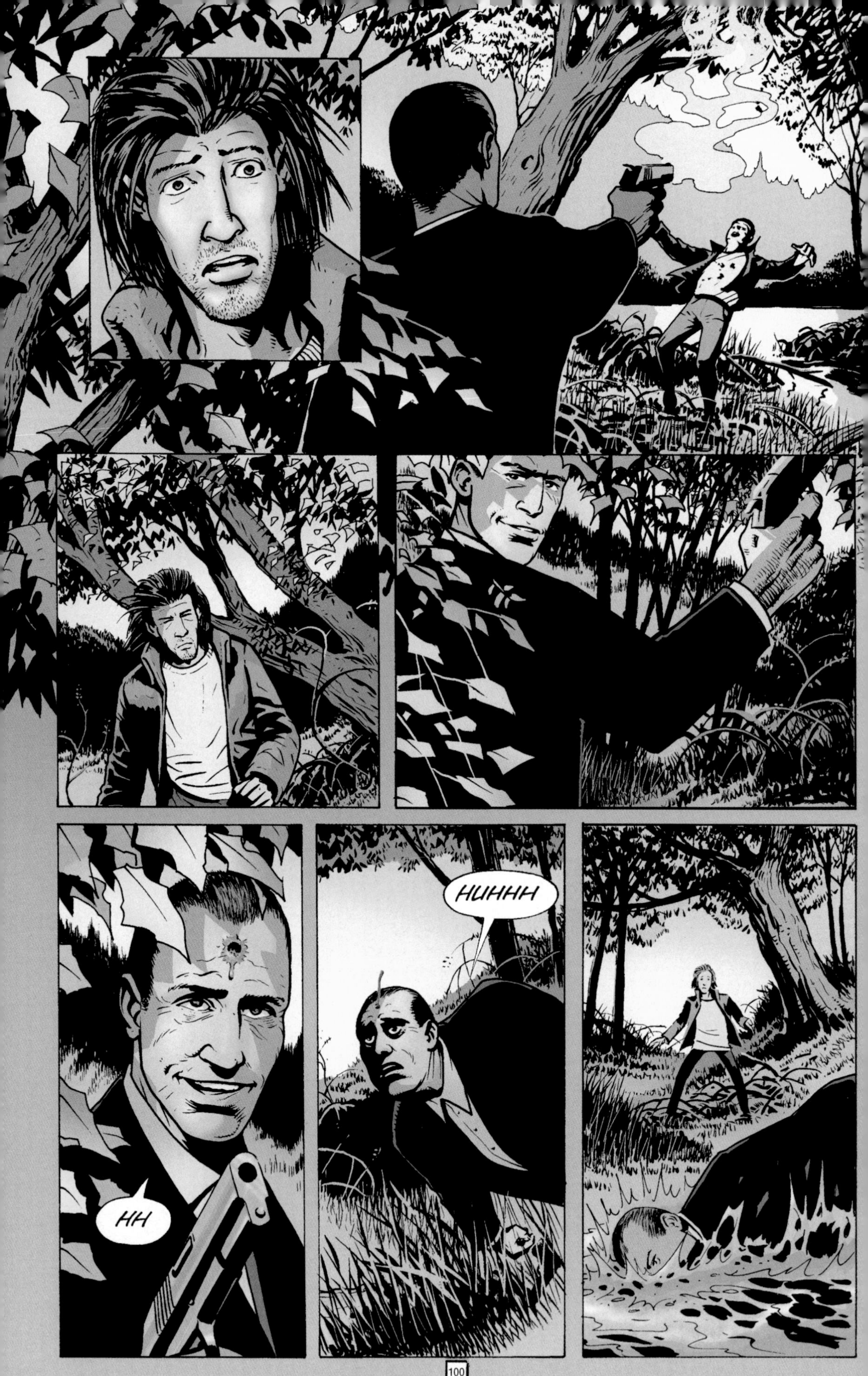
HH
HUHHH

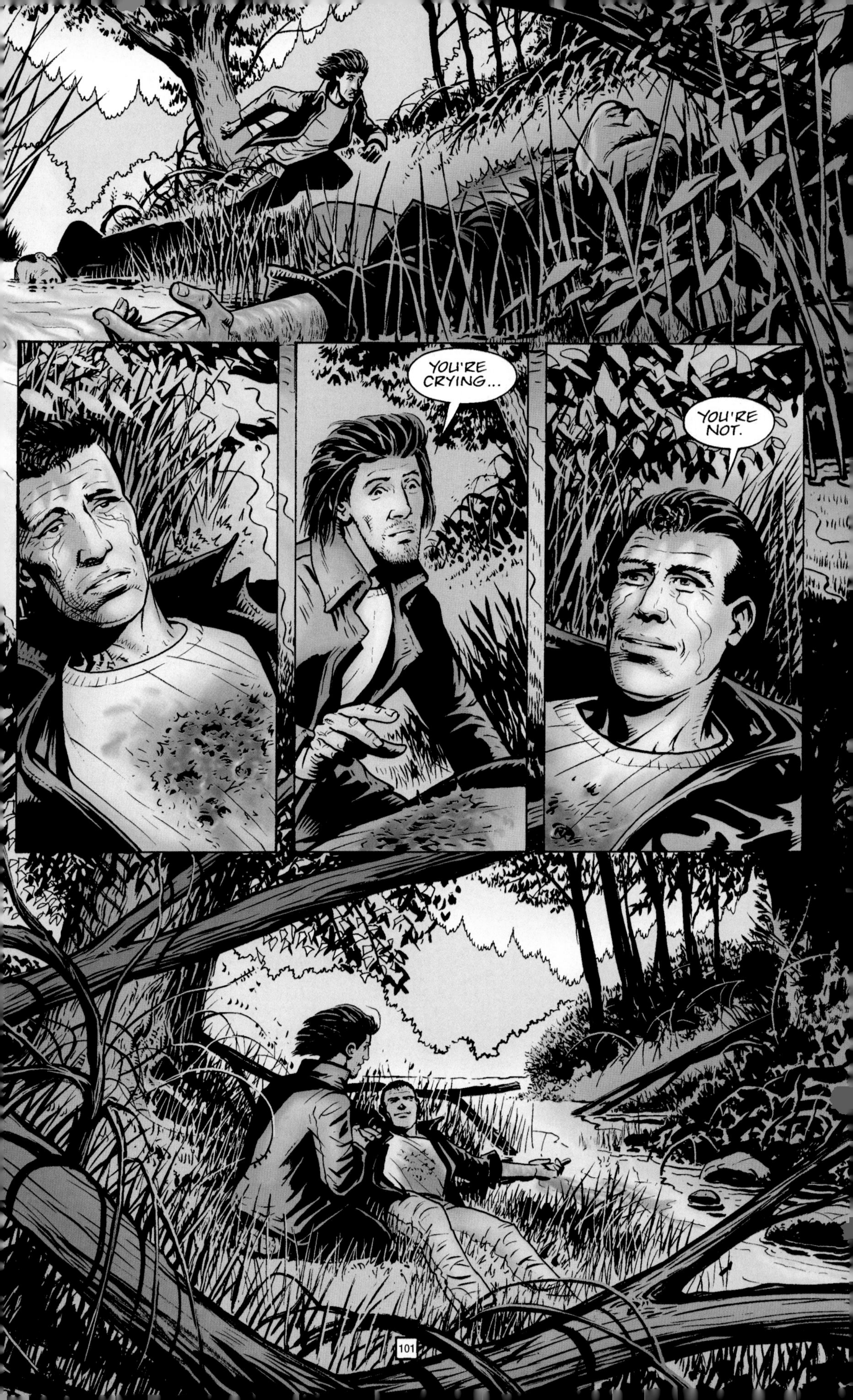
YOU'RE CRYING...
YOU'RE NOT.

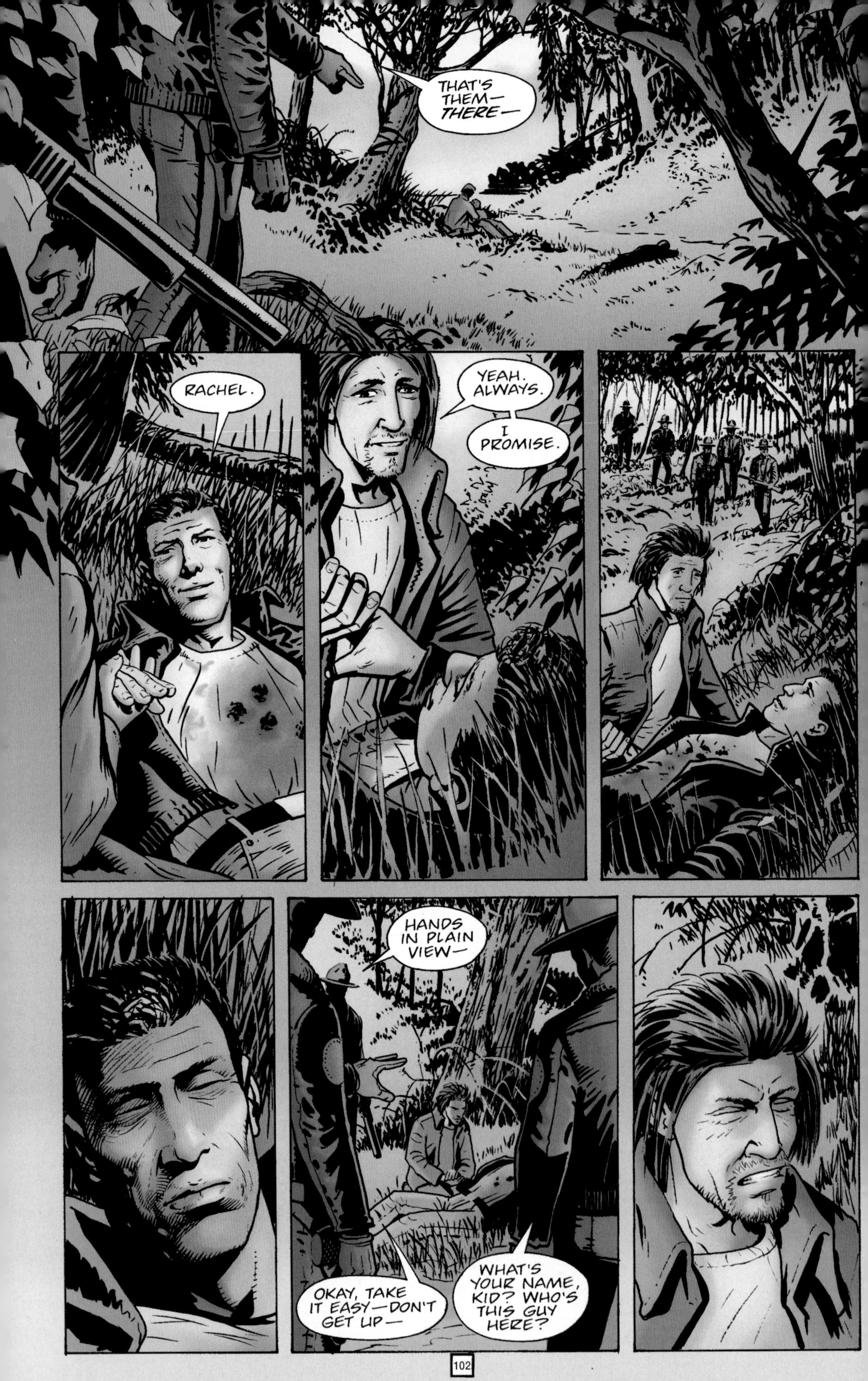
THAT'S THEM— THERE—
RACHEL.
YEAH. ALWAYS.
I PROMISE.
HANDS IN PLAIN VIEW—
OKAY, TAKE IT EASY—DON'T GET UP—
WHAT'S YOUR NAME, KID? WHO'S THIS GUY HERE?

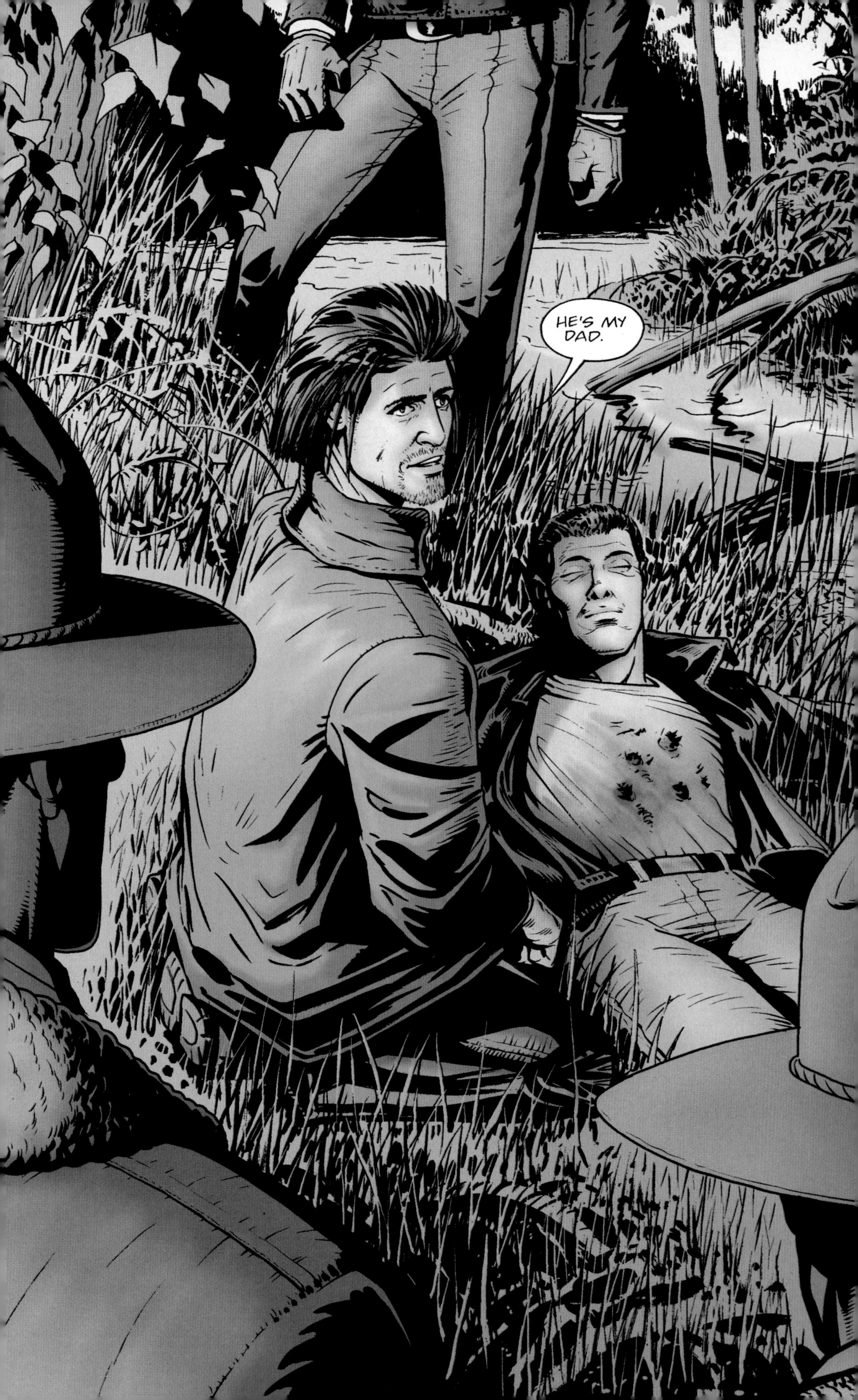
HE'S MY DAD.

GARTH ENNIS has been writing comics for over twenty-five years. His credits include *Preacher, The Boys, Hitman, Red Team, Caliban, Rover Red Charlie, Battlefields* and *War Stories*. Originally from Belfast, Northern Ireland, Ennis now lives in New York City with his wife, Ruth.

JOHN HIGGINS is best known for his color work on *Watchmen*. He has also worked as an artist—and sometimes writer—on such diverse characters as Judge Dredd, Batman, and Jonah Hex. At the end of the nineties, Higgins self-published the first issue of the acclaimed comic book *Razorjack*, for which he was the writer, artist, and colorist. Currently, he and writer Eric Kripke are working on the DC/Vertigo miniseries *Jacked*. Higgins has enjoyed seeing new life being breathed into *Pride & Joy* at Image Comics.